Third Base

JASON BLACKER

Copyright © 2015 Jason Blacker

PUBLISHED BY: Lemon Tree Publishing

Visit JasonBlacker.com on the web to stay up to date

Editing: Andrea Anesi

ISBN-13: 9781927623596

For you dear reader for shining the light of justice into dark corners.

Jason Blacker was born in Cape Town but spent most of his first 18 years in Johannesburg. When not grinding his fingers down to stubs at the keyboard he enjoys drinking tea, calisthenics and running. Currently he lives in Canada.

Under his own name he writes hard boiled as well as cozy mysteries, action adventure, thrillers, literary fiction, science fiction and anything else that tickles his muse. Third Base is the 3rd full length novel starring Anthony Carrick. This is in addition to the short stories featuring the same hard drinking, wise cracking PI.

Jason Blacker also writes poetry and daily haikus at his haiku blog.

You can find his haikus and other poetry at his website haiqueue.com.

To stay up to date and learn about new releases be sure to visit jasonblacker.com where you can find more information about his writing and upcoming projects.

If you enjoy space opera in the tradition of Star Trek then take a look at Jason Blacker's pen name "Sylynt Storme". It is under the name Sylynt Storme where you can find both sci-fi and vampire fiction written by Jason Blacker.

"Star Sails" is the space opera series and "The Misgivings of the Vampire Lucius Lafayette" is his vampire series.

CHAPTER ONE

Peer Into Promiseland

THE weather in Santa Monica in October was charming. It's the kind of place to be if you like a warm breeze in your face and a quieter beach. The tourists have gone home, having packed up their sunburns and umbrellas and screaming kids. Santa Monica is my town again. The highs are in the seventies, and the lows, well, let's just say the lows are crisp enough to keep you walking briskly home.

But today was a day to remember. I was sitting at the Mariasol at the end of the pier. But I wasn't alone. You'll remember the lovely Emily Stratham. One of our finest coroners in the city of lost angels. I had fancied some Creole fish, but she reminded me she was vegetarian. I guess the fish get a reprieve. We had just taken our seats. I had met her here. I had offered to pick her up but she declined. Maybe she was an independent woman or maybe she didn't like the look of my jalopy in her neck of the woods. I wasn't hurt. I still didn't know where she lived, and that was alright. How can you be hurt by a good-looking woman? Let me count the ways.

Things were quiet. Had been for weeks now. It was like the Santa Anna winds had swept all the trash into the Pacific. Either that, or the LAPD had no need for a grizzled, grumpy gumshoe like me. I liked to blame it on the Santa Anna winds. But I reckoned if there was some truth telling to be told that I was wrong.

Mariasol is a small place. But it has charm. Emily and I were out on the deck looking out over the ocean. Some surfers were out catching some waves in their wetsuits. They looked like anorexic seals. I guess the water was colder than the warm breeze in our faces suggested. Or perhaps kids nowadays just aren't as tough as they were back in my day.

I was thinking how I could use a case. I felt like I was getting rusty. There was only so much painting I could do. I didn't need the money. Alimony was paid up. Pirate was well fed, and I'd sold a couple of paintings in the last month. Hell, I was feeling like King of the world, and it was gonna end. I knew it, but more than that, I was getting itchy to clean up some dark part of this town. Sweep some trash out to sea. I didn't need Saint Anne helping nor the LAPD. You can tell I was getting antsy.

"Are you ready to order?" asked the waitress.

She was a Latina in a black dress and white blouse. She was stunningly beautiful and seemed carved out of coffee beans. She was young and bubbly and I bet she made more than me on tips alone. Emily looked up at her and smiled. Then she looked over at me, and I made sure I was looking at her and not the waitress.

"Are you ready, Anthony?" she asked.

I nodded.

"The lady will have the vegetable burrito and I'll get the carne asada."

The waitress nodded at me.

"And to drink?" she asked.

I was craning my neck to keep my eyes above her neck. It wasn't helping that her cleavage was thrust in my face like milk chocolate Hershey kisses. So I did what any noble man would do, I turned to my date.

"I'll have a lemonade," said Emily.

I smiled at her, and kept my eyes on her.

"Make that two," I said.

The buxom waitress trundled off, saving me from myself. And for that I was grateful.

"Do you see dead people?" I asked out of nowhere and then immediately felt weird about it. Emily looked at me and grinned and slowly shook her head.

"You sure are a strange catch of the day."

"I didn't know we were fishing."

She shook her head some more, but she wasn't upset.

"I'm sorry," I said. "I haven't, and I could use a case."

"It'll come," she said. "You're good at what you do, and as the saying goes, you can't keep a good man down for long."

"Yeah," I said, "but you can keep him in the dark indefinitely."

Emily laughed.

"We must be two pretty macabre people," she said, tossing her head back, and making me weak at the knees.

"How so?"

"Well, we both enjoy looking at dead people," she said with a bit of irony.

"Not true. It's not the looking so much as the figuring out that keeps me going."

She nodded her head.

"That's true. Same with me. It's rewarding figuring out cause of death and even more so when that leads to justice."

"Exactly," I said. "Nothing like good old justice, and vengeance."

"Vengeance?"

I tilted my head from side to side and turned up my mouth in contemplation.

"Yeah, in a way. Sometimes vengeance is better than justice," I said in all honesty. It was how I felt right at this moment in any event.

"You are a strange bird," she said.

"I'll take that over being an odd duck."

She laughed. In fact if she'd been maybe twenty years younger I might have called it a giggle. I smiled at her laughter.

"You see what I mean."

I didn't say anything. I looked out at the blue ocean. Surfers tumbling like small rags in the waves. Others riding them almost to shore.

"Have you ever surfed?" I asked.

She shook her head and followed my gaze.

"It looks fun," she said. "What about you?"

I shook my head keeping my gaze on the men out there. At least from here it looked like men.

"I'm not originally from here," I said.

"Really?" she looked at me with pinched eyebrows. "I don't think you ever told me that."

I turned to look at her, and smiled.

"I didn't. I moved with my mother when she divorced my alcoholic father. I started junior high out here."

Emily looked at me for a while like I might have just stepped on a kitten.

"You don't like it?" I asked.

She shook her head and rested her chin on her hands.

"It's not that, you're just really quite intriguing. Seems every time we get together I get to peel another layer from your onion."

"So long as I don't make you cry, we'll be alright," I said.

She smiled.

"Where you from then?"

"I rolled in a while back from the dustbowl," I said, grinning.

"No, where are you really from?" she asked gently.

"From Oklahoma, I'm an Okie but not from Muskogee."

I was still grinning but I wasn't selling it.

"Where?"

"You've probably never heard of it," I said. "Small little town, at least compared to The Big Orange, called Stillwater."

"That sounds lovely?"

"It wasn't," I said, my face now deadpan.

"Oh, you didn't like it there?"

"The city's alright. Your average mid-western city. It's small. By the time I left it had maybe forty thousand people."

"So what didn't you like about it?" she asked.

I was saved by the waitress. She came by and served up our plates. My steak looked good. Pink in the middle with nice grill marks and dark on the outside. Tasted great too. Emily's burrito didn't look too bad either, not for a vegetarian dish anyway.

I couldn't help but take a look at the waitress' cleavage. She practically shoved her breasts in my face as she leaned in to place my plate. That's one of the things I love about The Big Orange, the color. The color in the people. You've got the Mexicans and African Americans and Europeans and other Whites all intermingling, or trying their best to figure it out.

It sure ain't no Stillwater. Maybe that's why I didn't like it too much. Too much whiteness. No color, no culture. And we all know what happens to white paint as it ages, it goes gray and cold and

5

peels. Gets stagnant. Not that I knew downright racists in Stillwater, I was too young to really understand that. But folks were too conservative. Too untrusting of folks that didn't look like them.

I thanked the waitress as she went off.

"I like LA," I said. "There's a lot of color here. In the people, in the cultures. It's vibrant."

Emily cut a piece of her burrito and took a bite and chewed on it for a while. I did the same to my steak. Damn, it was good. But then I've always liked Mexican food.

"I know," she said. "I'm born and raised here. I love the culture, the vibe of this place and all the different cultures too. I guess Stillwater's not much like that?"

I shook my head and put my knife and fork down.

"Nope. I haven't been back in about forty years. But I don't remember it being particularly liberal."

"Then what made you so liberal?" she asked.

I looked around. It was quiet for afternoon lunch. But we were eating a late lunch and the tourists were gone. I sipped on my lemonade.

"My father," I said and picked up my knife and fork and started cutting at the slab of meat.

"He must have been a good man," she said, looking at me smiling.

I looked up at her and grinned. A piece of meat stuck on my fork.

"He wasn't," I said. "He was the biggest asshole I ever met."

I put the meat in my mouth and chewed on it. I had nothing better to do. I wasn't mad. The old bastard had been dead going on twenty years or so. I'd put him in his grave and left my anger there with him to keep him company.

"Oh," said Emily, frowning and looking down at her plate. "I'm sorry. I just thought..."

She didn't say anything. She went to eating her food.

"It's okay," I said. "I'm not mad. Not anymore. Just telling you the honest truth. That's what you want isn't it?"

She looked up at me and nodded.

"I guess, I don't understand then how the man who raised you, who you didn't like turned you so liberal."

"That's easy, M," I said. "It was because he was an asshole. When you're raised by the biggest jerk you get a soft spot for the downtrodden, those tossed away in the gutters of life. At least it gave me a soft spot. Gave me compassion, I guess."

"Tell me more about him... if that's alright?"

"It's not a problem. I buried him back in Stillwater some twenty or so years ago. Buried my hatred for him right there too."

Emily looked up at me and nodded. She smiled a smile as soft as kisses and warm as fresh caramel. She was the kind of woman I could meet the end with.

"Maybe if I'm feeling kind I could say the war did him in. The Vietnam war. My mother always said he came back different after that. I figure he was just always an asshole."

"So your mother met him before he went off to fight?"

I nodded and stuffed more meat in my face.

"Yeah, Stillwater was a pretty small town back then. Guess it still is. They were childhood sweethearts. That wasn't uncommon back then. Met in the eighth grade. She waited for him get back from the war and then they got married. She tells me the first few years were pretty good. Even when I was a baby she says he wasn't drinking too hard. I don't remember any of that."

"You only knew him as an alcoholic?"

I nodded again.

"Yeah. He thought I was a sissy because I liked art and liked drawing. My mother wasn't like that. But that was the start of it. The fights between them. Him telling her he was gonna make a man out of me. And he meant it to."

"I'm sorry," she said, sipping lemonade. Her eyes were sad. The saddest blue I'd ever seen. Deep blue pools where a man could drink for ages and never get tired.

"Don't be," I said. "He helped make me the man I am now. This bleeding-heart liberal."

I grinned at her, and raised my glass. She clinked with me.

"To the cracks in us," I said, "that let out the rainbows."

"That's lovely. I'll drink to that."

"I guess your childhood was pretty good, huh?"

Emily nodded.

"It was. I can't complain. I had two loving parents."

"Good for you," I said, and I meant it.

"But please go on," she urged.

I took a bite of meat and chewed for a while.

"When I was around five, at least this is when my memories start, he started to teach me how to box. That was his way of trying to toughen me up. Make a man out of me. He was a semi-pro boxer, just wasn't ever good enough to break into the pro circuit. He was a failed man in pretty much everything he did. He got a horrible job in Stillwater that he couldn't keep. He was in and out of more jobs than I've been in and out of fights."

Emily nodded. She had finished her meal and pushed her plate off to the side.

"My biggest memories of him are of his whiskey breath and his bad temper."

"He wasn't actually violent, was he, towards you and your mother?"

Emily looked at me, resting her head on her hands. Her face was placid but her eyes remained sad. I nodded.

"Yup," I said. "He beat the shit out of me regularly. Always used boxing as an excuse. It was worse when he was drunk though. He'd tell me it was time for a round in the ring to practice boxing, he'd say. What he really wanted was a moving punching bag."

"That's horrible," she said, turning her mouth upside down.

"Yeah, it was. Now I don't want it to sound worse than it was. I mean he never broke my nose or jaw, or anything like that, but he'd punch me hard. Harder than the other boys could punch at the boxing club he had me join."

"Wow, and your mother never did anything about this?"

"She didn't know any better. She just thought it was how we roughhoused. She probably suspected he was rougher than he should have been, but I got beat up in the ring plenty too, so you can't blame her. It softened me up, but it also toughened me up."

"How do you mean?"

"I learned a hatred for those abusing their power over the vulnerable, like my old man did by abusing me. That gave me my liberal views, and it toughened me up in that I learned how to take a punch. Whether literally or just to roll with the punches that life throws your way."

"Still, that's an awful way to learn those lessons for a child."

I nodded and finished up my food. The waitress came by and asked how everything was. It was great and I told her as much. We ordered a Mexican coffee for me and a regular coffee for Emily. She was back to work this afternoon and couldn't afford the tequila and Kahlua.

"It wasn't ideal. There are only two gifts my father gave me that I ever appreciated."

"What are those?"

"Boxing and compassion. Though that last one was probably the last thing he was trying to give me. He wasn't a compassionate man. I wouldn't say he was racist but he had prejudice. I know that for a fact."

"How?"

"Just the way he'd treat the less fortunate, especially any bums who happened not to be white. It was just the things he'd say to me after, that's all. Not outright hatred, but prejudicial."

"So what happened that caused your mother to leave him?"

"He happened. He'd been off work for several months. I grew up poor, and when the sole breadwinner is out of work for some months you get even poorer. I remember lots of weeks when the only meal I had was what I could get from the school lunch lady."

"That's awful," she said. "I'm so sorry."

"Not your fault. I'm not looking for sympathy. I'm just telling you how it was. That's all. I'm a big grownup man now. I've made peace with it."

Our coffees came back and mine looked like something that Emily would have liked with the cinnamon stick in it and the whipped cream. I offered her a sip and she took me up on it. The whipped cream stuck to her upper lip till she licked it off. Made her lips look like cherries with whipped topping.

"So I came home one day at the end of my grade seven year. I was twelve, coming on thirteen. He'd been hitting the bottle real hard. Come dinner time he was just looking for a fight and he found one with my mother. She'd done the best she could, but dinner was rice with some diluted tomato sauce. He wanted to know where his meat was. She told him she couldn't afford any on account of him not working all this time."

I took a break to take a sip of the coffee. It was damn good. I don't usually go for fancy coffees, but this one hit the spot.

"They got to arguing back and forth. He eventually slid the plate at her and it fell off the table and broke on the floor. He told her to pick it up and she told him to clean it since he'd made the mess himself. He smacked her so hard across the face she was bruised for weeks. It also knocked her down. I'd never seen him hit her before, and I don't think he had. Anyway, that was the straw that broke my camel's back. I got up and punched him in the nose. We got into it then, had a great old fight, it was the first time I'd been knocked out, but not before I got some good licks in myself."

Emily was shaking her head slowly.

"I can't imagine. This is one of the worst things I've ever heard. He actually punched your mother in the face in front of you?"

"No, he didn't punch her, he slapped her. Not much of a difference to the outcome though. The really bizarre thing about all of this was how proud he looked when I was coming too. Not proud of himself, but proud of me. He'd cracked my cheek, split my lip and broken my nose. Next morning when he went down to the unemployment office my mother got me to pack my bags and we left. No note. No anything. I wouldn't see him for almost ten years."

"And that's when you made it out here?"

I nodded and sipped on my coffee.

"Yeah, nothing but a few thousand bucks she'd squirreled away doing odd jobs in Stillwater. No job. I've got a lot of respect for what she did for us. I used to wish she'd done it sooner. But like I said, there're two things I got from my father that I'm now happy for."

"It must have been tough for you. I can only imagine," she said.

I grinned at her.

"You'd think so, but you'd be wrong. We were so poor in Stillwater that I might as well have been raised by a single mother. So coming out here wasn't that bad. Started having regular food on the table. My mother was working two jobs. Worked as a secretary for a used car dealership and then waited tables at a greasy spoon a lot of nights. Never had so much financial security as I did then. Best times of my life started when I got out here."

Emily nodded.

"But like I said, we were poor. But we had each other and we had peace."

"But the first few months must have been hard, coming out to a new state and a new school. Did you have any trouble fitting in?"

I chuckled under my breath and grinned at her.

"What's so funny?" she asked.

"My father got rid of most of my fears," I said. "By the time I got out here, I wasn't afraid to make friends or stand up to bullies. The first few weeks were awkward for sure."

"What do you mean by that?"

"You know kids, they can be unkind, mean. I was in Grade Eight and a couple of Grade Ten kids figured it'd be fun to tease the new kid about where he was from. So they got to calling me the Okie from Muskogee. I don't like being called Tony, but that's more of a personal preference. Now if you go insulting where I'm from, that's different. So the first time they did that at recess I knocked them both on their asses. Everything was gravy then."

I was grinning at Emily, and she smiled wryly at me.

"Fighting isn't always the answer," she said.

I nodded slowly.

"I learned that lesson the hard way. See, my father had only shown me that one language. And sometimes that's the language you've gotta use when talking to some folks, but I learned its better to walk slowly, speak quietly and only then use a big stick if necessary."

"How did you come to realize that?"

"Because there's always someone better than you," I said. "I joined a boxing club after I arrived here. My mother thought it would give me a sense of belonging and a feeling of home, like Stillwater. She wasn't very wrong. There was this club close by where we lived in University Park. It was called Moe's Gymnasium. Very old school. Anyway, the owner was Moe Hirschwitz. We all called him Hershey, because even though he was a tough son of a bitch he had a real sweet center."

"What was he like?" she asked, sipping coffee.

"Just like how you'd imagine a benevolent uncle. He was a Jew from Poland originally. Left with his folks during the war. They were lucky if you can call it that, in that they made it out alive, all of them. But they suffered a lot of hardships too, on their journey to get here. Plus, it wasn't easy the first years in the US either."

Emily nodded, holding her coffee mug between us.

"I can imagine," she said.

"When I met him he was in his fifties. He had thinning gray hair, eyes that bulged out his face, thin lips and a nose that had smelt too many fists. It lay against his face like a used gray hankie."

Emily giggled.

"You have a way with words," she said. "You're a poet, you know."

"Well, I don't know about that. It's just that's how it looked to me. Anyway, he was a great man. Really took me under his wing, but he took no crud. Not from me, not from anyone. But he offered respect and expected it in return. He boxed for the US in the 1960 Rome Olympics. Got the silver in the middleweight division, when he lost on points to a Russian. Incidentally, one of his teammates was Cassius Clay, since known as Muhammad Ali. Hershey said Ali was the best boxer he's ever seen, any way you look at it. I'd agree."

"You really like boxing," she said.

"I didn't, not at first. Not until about a year after I got here and Hershey really taught me all about the sweet science. What I was trying to say is that Hershey was a really great boxer, but more than that, a great man."

"If I can interject quickly," she said, and I nodded, "why is boxing called the sweet science? It seems brutally barbaric if I'm to be honest."

"I know, and it is. But it's also very tactical. It's fisted chess is how I like to think of it. You have to be very strategic, and you'll see that sometimes. Sometimes the best technical boxer is defeated by a less technically proficient but greater tactician. Anyway, it was coined the sweet science by an English journalist named Pierce Egan back in the early 1800s and it's sort of stuck ever since."

Emily lifted her eyebrows in surprise and also disagreement.

"Anyway, you were saying about Hershey," she said.

"Yeah, well, he was a great boxer and great man. He taught me about the nuances of boxing, the sweet part of it, the science. But he always instilled in us the fact that it was a sport and an athleticism, and that its ultimate aim was not about fighting for anger or aggression's sake. I didn't believe him of course, but I came around."

"How did that happen?"

"I was arrogant. I mean I was good, guess I still am, but I was cocky with it in my teen years. In my weight division at the state level I was unbeaten. It was different at the national level. I never won a national tournament. But that wasn't the only thing. I got the living crap kicked out of me one time by a bunch of thugs, and that happened mostly because I was too cocksure of myself. I was in the wrong place when I knew better and instead of backing down I went looking for a fight and it found me. That's when I learned the hard lesson that Hershey was trying to teach me."

Emily smiled at me.

"It sort of buffed out the round edges then, did it?" she winked.

I nodded.

"And how. But I got justice for the slight I encountered. These weren't good guys. But I had no place doing and being where I was at the time."

"Sounds like you really liked this man Moe, or Hershey as you call him," she said.

"I did. He was like the uncle, or really, like the father I never had."

I looked down at the last dregs of my coffee. I could still see Hershey smiling at me, his crooked grin and his wrinkled, beat-up old face.

"Is he no longer around?" she asked.

I nodded slowly, sadly.

"Yeah, he died some years back. Wasn't very old, seventy-something, but I don't think he would have wanted it any other way. He was still doing what he loved. Had a heart attack in the ring. Not boxing, teaching. There could be worse things."

Emily nodded.

"I love what I do, but I wouldn't want to die in my theater."

"That's weird too, not the dying bit, the bit about why it's called a theater. I never got it. You aren't actors performing a play."

I grinned at her and she laughed out loud.

"Well, we don't really call it that anymore here. I think that's maybe more British. But it used to be a theater in a real sense. Way back in the old days, students would literally watch the surgeons operate as if they were in a theater. In fact the set up used to be quite similar to current theaters but much smaller."

"Interesting," I said.

The waitress came back and asked if we wanted anything else. We didn't, so she put the check down in the middle of the table. I reached for it, but I wasn't fast enough. Emily slid it towards herself and smiled at me.

"Anthony, would you please let me get this one? You've paid the last bunch of times."

"And I'm happy to pay for this one too."

"I know, and I love it that you're a gentleman that way, but these are modern times and I'd much rather contribute."

I shrugged and sighed half heartedly.

"Sure, doll, but don't cheap out on the tip," I said teasingly.

She grinned at me.

"I never do," she said and put down some plastic over the paper, not even turning it up to look.

"I've been doing all the talking," I said, "when am I going to hear all about you?"

"I'm not all that interesting. Not like you," she said.

"But you're fascinating to me," I said.

"Well," she said, putting her purse back in her bag, "if you want to have another date then I'll tell you everything you want to know."

"Yeah, like where you live for starters," I said, grinning but also really curious as to why she hadn't shared that information with me yet.

"Next time," she said.

The waitress came by with a handheld card reader and gave it to Emily. Emily paid and left a pretty good tip, at least so I imagined. I walked Emily back to her Prius. Just before she got inside I took her cheek in my hand and kissed her on the lips. She tasted like cherries and coffee. Her mouth was warm and soft like sun-drenched plums. I could have lingered there all afternoon. But I'm a gentleman.

"I was wondering how long it would take for you to kiss me," she said softly, her words like a soft sigh. She caressed my cheek and got into the car. I had nothing to say. I had wanted to kiss that woman all my life, I just never knew it until I'd met her. And until now, if I'm gonna be honest I hadn't the courage.

I watched her drive off and I waved at the back of her car. I saw her wave back. For once in my life, I thought I might just have gotten lucky. I might just have found someone for the ninth inning of my life. I turned and took a walk along the beach. It was quiet and the waves lapped over the sand like the lolling tongues of playful dogs.

CHAPTER TWO

An Event Horizon

I was sitting on my couch in the living room. A new painting was drying off to the side. I was watching TV. There wasn't much good on. Never is. I had flipped around the channels for a while and got stuck on sports. I'm not a huge fan. I like sports well enough. More the playing than the watching. But it was coming up on the World Series. Why they called it that, I had no idea. It was only ever American teams, and maybe the Toronto Blue Jays on a lucky day.

But there it was, highlights from the season. The regular season was now behind us and we were watching highlights. The All-Star Game had been won by the Chicago Cubs, a team that hadn't played in the World Series since 1945. I didn't know any of this, it's what the television man told me. What was worse, or maybe thrilling, was that the Cubs hadn't won since 1908. Winning the All-Star Game meant they'd have hometown advantage, meaning all games would be played at Wrigley Field.

The crazy thing was, they were playing against the Baltimore Orioles. The television man said this was crazy 'cos they were the American League team that hadn't played a World Series in the longest time. At least of AL teams that had made it to the World

Series at least once. Last time The Birds had won was in eighty-three which was also the last time they'd played in the World Series. I could see the appeal. This was likely to be the biggest game in baseball history. Two teams that were the hungriest.

I could see that it would be a big event. Baseball has the largest audience of all the major American sports. That's also what the television man said. At least that was for the regular season. Seventy-something million sad souls glued to the television. That's about one out of every six Americans with nothing better to do.

And I had nothing better to do. I was gonna hang out with the lost souls, I figured, and spend some time drowning my life in that sink of baseball. There were better things to do of course, like paint some paintings, at least they could earn me some money. If any of them sold. And that was always iffy. But still, all work and no play made Anthony a dull boy. That was my excuse.

The thing about baseball is that it was relaxing. You could zone out on the couch and drink a few beers and kill some time. I had to kill some time anyway. Seems those killing each other didn't want my help, so I might as well help kill time. Become the hunter instead of the hunted.

I liked The Cubbies' sad story the best. Like I'd said, they hadn't won in over a hundred years. That's a dry spell. They'd seen the World Series ten times, only won it twice. I liked that, that was a sad and sorry story. I was a sucker for a sorry story, and they had one. I turned to Pirate whose head I was scratching. I could hear him purring like a diesel.

"We're gonna support the Lovable Losers," I said. "How does that sound?"

He looked at me, and if he was a teenager he might have been saying 'whatever'. But he wasn't, and he was another sad story that

I'd clung to. I took the last drag on my cigarette and leaned towards the coffee table that had just held my feet and I put out the cigarette in the ashtray. I picked up my whiskey tumbler and took the last sip.

"Yup," I said to nobody except Pirate, "I think maybe we'll even put a hundred bucks on them, what do you think?"

I didn't look at him, because nobody likes a gambler that can't afford to lose. But I felt a little flush. I hadn't had a loose Benjamin burning a hole in my pocket in quite some time. Yeah, times were lean, what of it. A man's gotta have some hobbies. And my hobby had all but dried up. It'd been a couple of months at least, so I reckon, since I'd seen the hint of a case. And besides, I'd sold a few paintings. Wasn't like Pirate was gonna go hungry or I was gonna go thirsty.

And who knew, I might even be able to make some money on the deal. I knew the Lovable Losers were the underdog and I'm a sucker for underdogs.

My phone vibrated on the coffee table. I looked at its face. It was my old friend and archenemy Johnny Rotten. It might be good news. The kind of news I hadn't heard of for a while. I picked up the phone.

"Johnny Rotten," I said.

"Please step out of the vehicle, sir, with your hands where I can see them," he said, and then burst out laughing.

"Jesus, I'm not in any vehicle, have you been drinking?" I asked with a smile on my mouth.

"Just having some fun with Anthony. How's it been?"

"Slow and lazy. I've been painting a lot. Painting more than I can sell."

"You've gotta get your gallery to fix that," he said.

He'd bought one of my paintings before. Maybe it'd be more accurate to say he stole it. I gave him a sweet deal, he really liked it. I'm a sucker for underdogs and friends. What you gonna do?

"They moved a couple this past month," I said.

"Great news, I guess I can hang up then," he said.

"Hey," I said, "I'm not that flush that I've forgotten my friends."

"What are you doing?" he asked.

"Watching the television man teach me about baseball."

"Ah yeah, the World Series is starting tomorrow. Should be a good game."

"I'm gonna put some money on the Lovable Losers, I think."

"I would hold off on that pal," he said.

"What you got?" I asked.

"I've got some good news for you, bad news for The Cubbies," he said.

"Yeah, what's that?"

"James Ensor is dead. Looks like murder," he said.

"Hmm," I said, "and I'm supposed to know who that is?"

"Any baller worth his mitt would know who that was," said Roberts.

"I'm not just any baller," I said, "in fact I'm not that up on the ins and outs of baseball."

"Might want to brush up," he said. "James, or Jimmy as he was known was their best hope at winning this thing. He's their star pitcher."

"Tell me more," I said, feigning interest.

"This World Series might have recorded his three thousandth strikeout, making him one of the few to reach that club. Less than twenty guys have done it. He's also pitched three no-hitters but not a perfect game."

"Yawn," I said. I could almost hear Roberts shaking his head.

"You need some culture, son," he said, and I could hear the warmth in his voice. "Let me put it to you this way, less than twenty guys in baseball's history, that's over a century, have record three thousand or more strikeouts. Only twenty-three perfect games have been thrown."

"Which he hasn't done," I said, egging him on.

"Yeah, but he was going to. He still had a good ten years left, maybe."

"Then how come the Cubbies keep losing, if their pitcher's so damn good?"

"Because," said Roberts, sighing like I'd popped his balloon, "baseball, in case you hadn't realized, is a team sport."

"Ah, I get it now," I said sarcastically, "so guys can come up with a whole bunch of excuses and blame it on their teammates."

Roberts laughed, he was hard to anger, but then he knew me well.

"Jeez, you sure are grumpy as hell."

"It's been a while since I've had something to do," I said.

"And that's why I'm calling you," he said. "A buddy of mine, the Captain of homicide in Chicago's Central Area needs a hand. Asked me if I knew anyone who could help out a high profile and sensitive homicide like this."

"And you told him I liked dead people?"

"I told him I knew a guy, who worked for peanuts, was a bit of a smart ass but had solved a homicide or two in his tenure."

"Yeah, who was that?"

"Bryce over at Hollywood Station, you ass," he said.

"Good to know, is he interested?"

"Fuck you, Tony," said Roberts, good naturedly. He was one of the few people who could get away with calling me Tony.

"So you're throwing me a frikkin' bone," I said, "thank you, anointed one."

"You're welcome, you ungrateful sonofabitch," he said.

"How's Jenny and the kids?" I asked.

"That's you being nice now," he said.

"Nah, not really, just reminding you never have me over anymore. Am I Quasimodo now or something?"

"You're something alright," he said.

There was a pause on the other end. I heard him talking to somebody else, but I couldn't make it out.

"Listen, pal, I've gotta run. Listen, I'll speak to Jenny about having you over if you do good up in the Windy City. I've vouched for you buddy."

"And I've never let you down. Thanks for the bone... really."

"Don't mention it, do me proud."

He hung up and I decided I needed another Scotch to mull things over. I hadn't been to Chitown in some years. Didn't much like the weather. It was the wind mostly. Wind makes any kind of day just a little shittier. I poured a fresh one, I wasn't counting fingers but it was a two-finger Scotch, a good two-finger Scotch like a Quasimodo pour.

I watched more baseball for the next fifteen minutes under the pretense of research. I came to appreciate the game more, especially that I might now have some skin it, to abuse the pun. If I was going to get paid to learn about baseball then I was the biggest fan. My phone rang and I looked at the screen. It wasn't a number I recognized, but I was answering anyway. It was a 312 area code. My best guess was that came from Chicago. I picked it up and put it to my ear.

"Hello," I said.

"Yeah, I'm looking for Anthony Carrick," said a deep voice that seemed to have travelled with heavy chains, all over the old cobbled streets and through the sewers to end up as deep and tired as this voice sounded popping up in my ear.

"Speaking," I said.

"Hey, Anthony," said the voice, not as tired anymore but still heavy with chains, "this is Captain Maurice Lane from Chicago Homicide. Your friend John Roberts gave me your number."

"Yeah, John's a friend," I said, "said you might be calling. How's things in the Windy City?"

The voice laughed in my ear and it sounded like those chains rattling all over sewer grates.

"Windy," he said. "The winds of desolation have descended upon us just before the World Series. You a fan?"

"I guess I am now," I said.

Again, the gravelly laughter.

"John tells me you work private. Is that right?"

"It is," I said.

"You interested in helping us with a high profile homicide?"

"That's my bread and butter. What you got?"

There was a pause on the other end.

"Listen," he said, "I'd prefer to talk about it one on one, you can understand."

"Discretion is the better part of valor," I said.

"Discretion is the better part of investigation," he said.

"I gotcha."

"But first, I need to know if we can afford you. Our budget's not quite as big as the LAPD's."

"I understand, hell, I'd do it for free, just to get back on the horse," I said, not lying.

"Roberts said you might say something like that," said the voice warm as thick honey. "Still, we will pay you, just need to know if it's something we can afford or am I gonna have to haggle you."

"Did he also say I'd need a slow dance and a pat on the back."

Lane laughed.

"Five hundred a day, plus expenses, you know, like a private plane to pick me up."

The voice laughed again, rattling chains.

"We can do that," he said, "plane's gonna have to be commercial, economy class."

"A fella's gotta try. I like it, when do you want me there?"

"On the next flight," he said. "You can understand this is time sensitive."

"I'll look into it."

Lane cut me off.

"It leaves at three thirty your time, I've already booked it for you."

"That's pretty presumptuous," I said.

"Nah, Roberts said there wasn't a way in hell you were gonna turn this down."

"Gosh darn it, can't we pretend you've been courting me?"

"That's just what I've been doing. I'll pick you up myself. See you later."

"Bye."

He hung up the phone. I stared at it for a while and then put it back on the table. I lit another cigarette and swigged on whiskey. I couldn't tell if I liked Lane or not. I decided I did like him. Wasn't his fault he knew I was going to take the job. Would have done it for free too. My phone told me it was just after one. I had a few things to do before I left and I had to be leaving real quick.

I called the cat sitter. Actually, I just went next door and spoke to Martha. She's a spinster who has two cats of her own. I've used her before. Pirate's always put on a few pounds anytime I leave him to her. She's got a soft spot for cats and him in particular. I can't complain.

Twenty-five bucks a day to take care of my roommate. Peace of mind and he gets fattened up. Only problem is, she's a talker. An old, lonely woman, teetering on crazy cat lady. I don't usually mind, but this time I had to cut her off short.

CHAPTER THREE

Chicago's Windy Blues

O'HARE International Airport goes by the airport code ORD.
Makes me think it might be ordinary. But it's not. The airport is the
busiest in the world at least by landings and takeoffs. I read that in
the inflight magazine. Something the inflight magazine didn't tell
me, but I'd overheard some young punks talking about while we
waited at LAX, was that over one thousand souls have been lost
flying into or out of ORD. That didn't put me at ease. What did
put me at ease were the couple of whiskeys I had on the plane.

We landed at Terminal 3. It was a nice terminal for an airport. I
don't live in them. For me it's just a corridor from one place to the
next, but for those who like to lollygag at airports apparently
O'Hare has won best airport in North America for ten years. I shit
you not. They'll give awards out for anything nowadays. I'm still
waiting for my hardest drinking PI award. Hasn't come in yet.

It was a chilly forty degrees when we landed at just before nine
thirty. No snow, clear skies. At least that's what the captain said.
And he shoulda known, he was flying through it. I made my way
down to the baggage claim. I only had the one suitcase besides my
carry on. I saw a big man holding a placard with what was

supposed to be my name on it. Only it was spelled wrong.

I walked up to him and nodded.

"Maurice Lane," I said.

He nodded and offered me a large meaty hand. I shook it. It was firm and warm. He had a few inches on me. I'd have put him at around six two, maybe six three, but he probably had close to seventy pounds on me. His head was bald and the color of lightly roasted coffee beans. I recognized the voice immediately. His lips curled into easy smiles and his eyes twinkled with mischievousness. They were warm and brown as chestnuts.

"Call me Morrie," he said.

"You butchered my name," I said.

"Yeah, sorry about that, didn't know how it was spelled."

"C A R R I C K," I said. "You were missing the last C."

He nodded.

"Won't happen again, Tony," he said, squeezing my shoulder with his big meaty hands.

"It's Anthony," I said.

He shook his head and then looked at me steadily.

"You're a tough sonofabitch," he said, "but I like your honesty. You don't like nicknames?"

"Just not that one," I said.

"I see," he said. "Listen, I'm a nickname kinda guy, so I'm gonna have to work on one for you."

"I'll give you a hand. I've only ever had one and it was from an old friend."

"Yeah, what's that?"

"Smiling Irish," I said, deadpan.

Lane nodded.

"Smiling Irish. I don't get it," he said, shaking his head back and forth slowly. "You don't look like the smiling type to me."

"I smile at funny things," I said. "More importantly, I smiled a lot in the ring, when I won."

"Alright, I can dig that. So you're a boxer, I respect that. I'm gonna call you Irish. Until I see you smiling, it'll just be Irish."

I nodded and walked over to the carousel where the bags were starting to come by in dribs and drabs. Lane walked with me. He was dressed smart. Looked more like a banker than a cop. He had on a navy blue suit with a deep purple shirt. A dark French blue colored tie with splashes of purple was knotted around his neck with a dimple that his chin had lost. A French blue pocket square stood proudly out of his jacket pocket like a roosters comb. He had on patent leather, shiny black shoes with socks that matched his shirt.

His cufflinks were silver. His Rolex was silver too. That gave me pause on a cop's salary. On his lapel was a silver medallion of some sort of saint.

"Who's that?" I asked, nodding at his lapel.

He touched it softly.

"Saint Jude," he said.

I nodded and turned up my mouth.

"The patron saint of lost and desperate causes," I said. "Is this an omen on the case?"

Lane let out his laugh. It was infectious and I liked to hear it.

"No, no. You're Catholic then?"

I nodded.

"Lapsed," I said.

"Aren't we all? No man, Saint Jude is also the patron saint of the CPD."

I nodded again and looked over at the carousel. My bag was

coming in. I reached in and grabbed it.

"Then perhaps he'll help us," I said. "I'm a sucker for lost causes."

"Let me get you to your hotel," he said. "We're making an early start tomorrow."

I walked with him until we got outside. I turned up the collar on my coat. It was cold. I knew that, I just hadn't felt it until then. Straight out front of the exit was a dark blue M5, similar color to his suit. That was his car. He walked me up to it and put my bag in the trunk. I got in on the passenger side. As we got going he nodded at the security guard patrolling the limited time parking.

"You've got fancy things on a cop's salary," I said.

"You like my car?" he asked.

"It's better than mine," I said.

"What do you drive?" he asked.

"Buick LeSabre," I said. "Some years old."

"American made," he said, nodding out the front windscreen.

"What can I say, I'm a patriot," I said, looking at him. "You like the Germans."

He nodded his head from side to side.

"I like them well enough, it's the engineering I'm really into. This car is the fastest production sedan on the streets."

And he hit the accelerator as if to prove a point. I was sucked back into my seat. A comfortable, warm leather seat, I might add.

"I get the point," I said.

He eased off and merged into traffic as we got out of the airport.

"You still haven't answered my question."

"What's that?" he asked, glancing a look at me.

"It's gotta be tough to afford things like this, even on a captain's salary."

He didn't say anything. I kept my eyes on him. He turned and looked at me briefly. He had his left hand draped over top of the steering wheel. His right was draped over the armrest between us, making him lean in towards me.

"I've got a question for you," he said, grinning. Then he opened up the armrest, looked down at it briefly and pulled out a toothpick which he stuck in the corner of his mouth. "You said you only had one nickname."

I didn't say anything. I remembered what I'd said.

"John tells me that he has a nickname for you to."

Lane looked over at me and raised his eyebrows and tilted his head.

"I still haven't heard any questions," I said, still eyeballing him.

Lane looked back out the window and moved the toothpick to the other side of his mouth using his tongue and lips.

"You're a tough nut," he said. "How come you told me you only ever had one nickname and yet I now know you've had at least two."

He glanced at me. I still hadn't taken my eyes of him.

"Must be I'm a pathological liar," I said, and then I smiled.

He saw it and grinned. Then he slapped his thigh, took the toothpick from his lips and rattled the chain in his throat that bubbled up in laughter.

"Hot damn, you are a sonofabitch," he said. "John told me you didn't take shit."

I didn't say anything. There still weren't any questions asked.

"Sid," he said to me, looking out the windshield, "Sid Vicious. I bet you earned that honestly."

"You can call me Irish or Anthony," I said serious as a punch to the face. I was still eyeballing him, and now my neck was starting to get tired.

"Alright, alright Irish, no need to get antsy about it. Let me ask you a question."

He already had.

"How do you think I got a car like this?"

"Well, you're a lawman," I said, "so you didn't steal it. You've either got a rich old lady or you're on the grift. Most times I've seen it, means you're on the grift. Plus, you aren't wearing no wedding ring."

Lane nodded slowly.

"You're a smart one alright," he said. "And you're right, I ain't married. Was once, didn't work out. Maybe again, who knows what the cards hold. But I ain't crooked, let's get that clear."

He looked at me earnestly. Maybe he was trying to intimidate me, threaten me. Didn't work. I'd been stared down and threatened by gangsters that could carry through and not been intimidated.

"Sure," I said, smiling like a Cheshire cat.

He shrugged.

"Shit, don't matter if you believe or not. I'm gonna tell you how it happened. My old man left me some money when he passed. Owned his own plumbing company. Sold it a while back, retired, then died a few years later. Probably 'cos he was bored. Anyway, left me a good chunk of change and I like to spend it."

I nodded and looked out the front window. Could be legit, could be bullshit. Didn't matter. I was here on the good people of Chicago's dime to investigate a murder, not crooked cops.

"Where's the hotel?" I asked.

"Got you in a Best Western up by Wrigley Field. Something nice but not fancy. Something the taxpayers wouldn't balk at, but at the same time keep you close to the game. Pun not intended."

Lane chewed on the toothpick and drove through the night. Soft jazz was playing on the radio, I recognized the current track as Wes Montgomery's Angel Eyes. It's never cut and dry. Lane might be a bullshitter but he had good taste in music.

"Tell me why I'm here," I said, trying to spark some conversation out of the wet and sorry-looking tinder between the two of us. Lane didn't look at me.

"To learn about baseball," he said, and grinned. "I'm just joking. I'm not a big fan myself. More of a football man."

He glanced over at me and looked me up and down real quick.

"You look like a hockey fan," he said.

"It's alright," I said. "I prefer to be in the game than watching."

"Yeah, I can dig that. That's me too. Though my football days are behind me. Bum knees."

I didn't say anything. Didn't particularly care.

"So James Ensor is the deceased," he said. "One of the best, if not the best, pitchers in the leagues at the moment."

I interjected.

"Almost got three thousand strikeouts, pitched three no-hitters. John gave me his stats."

Lane looked over at me, and nodded. He grinned his big wide grin. I liked it.

"Yeah, this ain't about his game though, this is about his murder."

"Tell me about it. I'm on the clock anyway."

Lane looked over at me again, the toothpick between his lips flicking around like the second hand of a clock.

"Shit man, really? You gonna charge the good people of Chicago for tonight."

"Well, this ain't a date, and if it was you'd be paying. I've been on your time since this afternoon. That's a half day I could've been sunning on the beach."

"Yeah, you white people trying to get as brown as a brother."

He shook his head.

"Looks good on you," I said, "might look good on me too."

Lane looked over and grinned wide.

"My man, you're alright."

"I'm just a brother from another mother," I said. It felt cute at the time.

Lane left out a little laugh. I'd have to try harder.

"Why is CPD looking for outside help on this one?" I asked.

"We need outside help on practically every one, only this one gets the news so the Mayor decides to throw some money at it. Originally he just wanted to bring in the help to cover other cases, but me and the Commander of Grand Central convinced the higher ups they needed to bring in good help to help with this specific case. That's how you got here."

I nodded at the windshield.

"That's awful nice of you," I said recklessly.

"Well, wasn't looking for you. I just trust my buddy John. He knows the best and told me that was you. He hasn't been wrong yet."

"Yeah, I heard you only clear around one third in a good year. That's pretty abysmal."

"You telling me. Is it true what I hear?"

"What's that?" I asked.

"You cleared all cases you were involved in?"

I nodded. Lane looked at me out of the corner of his eye.

"Hot damn," he said, slapping the steering wheel. "How many did you have? Two or three?"

He laughed at that. The joker, thought himself pretty funny.

"Two hundred and thirty-one so far," I said.

That shut him up. He went back to looking out the window at the bleak night sky.

"We got a lot of murders up here," he said after some time, "our guys are going from case to case. Hard to do them all justice."

I didn't say anything.

"Four, five hundred?" I asked.

"Probably over five this year. Not as bad as some years though."

"Worse than others," I said.

"Glass half empty kinda man, hey?" he asked.

"Glass halfway, anyway you look at it," I said.

We drove along for a bit in silence.

"Who found him?" I asked.

"James Ensor?"

I nodded.

"A teammate, later that evening. Went to see why he hadn't come in from practice. James was throwing some balls in the net at the field. Around nine thirty, Darian Stark comes by to look for him. Sees him dead on the field by the pitcher's practice net. Called it in."

"What position does this Darian play?" I asked.

"I know what you're thinking, sometimes it's the person that finds the body is the one that murdered the body. We know that."

"Yup, but that's not what I'm asking."

"Darian's a pitcher. Hasn't been getting a lot of play lately."

"Right, so this is gonna be a good deal for him," I said.

Lane nodded.

"Yeah, most likely. He's their second best one."

"What did your guys see when they got there."

"James Ensor, dead on the field. Double tap to the chest area. Probably close proximity, but no GSR on his clothing. Arm's broken pretty good too."

"Which one?" I asked.

"His pitching arm."

I nodded.

"Could be related," I said.

"Could be," he said.

"This would've been on Monday, right?"

Lane nodded. He pulled into the Best Western entrance and stopped the car outside the main entrance. It was a clean, unpretentious hotel. I was surprised to be getting any hotel this close to Wrigley Field this close to the World Series. Lane leaned in and looked at me.

"World Series was supposed to start tomorrow, but with this murder and all, they've postponed the start until Friday. It'd be nice to have this wrapped up by then."

I shook my head at him.

"Unlikely," I said. He shrugged.

"I'm giving you the pep talk the mayor gave us. Detectives Jeramie Jackson and Bradley Dykes will pick you up tomorrow at eight sharp. They're two of our best, and I figure you'll like working with them. You probably won't be seeing a bunch of me unless you're not getting the results we're expecting."

Lane reached into his inside jacket pocket and pulled out a business card and handed it to me. The toothpick was still stuck in the side of his mouth. I looked at the card. Then he offered me his hand and I shook it.

"Any questions?" he asked.

I looked at him for a moment.

"What was your father's business called?"

He looked at me and then looked away.

"Shit, man. Any questions about the case?"

I looked at him for a while and then slowly shook my head. He didn't answer mine. He was a lying sonofabitch and I wasn't sure why. I got out of the car and leaned in from the open door.

"Take care," I said, "you never know how long the good times'll last."

He looked at me and his eyes narrowed.

"John vouched for you," he said. "I'm hoping it wasn't misplaced, because that's on me. Just stick to your knitting."

I closed the door and went to retrieve my bag from the trunk. I watched him drive off without even the smallest wave. I wasn't sad about it. I just wondered how many times he'd be seen driving that fancy car when I was done with the Windy City.

CHAPTER FOUR

Green Grass Of Wrigley Field

I was waiting in the lobby of the hotel on Wednesday morning. It was seven thirty and I was reading the local paper. The front page of the Chicago Tribune didn't have much to say about the ongoing investigation of James Ensor. The paper was conservative, as most large citied papers seemed to be. The front page news had returned to world events, which I wasn't much interested in. Primarily because they were always so depressing but also because there wasn't much I could do about it. But maybe most importantly today, I was on the job, and my focus was finding out about James Ensor. I read the City and Sports sections. They had coverage on Ensor.

I didn't learn a whole lot more than what I already knew. Everyone was hoping for his three thousandth strikeout during the series. Fans were upset. Some even doubted the CPD would solve his homicide. That was amongst the more salty diehard Chicagoans. It was honestly earned. The homicide clearance rates would make a gangster rejoice and the Chief of Police cry like a baby. Not that I'd seen it.

The Lovable Losers played in the National League, what that

meant, I found out, was that the pitcher didn't get a designated hitter. Didn't mean much to me, but in many leagues the pitcher only pitched. I didn't get it, but there it was.

I also found out Ensor had won two Cy Young awards as well as Rookie of the Year and MVP. I had to admit I didn't know much about him. Heck, I hadn't even been familiar with his name. That was on me. I didn't watch much sports, but you knew that already. His career ERA was 2.49. This was putting him in a race with Clayton Kershaw of the LA Dodgers. That was a name I knew.

What the newspaper man was saying in effect, was that Ensor would probably go down as the second best ERA leader in the modern era of baseball. He was older than Kershaw by almost eleven years, and generally, a pitcher's ERA doesn't improve with age, it usually slips. I wasn't gonna get into any arguments about that. Baseball fans are hardcore and opinionated, I'd leave the arguments to the professionals. I was just learning the stats as they stood.

James Ensor wasn't a bad hitter either. At least for a pitcher. That was also in the paper. The writer I was getting most of this from was the sports writer Zak Brookes. I figured I might have a talk with him. He might have some information about the game and specifically Ensor that might come in handy.

I was just finishing up the paper when two badly dressed bankers walked into the lobby. They wore the gray suits of homicide cops. I don't know why they preferred gray. Maybe it was the color of dreariness that suited the job. Maybe it was a metaphor for murder, the gray area where most crimes are committed. Maybe I'm being too deep. Maybe gray suits are just more common and cheap. Yeah, that must have been it. They looked around the lobby looking for me. It was going to be hard. The lobby was busy. This was the start of the World Series after all.

I stood up and nodded at them. They walked over. They looked like the odd couple. Bradley Dykes, if I was to guess, was the white cop. It seemed like a white boy's name. He was tall. Around six two and thin as a rake. He also had his gun on his waist. I could see that through his jacket. He had orange hair, short cut and a pale face that was wrinkled more than it should've been. I'd peg him in his fifties, but he might have been forties.

Jeramie Jackson was the African American. I did that by exclusion. These are the detective powers I have. He was average height but thick. Thick with muscle and fat. He had short hair closely cropped so it looked like not much more than a frame around the top of his head. The way he carried his left arm slightly away from his body meant he carried his piece in a shoulder holster.

Bradley gave me his hand and I shook it. He didn't smile. He didn't have to. I saw his badge on the front of his waist. His name was spelt D Y K E S. I grinned, and looked him in the eye.

"Detective Dykes," he said. He was sucking on a mint.

I nodded and shook his hand. He had a soft handshake like clutching a small bean bag.

"I didn't get that from the spelling," I said, smiling. He had pronounced it like everyone had up to this point as 'Dax'.

He didn't smile, but Jackson let out a chuckle. Dykes looked over at him unimpressed, then he looked back at me.

"It's pronounced, 'Dax'," he said like it was a fact he'd known all his life.

"I get it. I mean where else could you go with it. Dykes obviously won't work, 'Dicks' is just as bad, but 'Dax', now that's a stretch."

"If you're going to keep taking the piss out of my name, we're gonna have a problem, me and you. It's Norwegian," he said, "of Viking origin." We weren't holding hands anymore.

I nodded, pretending to be impressed. Jackson had a big smile on his face. He also had a gold tooth that was his left upper incisor.

"Detective Jeramie Jackson," he said, "he's Bradley by the way."

"I got that, thanks," I said, shaking his hand.

Jackson had a plain face. It was round and undistinguished. The only thing that stood out was his haircut and his incisor. He looked to be in his forties.

"How long you been on the job?" I asked.

Jackson was the chatty one.

"Almost twenty-five years for both of us. Bradley here's been in homicide six years, this is my fifth."

I nodded.

"You ready to go?" asked Dykes.

I nodded, and I walked with the three of them out the front door to their obviously unmarked police Crown Vic. It was the same shit brown as my LeSabre. I felt sad for some reason. Dykes got into the driver's seat. He pulled out a roll of Lifesavers and popped another one in his mouth.

"Dykes says he never got teased about his name in school," said Jackson. "Apparently his family has been pronouncing it 'Dax' for a long time."

"That's the proper pronunciation," he said. I detected no emotion in his voice.

Jackson was turned around to look at me in the backseat. Dykes was driving. I nodded at Jackson.

"I get it," I said, "nobody calls me Tony except my mother, and that's only when she's happy."

Jackson laughed out loud, and turned around to face the front.

"You guys been partners long?" I asked.

I saw the back of Jackson's head nod up and down.

"Since I got on homicide," he said. "Dykes taught me everything I've since forgotten. Lane tells me you're the best."

"The best at what?"

"You've got a good record. That's why they've paid for you to come out here."

"I did alright, when I did my dime in LA."

"Ten years in homicide?"

"No, seven years. Had to work the street for three years."

"Shit, man, you serious?"

Jackson turned around and looked at me. He was still grinning at me with that gold tooth. I nodded at him.

"Man, I never heard of that." Then he looked over at Dykes. "You ever heard something like that?"

Dykes shook his head. Jackson turned back round to look at me.

"Took me nineteen years to get into homicide," he said. "Seven years on the street, then vice, then domestic violence, then major crimes and then and only then I got onto homicide. What did you do?"

"I guess I got lucky," I said. "I'm good with puzzles."

"Or you kissed the right ass," he said.

I gave him a look, that told him I'd kiss him with a knuckle if he didn't mind himself.

"I'm just kidding with you. Just never heard nothing like it."

I didn't hold any hard feelings.

"Neither had LAPD, haven't since either."

Jackson was facing forward again.

"So what happened after ten years?" he asked.

"I fell out of favor with the brass."

Jackson nodded his head thoughtfully.

"You a fan of the game?"

"Not really, but if it means anything I was gonna put a Benjamin on your team here."

Jackson nodded.

"Why's that?"

"The Lovable Losers had the sorriest story I'd heard. I'm a sucker for sad luck stories."

Jackson laughed again.

"Yeah, well it's gonna be a good one, though we'll probably lose because of this murder of The Baller."

"The Baller?"

"Yeah, that was Ensor's nickname."

"I thought it was someone who played basketball?"

"Yeah, it is, but it's also been used to mean anyone making it out of the streets and into the pros at baseball too."

"So Ensor came from the wrong side of the tracks?" I asked.

"No man, it's just a nickname. Starts off from that meaning but then just comes to be a nickname. He's made a good living out of playing ball, but he's also known for his strikeouts, and you know how a batter doesn't usually strike at balls, well, because he's got, had, so many strikeouts fans started figuring that batters thought they were seeing balls. So he became The Baller. Anyway, shit, takes the magic out of it having to explain it to you."

"So you're a big fan?"

"Nope, just know the game a little."

"What about Silent Red over here, the Viking?" I asked.

I saw Dykes look over at me from the rearview. He didn't have an expression on his face.

"He doesn't much like nicknames," said Jackson. "But damn if I

46

don't like Silent Red the Viking."

Jackson laughed. Dykes didn't say anything.

"You mad at me?" I asked the man in the rearview mirror wearing black cop shades. Still nothing.

"He ain't mad," said Jackson, "he just doesn't say much 'til he's sussed you out."

"I figured you might be mad they're bringing in outside help to piss on your parade."

"Nah man, that's all good. Gonna be our collar anyhow."

"True."

We sat in silence the rest of the way. That wasn't too long. Already by the time I'd shut up, I could see Wrigley Field's stooped shoulder up ahead. It looked like the home of a team that had gotten used to being the bridesmaid, and never the bride. Dykes pulled into the parking lot off of North Clark Street. We all got out. I looked around. This was hallowed ground, if you were a baseball fan. I wasn't. For me, this was a crime scene. I took it all in, just like any other crime scene.

Problem with this one was the location. Outdoors, a huge place. Dollars to donuts evidence would be hard to come by. We walked towards the main entrance.

"We're gonna show you the scene first. That cool?" asked Jackson.

"Cool," I said.

Jackson walked with an easy gate. Dykes walked like he was a robot.

"So you never lost a case?" asked Jackson. "That's what we heard."

"I've lost plenty, if that's what you mean. Sometimes the DA has his head up his ass. Never left a case unsolved if that's what you mean."

"Yeah, that's what we heard. Over two hundred. Is that right?"

"This'll be two hundred and thirty-three, all going well," I said.

"If we get the collar," said Dykes.

"He speaks," I said, grinning at him. Nothing. He was going to be a tough nut to crack. Jackson was all smiles. He was easy.

"Hot damn," Jackson said, "two hundred thirty-three. We'll make sure this one gets solved."

"It will," I said.

Dykes stopped as we got into the entrance. He turned to me, taking his shades off and looking me straight in the eyes with pale blue eyes that looked the color and distance of lost skies.

"How can you be so sure?" he asked. "If there's something I hate worse than murders it's arrogant cops."

"It's not arrogant if you can back it up," I said.

"Look," I continued, standing and looking up at him. "You guys are overworked, chasing leads all over this Windy City as the direction changes. I get it. But ninety-nine times out of a hundred murders happen for simple reasons. And thank God for that. Very seldom are we dealing with random events. And when we are, you've just gotta find the impetus that pushed it."

"So you think you've figured this out already?" asked Dykes.

I nodded.

"Somebody had a beef with Ensor," I said. "Likely a whole bunch of people. We've just gotta figure out the best beef with the best sauce."

Jackson shook his head.

"Sauce?"

"Yeah," I said, turning to look at him. "Sauce. The person with the beef but also the spicy temperament to follow through. Let's see what we got."

I turned to go. Dykes and Jackson led me through the concourse and out onto the field. Wrigley Field wasn't designed to be anything other than a baseball field. As such, it was nothing but concrete and steel and urinals. Plus the prerequisite cameras in this age of surveillance and the nanny state.

We got out onto the field and walked towards the catcher's box. I looked up towards the pitcher's mound.

"That's further than I realized," I said, looking towards the pitcher's mound. Jackson followed my gaze.

"Yeah. Sixty feet and six inches from the back of home plate," he said.

I looked at him and grinned.

"You are a fan," I said.

He turned and grinned at me.

"I having a passing interest," he said.

"How high is it?" I asked him.

"Can't be more than ten inches higher than home plate."

"Why do they call it home plate?" I asked. "Guys eating lunch here before they go to bat?"

I grinned at him. He slapped me on the shoulder.

"I have no idea, but that's actually a pretty good question," he said.

We walked off towards the left, towards third base where the Lovable Losers had their dugout. Just before we got there, Dykes stopped and turned towards the stadium, where the fans would be gathered in a couple of days.

"This is where Ensor was found," he said.

I looked at the grass. There was nobody there. There was also no chalk outline. I sighed.

"I don't see anyone," I said.

"You've got to imagine," said Jackson. "We all see dead people."

I game him a sad soft smile. It was a try, but it wouldn't have made it to home plate.

"Hell, I don't even know what the guy looked like except what I've seen on TV and in the papers."

"That's what he looked like," said Dykes.

I grinned and nodded.

"That's helpful," I said. "Case solved. It was really James Ensor who was found here dead. Great."

"Walk me through the scene?" I asked.

Dykes took a few steps forward.

"He was lying here face up. His face was towards the dugout here, almost parallel with it. His right arm was twisted at an odd angle due to it having been broken. His head was looking off that way."

Dykes waved towards the stands.

"His right knee was pointing towards the stands too. His left leg was straight out. A baseball was found a couple of yards from his right hand. His baseball hat was off to the right of him too. Double tap in the chest. Close range but no GSR. Either shot would have been fatal from what the coroner tells us."

Dykes looked over at me and then at Jackson.

"Anything else?" he asked his partner, as he stood with his hands on his sides.

Jackson shrugged.

"What else was around here. I figure he was out practicing, right?"

Dykes nodded, and pointed off to our left, away from the dugout.

"Right. About seventy feet away was a pitcher's net. It had around a dozen balls dotted around it."

"So he was practicing. How many balls exactly?" I asked.

"Is that really important?" Dykes asked.

"Probably not," I said, "but it tells me how diligent your people are."

Dykes shook his head and looked over at Jackson.

"We're thorough, that's why we're amongst the best in homicide," he said.

"That's swell," I said, "so we're all the best standing in Wrigley Field having a pissing contest."

Dykes nodded at Jackson who took out a notebook. Jackson reefed through a few pages.

"Baker's dozen," he said.

"What?" I asked.

"Baker's dozen, thirteen, that's how many balls were by the net."

"See, that wasn't hard."

"You could have counted them yourself with the photos," said Dykes.

I grinned at him.

"Except I haven't been hired as your accountant."

Dykes didn't say anything. He was tough as Brazil nut shells and just as smooth. He looked back down towards his feet.

"Blood on the grass suggests he was shot here and not moved," he said.

He looked at the ground as if Ensor might as well be lying there. He wasn't. I checked. In another location we might have been a couple of clowns kicking tires and talking cars. But we weren't.

"What kind of bullet did we find?" I asked trying to join the conversation with the royal and archaic we. Dykes looked up at me.

"Nine millimeter Luger."

"Type of gun?"

"Don't know that yet," said Dykes, taking another Lifesaver spearmint candy from the roll and popping it in his mouth. The roll was half eaten by this point. He hadn't offered me nor his partner any. I nodded at him.

"And what time was this at?" I asked.

"Lane never told you?" asked Dykes.

"I'm asking you."

Dykes nodded at Jackson and turned round and kicked at the grass where the imaginary Ensor was. Jackson didn't need his notebook for this one.

"Coroner puts it between eight and nine pm."

I nodded at him.

"That was Monday night right?"

Jackson nodded.

"Nobody was here when he was found?" I asked.

Looked like Jackson and I were having a private conversation now.

"Not that we know of. Most of the guys were leaving when Stark..." Jackson looked at his notes again. "Darian Stark came out to see if Ensor was gonna join them at the bar that evening."

"You took his statement?"

Jackson nodded again.

"Says what you'd expect from him. Found the body like Dykes says. Checked for pulse and then placed the 911 call."

"What time did that call come in?"

Jackson glanced at his notes. Flipped his pages back and forth a bit.

"Nine thirty-three."

I nodded.

"And he has an alibi?"

Jackson shrugged.

"Haven't looked into that yet. Haven't interviewed any of the teammates yet. You think he's a suspect?"

"Everyone's a suspect Jackson, until they alibi out. Plus, I bet he's got skin in the game too. What position did he play?"

Jackson didn't have to look at his notes. He's not a baseball fan, you understand, but he knows some things about the game.

"He's a relief pitcher. A left-handed specialist. The Cubbies like to bring him in sometimes when Ensor needs a break and it throws the other team for a loop."

"How's that?"

"Well, he's a leftie. Ensor's right-handed, so it takes a bit of an adjustment to hit against a leftie."

I nodded, and turned to look towards Dykes.

"This is the only practice area here. Right out here at this iconic field," I said, waving out towards the stands and towards the main entrance behind the pitcher's box.

Jackson grinned at me.

"Nah man, you're thinking about the bullpen. They moved that under the bleachers. You enter up there."

He pointed to it with the notebook in his hand. It was way off to the right of us at the end of the bleachers.

"You want to see it?"

"Not unless it's part of the crime scene."

Dykes turned around again, his black aviator glasses still on his face. I was squinting at him. I could have used a pair of sunglasses but I didn't have any. I should have brought my fedora, but I forgot.

"It's not part of the crime scene," said Dykes.

He pulled out his diminishing roll of Lifesavers and carefully unwrapped the outer layers from it. He thrust it out at me.

"Take one," he said.

I did. I was polite that way. Jackson smiled and nodded.

"Alright," said Jackson, "we can all be friends now."

I looked at him as Jackson took a spearmint candy with the hole in it.

"When he offers you a spearmint that means he likes you."

Jackson was smiling big and wide like he was proud of the two of us. I nodded at Dykes. He nodded back. I felt special. Almost like I'd been invited to the prom.

"How do you know the bullpen isn't part of the crime scene?" I asked.

"Because we looked, and CSPU looked and found nothing," said Dykes.

"CSPU?" I asked.

"Crimes Scenes Processing Unit," offered Jackson helpfully.

"SID," I said.

"Huh?" grunted Dykes.

"Scientific Investigation Division at LAPD. Same thing," I said.

Jackson nodded. Dykes looked at me as if I'd spoken something in Greek which had just wasted a moment of his life.

"So Stark would do better if Ensor wasn't in the picture. Is that fair?" I asked, looking at Jackson. The fan who wasn't. He nodded.

"Yeah, you could say that. But you could say that about any of the pitchers for the Cubbies," he said. "They'd all have better chances of getting noticed."

I frowned at him.

"How many pitchers do they have?"

"Over twenty last I counted."

I looked at him as if he'd just told a bald faced lie to a priest during confession.

"Nah man, that's serious. For games they'll have half of their players on the roster being pitchers. Pitchers is the meat and potatoes of baseball. Check this out. Our deceased, Ensor, he cost the Cubbies around twenty percent of their player payroll."

I shook my head sadly.

"But a good pitcher is worth every penny," said Jackson. "It's much harder than it looks. It's hard on the body, the arm especially, and they've gotta be good each and every game to earn their keep. Plus they've gotta be diversified with the kinds of balls they can throw..."

I'd heard enough.

"And you say you're not a fan," I grinned at him.

"Man, you should hear some of the fans," he said. "They've got all the opinions and they're always right. At least so they think."

I looked around.

"And how much did Ensor make?" not really wanting to know the answer as soon as the question had come out of my mouth.

"Twenty-five mill last year, but his contract was being renewed. Some were putting him at double that for the next three years."

I shook my head. Dykes had been watching us back and forth.

"Not worth it," he said.

Jackson looked at him.

"Worth it if the fans pay it," he said.

"Really?"

"Really."

"You're not a fan then?" I asked Dykes.

"Nah man, he's just sore 'cos he never made it to the big leagues," said Jackson.

55

"You were a player?" I asked.

Dykes nodded.

"Got injured in college. My shoulder. I was a pitcher and I was being scouted. Problem as I see it, is you throw all this money at these guys and ninety-nine times out of a hundred they choke the next year. It makes them soft."

"That's not always true," said Jackson.

Dykes looked at him.

"That's why I said ninety-nine times out of a hundred."

"I appreciate you guys want to argue about baseball. I frankly don't care. What I do care about is wrapping this up so I can go back home to where it's warm and drink my Irish whiskey and watch girls roller blade along the boardwalk in bikinis."

They both looked at me. Then Jackson looked at Dykes.

"Sounds like a pretty good deal to me. Is the LAPD hiring?"

"I wouldn't know about that," I said. "Tell me something though, before we move on. How come a guy that earns twenty-five million a year can't win a World Series. Seems to me he's overpaid then."

I was looking at Jackson.

"That's what I'm getting at," said Dykes.

Jackson shrugged.

"How many murders do you think can remained unsolved before you get booted off homicide. Could you go ten unsolved homicides in a row and still keep your job?"

Dykes shook his head.

"Probably not, but then again, this is Chicago and solving homicides hasn't seemed to be a priority for brass."

He grinned. It was the first time I'd seen him grin.

"That's not exactly true. We just haven't had the political will or the money," Jackson said.

"Your budget's almost as big as LA's," I said. "And you've got about twenty percent more officers. And LA has about fifty percent more population."

I looked at them then for a while. I'd done a bit of research before I came out.

"And to rub salt in your wounds, you had about a hundred less homicides last year than we did."

I grinned at them like I'd won first prize at the Science Fair. Jackson shrugged. He wasn't feeling so chipper anymore.

"That's a fair comment," said Dykes. "Though we clear greater than sixty percent of our cases. And that's good for CPD Homicide."

"I never said I believe that Ensor deserved the money he's getting. I'm not necessarily a fan, but if that's what the market will bear, then what you gonna do?"

"Except that's not what the market will bear, because all these owners keep getting public funds to renovate, build their stadiums, repair infrastructure. I've seen it all the time. It's bullshit. But I don't want to debate it with you. Let's get back to the homicide."

Dykes grinned at Jackson.

"This guy's alright," he said. "What do you want to do now?" he asked me.

"I noticed a whole bunch of surveillance cameras when we walked in and out here in the stadium. Did you get any footage off of any of it?"

Dykes shook his head.

"The cameras aren't on twenty-four seven. They only roll them on game days."

"That's helpful," I said.

"Not really," said Dykes.

He pulled out his roll of Lifesavers and offered me one again. I declined. Jackson took one though.

CHAPTER FIVE

CPD Headquarters

THE City of Chicago Public Safety Headquarters is an uninspired municipal building built by politicians without any sense of the creativity you might find in architects. It's five stories high and is located on the corner of eighty-fifth and Michigan. Dykes parked on the street and we all walked into the dour facade. It was faced with a few trees and a square or two of green grass. Other than that it reminded me of all the bureaucratic uninspired government buildings you'd find in any city in this overly bureaucratic country.

We went up to the fifth floor and into a large office space dotted with desks that looked like the floating wreck of an old ship on the ocean of black tile. At the one end was a room we walked into that looked like a small conference room. A table and some chairs were in the middle. Against the length of one wall was a whiteboard and opposite it was a bank of windows that looked out over Michigan Avenue. The whiteboard had all the details about the homicide of Ensor that CPD had gathered to that point.

"That's what we call the puzzle box," said Dykes.

"I call it a whiteboard," I said. Dykes smiled at me.

"Better than a murder board," he said. "We know what we're

investigating, right?"

He was looking at his partner. Jackson grinned and nodded.

"Yeah," he said, "those Hollywood shows always like the extra drama. Am I right?"

He was looking at me. I shrugged.

"I don't work for Hollywood," I said. "But they don't always like to stick to the facts. Can't blame them. Sometimes the facts aren't dramatic enough, I suppose."

Times must have been tough for Chicago PD. Green marker had been used to divide the whiteboard into ten vertical strips. I counted them and that's how many there were. All strips had the name of the homicide victim on them as well as a case number. Ours was the latest case and as such, next to the door.

"These all yours?" I asked.

Jackson nodded.

"Yeah, but this is the one we're working on now. The others are on hold on account of how important this particular case is."

I was looking at mostly white space. At the top left of the little rectangle was a picture of the dead Ensor. A picture that the coroner probably took without much forethought for lighting or even makeup. If you thought DMV pictures were terrible, you ain't seen nothing until your dead mug is captured.

There was a short timeline at the bottom that started at eight pm on the previous Monday night. The times between eight and nine were bracketed and above the bracket was written 'TOD'. Next on the timeline was nine thirty-three, the time Stark called 911. Other than that the board was clear.

"What have you guys been doing?" I asked.

Dykes looked at me.

"Been waiting for the hotshot from LA," he said.

I grinned at him. He didn't say anything else, so I looked at Jackson. He was looking at me.

"We've got a file on the case. Let me go get it."

He got up and left.

"I think if we used one of his official headshots from the team it might brighten this place up a little," I said to Dykes.

"We work with what we've got. I'm not wasting time hunting down a prettier picture of the deceased because the one we got hurts your eyes."

"I didn't say it hurts my eyes," I said as Jackson walked back in carrying a manila folder.

"What hurts?" he asked.

"Carrick figured we should get a prettier picture of Ensor. One of his headshots from the club," said Dykes.

Jackson nodded his head.

"That's a good idea. I like it," he said. "I can probably arrange that."

I looked over at Dykes and smiled some more. Jackson put the manila folder on the table in the middle of the room and opened it up. There was a picture of Ensor, like the one on the whiteboard. There was a picture of Stark, taken off the website of the Cubs most likely. It was a prettier picture as Dykes had called it. There was also a yellow page of loose notes. I took a look at the notes. There wasn't much on it that impressed me.

It was handwritten in either a doctor's or a lawyer's scribble, and yet it was likely penned by either Dykes or Jackson. It was terrible handwriting for a cop, and I'd seen bad cop penmanship. Every couple of lines on the page was a one word question. 'Who?', 'What?', 'Where?', 'When?', 'Why?' and 'How?'. The how, what, where and when were filled in.

Ensor was shot with a nine millimeter Luger bullet. That partially answered the how, and maybe a bit of the what. As in what happened to him and how did it happen. We needed more, like what kind of gun we were looking for. The where was obvious. He was shot in Wrigley Field and that was the answer to the question, written down on the yellow page. We also knew the when which was between eight and nine on Monday. We needed to know who killed him and why they killed him. Knowing the why might help us tease out more of the what. As in what transpired to cause his murder.

"We need to start shaking some trees," I said.

"How's that?" asked Jackson.

"These notes are sparse," I said, trying to be kind. "We need to start talking to people and finding out the whys. We need motives and means and reasons for this treason."

Jackson shook his head as he looked at Dykes. Dykes shrugged.

"Who have you spoken to besides Stark?" I asked.

"We're setting up interviews over the next few days," said Jackson.

I shook my head.

"No, that's not gonna work. We're going to start interviews right now. Jesus, we've got a homicide here, we lead the investigation, we don't allow anyone to get their bearings. We grab them at inopportune times to keep them unsteady and under pressure."

"Well, we've got the wife coming in this morning. She should be here any minute actually," said Jackson, looking at his watch.

"After that," I said, "I'm going to start rattling the batting cages. I want to speak to the coach, the manager and the bat boy. And I want to do that today."

Dykes nodded with an upturned mouth.

"Sounds good," he said. "In the meantime, why don't we get a coffee before the wife comes in."

I nodded. Seemed fair enough considering she'd be here any minute and I wasn't going anywhere.

CHAPTER SIX

What's For Money Honey?

WE sat around talking shop for a while in the conference room, staring at pictures of dead people and drinking coffee. The coffee wasn't half bad. Dykes and Jackson were coffee snobs and the little place round the corner was an independent business selling fair trade and organically grown coffee. Dykes brought for everyone. He hadn't been eating Lifesavers since we got to headquarters after leaving the ball park.

She was supposed to be here by noon. It was noon thirty before she showed up.

"This is why you lead the investigation," I said to deaf ears as we walked out of the conference room to greet her. She had been chaperoned up by a uniformed member.

She had an air of entitlement around her that reeked worse than her expensive perfume. I didn't like her and I hadn't even met her yet. Yeah, I judge like that sometimes. And I can't remember the last time I was wrong. We walked up to her. Dykes in the middle, Jackson to his left and me to the right, slightly back. I preferred to observe. There was a balding, older man with her. His hair had fallen to the sides of his head were it clung precariously to the white cliffs of his scalp. The hair was the walnut brown you only see on walnuts or hair dye products for men. The bad kind. He was too old to have naturally brown hair. But both his tufts on the side and the wispy eyebrows above his eyes were dyed with the very same paint. He had on round glasses that were too big for his face and a beige suit that fit well. He was slim except for a belly that he carried like a pregnant woman.

Dykes offered his hand to the woman. She didn't take it. She clasped her hands in front of her. I noticed they were heavy twigs to show off the gold and diamonds. It was hard to tell which hand held the engagement ring. Both her left and right ring fingers had obscene crystal and gold on them. She was a pretty, leggy blond and she looked me right between the eyes. She was tall, but she wore high heels even though her red T-shirt and blue jeans offered a more casual look.

I didn't know much about fashion, but I figured she probably wore over a thousand dollars in just the clothes. Add to that her handbag, and shoes and she was wearing more money than I'd seen in several months of hard work. Throw in the earrings, rings and necklace and she could have bought me outright. If I was for sale.

The older man with her stepped up and shifted his brown leather case to his left hand and shook Dykes' hand.

"Frederic Salisbury," he said, "without the k. I'm representing Celia Ensor."

"Detective Bradley Dykes," said Dykes, and then pointing to Jackson. "This is my partner Detective Jeramie Jackson."

Salisbury and Jackson shook hands. Then Salisbury looked me up and down like I was the catch of the day.

"That's Anthony Carrick, he's a private investigator from LA we've brought in to help us with the case."

"I see," said Salisbury, looking at me, but talking to Dykes. "You're hoping for better luck on this one."

We shook hands. He had a surprisingly firm handshake for someone who looked like a nerd filled douchebag.

"Please come this way," said Dykes.

I turned to let the two of them follow Dykes and Jackson. I followed them. Celia was a slim woman with a bum as firm and as tight as sun baked plums. She was the kind of woman who'd never notice a fella like me. She had a laser focus and that focus was dialed in to money. She was expensive arm candy and I wondered if Ensor knew it. She must have cost a small fortune. Watching her pass by me without any indication that she knew I was there, I wondered if anything about her was real. The only thing I came up with was her arrogant air of entitlement. The rest was plastic and wax.

We entered a separate conference room that was plain and held no whiteboard. It also had a digital camera in it on a tripod. I was happy for that. In the middle was a desk. Dykes gestured for the two of them to sit on the opposite side of the camera. Dykes and Jackson took the two seats in front of them. I stood to the side. Dykes reached over and turned on the recorder.

"Detective Bradley Dykes, Detective Jeramie Jackson, consultant Anthony Carrick," he said, turning the camera on each of us in turn.

"This is the first interview of Mrs. Celia Ensor and her legal representative Frederic Salisbury..."

Dykes went on to add the date, the case number and both his and Jackson's badge numbers. In front of him he had a pad of paper. Jackson had his notebook, and both were ready to take notes.

"As you can imagine," offered Salisbury, "my client is here to help, even though she is deeply devastated by the death of her husband."

"I can see that," I said sarcastically. I should have kept it in my mind instead. Nevertheless, she shot me a look with cold blue eyes. She wasn't sad. If she was, I'd never seen anyone express it so vacantly as she was. Salisbury looked at me like he was the principal at the school where I was the insolent SOB schoolboy. Then he turned to look at Dykes.

"Unless you're willing to charge my client with something, please let me remind you that we are here at our leisure and not yours."

He smiled thinly at Dykes. Dykes nodded.

"I do apologize for the help. He's not used to the professionalism that the CPD affords people of your stature."

Dykes said it sincerely. But I'd already known him well enough to realize he was dripping with sarcasm. He was good. It made me sad for his close rates. Salisbury nodded.

"With respect," said Dykes, "we'd just like to ask Mrs. Celia Ensor a few questions related to the death of her husband."

Salisbury looked at his client and nodded at her.

"Please call me Celia," said Mrs. Ensor to Dykes, in a breathy voice I'd only ever heard on commercials for late night chats with lingerie dressed women at a dollar ninety-nine a minute. I'd never called them myself, mind you. But you got the flavor of it in the commercials.

"We're sorry for your loss," said Dykes as if he were juggling a hot potato in his bare mitts. She smiled at him and looked down and frowned pretending as if she might cry. She didn't. Of course she didn't. I even wondered if she could. Maybe she was a new model of android without the duct work for tears. I didn't like her. But I knew that already when it turned twelve oh five. But did she kill her husband? That was a tougher call to make.

"May I ask you how long you and James were married?" asked Dykes.

Her bottom lip quivered as if it were strung to tight.

"James and I..." she said before looking down and squeezing her eyes shut a few times before a tear trickled down and she made a motion of reaching in her handbag for a tissue.

We all sat, I stood, and watched the performance. It might have passed for a low budget porn shoot with vapid storyline but she wasn't winning Oscars.

"I'm sorry," she said, looking back at Dykes and batting her eyes at him. He smiled at her warmly, but there was no real interest in it. "It's just still so real."

Dykes nodded.

"I understand," he said. "Take your time."

She dabbed at her dry eyes again. Not even her mascara had been fooled by the fake tears.

"Jimmy and I had just had our second anniversary in July."

Dykes and Jackson smeared blue ink all over their papers and notebook. I just watched from the sidelines.

"You must understand that in our line of work we have to ask difficult questions," said Dykes.

Celia nodded and looked down at her lap while she fiddled with her tissue.

"Was your marriage happy?" he asked.

She looked up at him. She wasn't offended. She nodded her head.

"We were very happy," she said. She put her tissue into her

handbag and put her hands palm down on the table in front of her. "Jimmy brought me a matching set of rings for our second anniversary. They're identical to my engagement and wedding ring."

Looking at them side by side, they did indeed look identical. I didn't smile. Dykes offered a smile as weak as last Sunday's tea.

"That's very generous of him," he said.

Celia smiled. It was insincere. You could tell by the lack of warmth in the eyes. The lack of smile at the corners of her eyes. The creases were the eyelids meet and crinkle. Some people call them wrinkles. I call them the irony of years. You have to smile to get through even a few months, let alone the monotonous and dreary foot soldiers that some call the years.

"How did the two of you meet?" asked Dykes.

He was a talkative fella now. Jackson sat almost mute. Perhaps Dykes liked her. Though I hadn't seen him offer her a Lifesaver which he had just recently popped into his mouth. The roll was down to two, maybe three holy mints. I couldn't tell. But then he hadn't offered me another one either. Maybe we were no longer friends.

"I've always been a fan of baseball," she said. "We met through mutual friends as it happened."

Dykes nodded and bled ink all over the page.

"Did your husband have any enemies?" asked Jackson, taking a swing for a change.

She transferred her gaze to him. She shook her head slowly.

"No, no one that I can think of. He was a very sweet man. Very kind. Very generous to everyone. His family, friends. Everyone."

Jackson smiled and nodded at her.

"So you can't think of anyone who might have wanted to hurt or kill your husband?" asked Jackson.

Celia shook her head.

"No," she said. "I'm sorry. Really I am. I wish I could offer you more help. I really want you to catch whoever did this."

More nodding bobble heads from Jackson.

"Did your husband have any financial problems?" asked Dykes, getting back up to bat. I'm sorry, I can't help myself. This is about baseball after all.

"Not that I was aware of," she said. "He made a lot of money, and his only extravagance was me."

"I'd say," I said under my breath. Nobody heard. Just as well.

"Though now that you mention it, I do remember him having a heated telephone argument late last week."

"Who was that with?" asked Dykes.

"His agent, Sunny MacKsay."

"Do you know what it was about?"

Celia shook her head.

"No, not really. I asked him about it. He just waved it off saying he was having a disagreement with Sunny over the upcoming contract renewal."

"Word on the street is he was looking for fifty million a year," said Jackson.

Celia nodded.

"He was worth it. The injuries he's taken. He probably only had a few more good years left. I don't know how much he was asking or what he was negotiating, but he did say he was worth at least fifty million for the next three years."

"Who takes care of your husband's money?" asked Dykes.

"You mean our money, Detective," said Celia.

Dykes nodded his head.

"That's exactly what I mean," he said.

"Dennis Blaney," she said. "He's a fund manager for UHNW individuals."

"UHNW?" asked Dykes.

"That means Ultra High Net Worth, Detective. You have to invest a minimum of twenty-five million with Blaney, and he needs to know that you're worth at least twice that with all your assets."

"And why does he need to know that?" I asked.

Celia shot another cold look at me, and shrugged.

"Because he only deals with UHNWs," she said.

"And how is that helpful to you?" I asked.

"Last year, Mr. Carrick," she said. "Blaney managed thirty-three percent on his AUM, which is assets under management."

"And what percentage of that did you and your husband make?" I asked.

I'd been around some high net worth individuals in my time. Mostly as clients. I wasn't exactly unaware of what hedge funds were.

"We got seventy-five percent of it."

"So you made around twenty-five percent on your money?"

"Twenty-four point seventy-five percent if you must know," she said, looking down her nose at me. "How much did you make on your money last year?"

I shrugged and nodded my head from side to side.

"I wasn't in the market last year," I answered. "I keep my hundred dollars under the mattress."

"And your husband was satisfied with this Dennis Blaney?" asked Dykes, getting back into the game. She transferred her gaze to him.

"I didn't hear him complain about him. Though I wasn't a personal fan of Dennis Blaney."

"Why was that?" asked Dykes.

"He didn't seem to take the wives of his clients seriously and I thought he took too much money."

"I'd agree with you there," I added.

She looked at me and then back at Dykes.

"It wasn't his performance fee of twenty-five percent, it was his management fee which is five percent."

I whistled.

"A fool and his money," I said, looking over their heads at the empty whiteboard.

It wasn't a question and no one spoke, though I could feel all the eyes on me.

"Did your husband have a will?" I asked. I was feeling my oats.

"Of course he did," she said.

"And who benefits?"

"None of your business," she said coldly.

I looked at her lawyer. He wasn't looking at me.

"In my experience," I continued, "the person most benefiting from a death is oftentimes the one most benefiting from that death."

It made sense to me. Salisbury looked over at Celia and nodded at her. She sighed heavily, her bosom heaving like the first moons in the night sky over Makeout Point. But that was a long time ago, and I digress.

"If you must know," she said. "In the event of Jimmy's death..."

She paused for good measure and quivered her bottom lip but she didn't cry. I think she was all out of tears, and I was all out of beers which was something I fancied this very evening.

"Now that he's dead," she continued. "I am the sole heir to his estate."

"That's what I figured," I said. "I thought you were money the first time I saw you."

"And what's that supposed to mean?" she asked.

"It means you don't believe in fairytales and sugar and spice and all things nice. Rather you fancy a man with a certain heft... to his wallet."

"Mr. Carrick," said Salisbury, "I'd rather you showed my client a modicum of respect at this difficult time. We are here at our pleasure and it is turning into displeasure."

I smiled at him.

"Did you and your husband have a prenup?" I asked.

"That's it," said Salisbury, standing up, "we're leaving. Are you charging my client with anything?" he asked Dykes.

Dykes shook his head slowly.

"Nothing except gold digging. But that isn't a crime, is it, Ms. Ensor?" I asked her. The smile was still on my face, as she got up.

"Those documents are easy to come by," I added, "and you'd do well to come clean."

She stopped by the door and stared at me with that frigid look I'd been getting from her all day.

"Yes, but he loved me," she said.

Salisbury put his arm around her waist and pushed her onward. I had the distinct impression she might want to say something else but she didn't.

"I'm sure he loved something about you," I said after her, but she likely didn't hear that last bit.

Dykes stood up and turned towards me when they were gone.

"That went well," he said, and he offered me one of his last mints. I took it. He offered one to Jackson who accepted and he popped the last one in his mouth, scrunched up the wrapper, took a three pointer for garbage can, and he made the shot. I was impressed.

"I think that went very well," I agreed.

"The rim shot?" he asked. I nodded.

"So you think she's good for it?" asked Jackson.

I shrugged.

"Maybe, she's definitely not the grieving widow I was expecting," I said.

Dykes nodded, then turned towards me.

"And that prenup. I'd like to see what that says."

"Me too. You have any friends with the DA?" I asked.

"As sure as God made little green apples."

I nodded, looking out the door that Celia and Co. had just walked out of. She was long gone, but that stench of her fakeness lingered like cheap perfume. Or maybe it was cheap perfume I was smelling.

"I'm going to the ballpark," I said. "Anyone want to join me?"

Jackson and Dykes shook their heads.

"We've got paperwork to do and I want to speak to the DA about a warrant for that lawyer of hers. I bet he has the prenup papers."

"I bet he does," I agreed.

CHAPTER SEVEN

A Piece Of Israel

THE taxi man dropped me off at the front entrance. He was all talk about the upcoming games. Wanted to know who I was rooting for. I told him the truth. But I would have lied. There was a real fervor in the air and if I didn't feel a soft spot for the Lovable Losers I would have pretended to root for them regardless.

He was an interesting man. He was recently from Pakistan though his English was impeccable. He was an engineer he said, but was taking courses to upgrade himself in order to train as an engineer here in the States. That wasn't the interesting bit. The interesting bit was he didn't think the Cubbies would win. He thought losing was in their blood, their genes. And what with the star pitcher murdered, he had lost all hope. But still, he would be watching the games. He urged me to find the killer. They always do that. As if I wouldn't be able to solve the crime without their serious urging.

But still, it was tender and heartfelt. So much so that I asked him if he knew Ensor. He said yes. I had to clarify. Had he ever had the man over for drinks or dinner. Of course not. But he knew him. These are the fans for you. The true fanatics. He knew a guy he'd never met. Then again, so did I. I knew Ensor, and I was getting to know him more as each moment passed, through the people who knew him.

What I knew so far was that he was a kind man. A homebody and a dutiful husband. But the witness giving that account was unreliable. I was gonna shake some different trees. See if some bruised apples fell from them. I walked into Wrigley Field like I owned it. I didn't. And a security guard was the first to point that out, until I told him I was with CPD. Didn't even need to show a badge. That was a good thing, because I didn't have one. Not one from CPD and not one from LAPD. Not that they respect that badge out here. Though collegial courtesy often goes a long way.

The security guard pointed me in the direction of the change rooms. They had been recently renovated. Supposedly quite fancy now. I'd be the judge of that. They weren't. I'd been lied to. Or perhaps I'd misheard. Maybe they were going to be renovated in the near future. I didn't care. Didn't affect me and I wouldn't be around to check them out anyway.

I walked into the wrong one. It must have been the visiting team's change rooms. How did I know this? Maybe the sign I saw after I exited that said 'Baltimore Orioles'. Hadn't noticed that when I walked in. It was empty when I got inside, and it was smaller than my ex-wife's bathroom. But she'd married into money. Still, a small place for a couple of dozen or more guys. I found the home team's change rooms. They were better, but nothing I would have bragged about. It too was empty. I walked back the way I came. I found the same guard.

"I was looking for the team," I said to him. I wasn't happy.

He shrugged at me.

"You said you were looking for the locker rooms."

That is what I had said.

"Well, I'm looking for the team," I said.

"You might want to check out the bleachers," he said, and he nodded behind himself towards and exit that led to the covered open air bleachers.

I walked past him without a word. I didn't like him. But maybe it was my mistake. I didn't care. The game was starting in a couple of days and I'd like to have things wrapped up before then. Outside it was still sunny. Smudges of gray and white clouds hung lazily in the sky watching The Birds practice ball, just like the Lovable Losers were doing. They were all dotted about in clumps not dressed in uniform. I found the older out of shape guy amongst them and figured he must be the manager. He was talking with Stark. I walked along the aisle towards them. They were standing up against a railing. Stark saw me coming and nodded at the manager who turned around and looked at me. They shifted and stood facing me as I came upon them. I grinned a real friendly smile.

"Anthony Carrick," I said, holding out my hand to shake the manager's. "You must be the manager," I said.

He nodded involuntarily like folks will often do when you catch them off guard.

"Yeah, that's right," he said. "Israel Kreyling. Press aren't invited in yet. I'm afraid you'll have to leave."

I nodded.

"I'm not press," I said. "I'm here about the murder. I'm consulting with the CPD on this homicide."

He nodded more slowly this time. He was wearing a windbreaker over a striped shirt with blue jeans. He was shorter than average with curly graying hair. He had a couple of days stubble on his face and time had clung to his lower lids like a scared man clutching the balcony from the twenty-first floor. His eyelids themselves had formed jowls. But real jowls he did not have. He was probably fifty pounds overweight and the fat gave his face a youthful look save for the lower lids. He seemed like a hairy guy, the tufts of hair on the backs of his hands and fingers gave that away.

"I've already spoken to the police," he said.

I nodded, still grinning.

"Right, but you haven't spoken to me. And I'm not the police."

Stark leaned on the railing with his one forearm. He was my height on the lean, which meant he probably had two or three inches on me standing tall. That put him at around six, six one. Israel was not leaning on anything and he was still shorter than me.

"Well, what I can do to help you then?" asked Israel.

"Did you find him out on the field here?" I asked.

"What, you mean a couple of nights ago?"

I nodded. Israel shook his head.

"No, that wasn't me. It was Darian," and he nodded his head back towards the leaning man. I nodded at him too. He just stared blankly at me with his eyes in the shadow of his ball cap.

"I also understand that Ensor was having financial troubles."

Israel squinted at me for a moment and then shrugged. I liked to make stuff up. See who knows what without telling them the what I know.

"Hadn't heard anything like that. He was looking for more money though. But that's not uncommon for a pitcher of his calibre."

"I bet everyone around here is looking for more money," I said, looking past Israel and grinning at Darian.

"Yup, but they're not all worth it."

"You think Ensor was?" I looked back at Israel.

"Worth it, you mean?" I nodded. He nodded, we were two bobble heads in the back of a senior's car on his way to Florida. "Yeah, he was worth it. A rare talent. I haven't seen talent like that up close in many years."

I tilted my head and shook it ruefully.

"Still," I said. "Fifty mill, that's a lot of money, I don't care how talented you are. How do you legitimize something like that?"

Israel reached into his back pocket and pulled out a ticket. He shook it in front of him.

"With this," he said. "I take it you're not a fan?"

"I wouldn't say that," I said. "I have money on the Cubbies, I just don't share the fanaticism of some. What is something like that worth?"

He handed it to me. I looked at it. It was Field Box 111. I handed it back to him.

"That's twenty-five hundred," he said, and put it back in his pocket.

"That's a salary," I replied.

He nodded.

"That's what fans will pay," he said.

"Really?"

He nodded again.

"Last year, average prices were around a grand. This year they're going to be fifteen hundred to two thousand. This is a historic baseball event. Never before have we had two teams from each league get into the series with such a long losing streak on both sides. Fans want a piece of that. Already I've heard tickets are selling on eBay for ten grand."

I shook my head and whistled through my teeth.

"I'll take that one if you're offering," I said.

He shook his head.

"Nah, this one's taken, but if you're serious, I can get you a ticket for the final in the Club Box if you're interested."

I nodded sincerely. I immediately liked Israel. His generous spirit and friendly gesture.

"I'd like that," I said. "If it's not an inconvenience."

"Not at all, perhaps it'll be an incentive of sorts."

He smiled at me.

"I don't need an incentive," I said. "We'll find out who did this."

Israel looked out over the field, watching The Birds toss balls around. Watching the pitcher throw some balls at the batter. They were soft balls. Even I could tell that. No way in hell they were showing their best stuff out there while the competition looked on like vultures on carrion.

"But," I said, returning to conversation. "Even a full stadium at two grand a pop is not gonna pay salaries."

Israel turned back to me and nodded.

"True, but you have no idea how much the TV rights go for, and the merchandise. This is a billion dollar business, just the Cubbies," he said.

I nodded.

"Plus we have sponsors and probably a dozen other streams of income that I'm not fully aware of. Put it this way, when the owner bought the team back in oh nine, he got it for seven hundred mill. That was about five times revenues. Businessmen buy these teams because they love the sport, but also because it's profitable. This is capitalism as a well oiled machine."

I looked out a the field again.

"How much is a team like them earning in salaries?" I asked, nodding my head at The Birds on the field. Israel followed my eyes.

"Over a hundred mill," he said. "Same as our guys. Our player salary expenses are a little higher at around one hundred thirty."

I nodded.

"That's a lottery win," I said.

Israel nodded.

"Yup, but for most of these guys, it's like winning the lottery," he said. "There's a lot of kids out there dreaming and hoping to make it to the majors. The odds are against most of them."

"Which is the most valuable team in the MLB?" I asked, more curious than anything, and taking a side road away from the task at hand.

"That would be the New York Yankees. Worth over twice what we are."

"And I assume they've got the biggest payroll as well," I said.

"You'd assume wrong," said Israel, "that would go to the LA Dodgers, though the Yankees come up a close second."

I nodded.

"So with Ensor out of the way," I said, "who has the most to gain?"

Israel looked at me steadily for a moment. Then he looked out at the field as a batter hit a fly ball that the catcher caught.

"You're asking me some hard questions."

"Probably asked by the CPD too," I said.

Israel nodded and then returned his gaze to me.

"The pitchers have the most to gain."

"Anyone in particular?" I asked, looking at Stark.

Israel looked down for a moment.

"That would be Stark, but I don't think he'd do it."

"Why's that?"

"He's a good guy. I just can't see it. If you've known him as long as I have, you'd think the same."

That wasn't half as reassuring as I was hoping it'd be. Generally, character witnesses don't stand in for alibis.

"How much you paying him?" I asked.

Israel and I had moved up a bit from where Stark stood. He might not have been able to hear Israel, but he could sure as hell read my lips.

"Around five mill per year. His contract's up this year. He'll want more."

"You've just given him motive," I said, smiling as if I'd just been handed a million bucks.

"I suppose, but I don't see it."

"He's getting a fifth of what Ensor was earning, right?" Israel nodded. "And now that Ensor's out of the way he's got the most to benefit. Am I right?"

Israel shrugged.

"I suppose."

"Well, the way I see it, he either does or he doesn't. Is there someone else that you're gonna replace Ensor with who isn't Stark?"

"There are a lotta good guys out there. But you're probably right, Stark might be the best we can afford at the moment."

"So he bumps up to top dog and a pay raise. Maybe ten mill, and you're no better at winning, but the math looks better."

"Yeah, he'd probably get bumped to ten or so," agreed Israel.

"Now I've given you motive," I said.

Israel laughed and shook his head as if I'd told him a funny off-color joke.

"That's outrageous," he said, but he showed no anger. "With Ensor we had a good chance of winning. You probably already know that if you've put money on us. But with him gone, we're the underdog for sure."

"So you didn't do it?"

Israel shook his head at me like I was a chump.

"No, I didn't. Let me tell it to you real easy so you can understand. I make seven figures a year. I'm happy with that. I was never gonna be a ball player, but I can manage. With Ensor gone, my contract's not looking good, which is also up this year. Like I said. If we had Ensor still, I'd put money on my own team. More than that, my contract would be renewed, one hundred percent, and there's an incentive bonus of five hundred grand for me personally if we win this World Series. So tell me again, in what universe does me killing the golden goose make any sense?"

"Maybe you didn't like him."

"I liked him just fine. Some of the others not so much. Some of them have got big egos. Ensor wasn't like that. He came from humble beginnings and he never forgot that."

"Did he have any disagreements with his team mates?" I asked.

Israel looked down at the ground between us and then back up at me.

"Yeah, he did. Him and Stark didn't always see eye to eye."

"Why's that?" I asked.

"You talk to him and you'll figure that out real quick. But the salary difference was one thing."

"Anyone else?"

Israel shook his head.

"Nothing that would give me pause. You know how it can be with some of these guys. Our left fielder Vance Gibb has a hot temper. He's a good hitter. Over five hundred and fifteen runs so far. Some think he might beat Bonds' record. I'm not one of them, but he and Ensor didn't often see eye to eye."

"Why don't you think he'll beat the record?"

"Well, he's got enough time to do it, but he doesn't have the temperament. He keeps blaming everyone but himself. But he has just as many at bats as any other player in the league."

I nodded.

"I see," I said.

"Plus, he thinks he should be the highest paid player on the team."

"What does he get?"

"Just over six million. But his contract's not up for another couple of years."

"And he'll bail, I guess?"

Israel shook his head and chuckled.

"You're not a big fan, I can tell. That's all right. Gibb will be lucky to have his contract renewed if he continues the way he's going. He's good, no doubt about it. But his shine has come off quick. Three years ago, he hit four oh one. That's phenomenally impressive. He did it over half a season, and he still brags about it..."

"Four oh one?" I asked.

"Yeah," said Israel, nodding his head. "That's his batting average. The number of hits divided by the number of at bats. Over four hundred is hardly ever seen anymore, at least for as long as a full season. A good batter is over three hundred. Currently, his career average is at three oh three, still really good. But it's heading in the wrong direction and he's still got years left. In fact, this season he's heading towards the Mendoza line."

Israel smiled sadly at that and looked down again.

"Mendoza line?"

"Yup, named after a short stop, a good one, who couldn't hit a rolling beach ball with a tree trunk. It's considered an average of two hundred or less, though the real Mendoza managed around two fifteen I think if I remember correctly."

Israel smiled again, looking down, before looking back up at me.

"In fact, that's becoming his nickname around here, Mendoza."

"So what's his average?"

"Two oh seven this season and likely to break under two hundred in these last games if he doesn't get his shit together."

I looked back out over the bleachers looking for a man I knew nothing of.

"Who is Gibb?" I asked.

Israel looked down the stadium and pointed at an African American leaning against the last railings of the first row seats. He was by himself. I nodded.

"I don't get how the death of a pitcher would help him," I said.

Israel shrugged.

"I don't see it either. You just asked me who Ensor had grievances with."

I nodded and looked back down at Vance. I could only see the back of him. Then I looked back at Israel.

"What about your bat boys?"

"What about them?"

"I don't see them," I said, scanning the bleachers for what I already knew wasn't there.

"It's a school day," said Israel. "Junior O'Riley will be here around three after class. Starting Friday he's got special permission to miss school during the event."

"Junior O'Riley?"

"James, Jimmy, but we call him Junior O'Riley. His father is James O'Riley."

Israel said that like we'd been high school pals and he was talking about the principal. I shook my head.

"Who?"

"Right, you're not a big fan. James O'Riley played for us from ninety-three to oh three. Junior is his kid."

"And that's how you become a bat boy. You need an inside hand?"

"It helps," said Israel.

"And the pay's good?" I asked.

Israel laughed again and shook his head.

"Nope, but the kids want to do it. We have some kids been on the waiting list for three years. They'll never be a bat boy, or girl."

"How come?"

"Well, you've gotta be fourteen at the youngest. If you've been waiting three years that puts you at seventeen, and there's still another six names ahead of yours. And between me and you, that list is meaningless. The only way you're gonna get on is if you have an inside track like you said."

"And how many of these lads do you have?"

"Six boys. Though the five of them get the scraps that Junior doesn't want."

"They don't see many games?"

Israel nodded.

"So if it doesn't pay well, why do it?"

"Why do men seek to earn lots of money and date beautiful women? Why do we do anything?"

I shook my head. I wanted him to answer his own questions.

"Prestige, plain and simple. If you were going to buy a car logically you'd buy something Japanese and likely a midsize sedan. They're just the most reliable and economical. Plain and simple. But guys like us, we'll buy a Mercedes or a Caddy. Why? We'll pretend it's because of all the high end features and other crap, but honestly, it's because we seek prestige. That Camry will get you home just as well, and probably more reliably, but we're monkeys at the end of the day and we want to show shiny things off to others. Bat boys get around twenty-five bucks for a days work. So why else would they do it?"

"Not because they want to buy a Mercedes," I grinned at him.

"Because being a bat boy if you're into baseball is like owning a Mercedes."

"You've sure been helpful. Anything you can think of I might want to know?"

Israel shook his head.

"Nah, I'll let you get to Stark, but I think it's a smart move to talk to Junior though."

"Why do you think that?"

"Because they're treated like the hired help. I don't let the players haze them or anything like that, but they're not really seen, and when you're not really seen, what you can overhear is probably interesting. That's all I'm saying. I like to stay out of my player's business. It's better for me that way."

I nodded.

"So the cops are looking into speaking with Junior then too?"

Israel shook his head.

"Nope. Didn't even bring it up. Maybe that's why the Windy City has the homicide clearance rate it has. At least it's good to see they brought in a real professional for this one."

Israel went to walk past me and give me some privacy to speak with Stark. Before he did, he put his hand on my shoulder.

"Just between me and you. I haven't been this confident in the CPD in years. Where can I get the tickets to you?"

I told him where I was staying. It was walking distance from here.

CHAPTER EIGHT

In Stark Contrast

I walked up to Stark. He was leaning on the railings with both forearms. I had my hands in my pocket. I also had on a light windbreaker. It was warm in the stadium with the sun shining down. The breeze had neglected the field, perhaps skirting around the edges of this murder scene. Afraid to ask the hard questions. I wasn't. Stark folded a long rectangular piece of gum into his mouth, crunched the wrapper into a ball and flicked it into the seats in front of him. I didn't like that. There was a trash can just a few feet from him.

He didn't look at me as I walked up and leaned on the railing, mirroring him. I looked over at him. He didn't look over at me. He had a thick black mustache across his upper lip that drooped on each side of his mouth. He chewed with his mouth open like a cow. I disliked him even more. From his profile his nose was as hooked as a crack prostitute giving blowjobs for a hit.

"You Stark?" I said, starting the conversation. He still didn't look at me.

"What's it to you?" he said.

"Seeing you live up to your name," I said. "I'm liking you for the murderer right now, that's what's it to me."

He turned towards me and leaned on the railing with his left hand and sneered at me.

"Fuck off," he said. "I don't feel like talking to you."

"That's too bad," I said, "because I'm in a chatty mood and I aim to talk your ear off."

Stark stood up tall, trying to tower his couple of extra inches over me. I moved closer. This was getting fun.

"I'm not interested. Unless you've got a warrant, I'm not talking to you and you're no cop."

"You're not the sharpest knife in the drawer," I said, smiling at him. He was still sneering and looking down at me. He moved a little closer. We could have reached out and embraced each other for the fox trot. But I felt a different dance coming on.

"What you mean?"

"Nobody needs a warrant to talk to someone. You need a warrant to obtain evidence. What you mean to say is that you're gonna plead the fifth. See, it's the fifth amendment that gives you your right to silence, or more specifically not to incriminate yourself. But that's usually when speaking to police or other arms of the government. Like you said, I'm not police so it doesn't apply."

Stark shook his head angrily.

"You're a douche bag," he said, pushing me with his hand.

"I wouldn't do that if I was you."

"I told you to fuck off, gumshoe, get the real police here if you want to ask me any questions."

He did it again. The fucking idiot pushed me again. I stepped back and gave him a right straight to his beak of a nose. It didn't crack. I hadn't wanted to break it. That was more trouble than I was willing to get into. I wanted to give him another but he wasn't expecting it and stumbled back and fell flat on his ass. He brought his hand to his nose and looked up at me in surprise.

"Shit, man, there was no need for that," he said.

I walked over to him and offered him my hand and helped him up.

"If you talk to me there'll be no need for any more of that," I said. "So long as we can have a civilized conversation."

Blood had started dripping down his nose and onto his nice Chicago Cubs windbreaker.

"Where do you keep the ice?" I asked.

"There's some in the locker room," he said.

"All right, let's go. Pinch the bridge of your nose and tilt your head back, it'll help."

"Why'd you do that?" he asked, genuinely interested. "You broke my nose for fuck's sake."

"I didn't," I said. "And if you've got to ask why, you're dumber than a bag of baseballs."

We got into the locker and I found some ice. I put it in a cloth and handed it to him. I also wet another cloth for him to clean up the blood. I gave that to him too.

"Put that ice on the bridge of your nose. It'll help the swelling."

He did like I told him.

"Now are we gonna have a nice and pleasant conversation?"

He didn't say anything. But the look he gave me was less angry this time. He had simmered down a bit. A surprise punch on the nose will do that. I sat on a bench opposite him. He wiped at the blood on his nose. He tilted his head back slightly and placed the cold ice on the bridge of his nose. Already his nose was giving up leaking blood.

"You must have heard what Israel and I were talking about. He said you had grievances with Ensor."

"So did most of the other pitchers," he said.

"But looks like you've got the most to gain."

He shrugged and I leaned in towards him on my elbows.

"I mean you do, right?" I said, it wasn't so much a question as a statement. "With Ensor out of the way you're going to be the Ace pitcher, no?"

He shrugged again.

"Yeah, so?"

"So, that gives you a good motive to kill him. What's more interesting is that you found him. That often means you killed him. You know, finders keepers and all that."

He shook his head.

"That makes no sense. Finders keepers. What the fuck is that about?"

"Do you own a gun?" I asked.

He looked at me down the bridge of his nose.

"No," he said.

His hand was holding the cloth of ice against the bridge of his nose. It looked like a trunk sprouted from between his eyes. I bet it felt nice. Better than the straight he took earlier.

"So tell me how you found him?" I asked.

"It's like I told the cops. We were leaving to head on over to The Red Herring. That's a bar we sometimes go to. A sports bar. Ensor had gone out earlier to throw some balls. Keep his arm oiled as he liked to say. I went to get him, to tell him we were leaving. I found him laid out on the grass up by the dugout."

"Describe how he was to me?"

"What do you mean?"

"What position was his body in? What did you notice? That sort of thing."

"Well, he was lying face up. His head was pointing towards the dugout and his feet were towards home plate. There was blood on his chest. He had been shot."

"How many times?"

"Twice," he said.

"How do you know that?"

Most times, it's hard for witnesses to determine how many times a body has been shot if it's center mass. They're just too confused, not thinking straight, the blood has darkened most of the front. It's not a pretty sight. Not like how it looks in movies. So I was curious how he knew that. If he had truly found Ensor he probably was in shock and not noticing those kinds of details.

"That's what the police said when they arrived."

"Or is that what you saw?"

"Man, I don't know. Maybe, I can't remember. This is the first time I'd seen a fucking dead body, alright?"

"So what did you do when you saw him?"

"I freaked out. I looked around a bit. I dunno why, maybe I was looking to see if the killer was still around. Then I checked his pulse. I mean there was blood all over him. I couldn't feel a pulse so I called 911. Then I went back inside and told everyone else."

"Was his baseball cap still on when you found him."

Stark took off his cloth of ice and frowned at me.

"I don't fucking remember. Jesus, man, what are you thinking, that I was taking notes?"

I shrugged.

"Maybe. Or maybe you killed him, went someplace to bury the evidence and then called 911."

Stark shook his head.

"That's bullshit. I didn't kill him."

"Was there a baseball in his hand when you found him?"

"I dunno. Fuck, man, I told you, I don't remember that sort of stuff. I mean, I know he had been throwing some balls. There were balls by the net, but I don't remember exactly how he looked."

"What did you do after you'd told everyone?"

"Well, they all left to go see for themselves while I took a shower."

"Why'd you take a shower?"

"I felt sick. I felt pretty fucked up, unclean. I dunno, I just wanted to wash off what I'd just seen."

"Or wash away any evidence."

More head shaking.

"I told you, I didn't kill him."

"Did they swab your hands?"

"For what?" he asked with a squinted face.

"For gunshot residue," I said. "Though that would have been the whole purpose of taking a shower I suspect."

He shook his head.

"No, they just took my statement."

I nodded. It was quiet in the locker room. Cold too, like a meat locker. Stark's nose had stopped leaking. He'd probably have a bit of bruising around an eye or two, but nothing to prevent him from playing. I started thinking that maybe I shouldn't have punched him. But come on, he had gone begging. And I could see now how he might not have been the most liked. He was an arrogant prick. Self entitled.

"Tell me about the beef between you and Ensor."

"What beef?"

"Now you're just playing coy with me. Don't do that. You're

wasting my time and I get upset when that happens. Everybody knows you two didn't get along."

Stark looked down, his wet, bloody cloth in his right hand and the ice cloth in his left hand.

"Don't do that," I said.

"What?" he asked, looking up at me.

"Don't look down, your nose will start leaking again."

He thrust his chin up towards me and looked at me down the barrel of his nose. He put the ice cloth back on the bridge of his nose.

"All right," he said, "I didn't much care for him."

"Why's that?"

"He was an arrogant asshole," said Stark. I was thinking the kettle was calling the pot black.

"Tell me about that."

"He thought he was one of the best pitchers out there."

"Well, from what I've heard of him and his stats, he was."

Stark wagged his chin at me as he looked down. He was trying to shake his head. It looked odd at this angle.

"Yeah, he was good, but he was also not giving me a chance to build my career. He was hogging all the games, going for more and more strikeouts, looking for that elusive perfect game."

"Those sound like things that help the team," I said.

"Help him more than us."

"School me."

"He wasn't going to get a perfect game. They usually happen earlier in a pitcher's career or maybe mid career, but not later in the career. Not usually, and at thirty-seven, Jim was getting old. Most guys peak in their early to, maybe, their mid thirties. Most are retiring by forty."

"But there's always the exception to the rule."

Stark nodded.

"But not with Jim. He was slowing down. This season you could really see it, but he wanted to play it out because his contract was coming for renewal and if you look at his last, say five years, it looks good. But the last year has not been as good. He was trying to keep himself on life support to get more money than he was worth and that pissed me off."

"Why?"

"Because he was a selfish asshole. I mean come on. He was making twenty-five mill a year and he was hungry for more. Greedy asshole. Yeah, he might have been a better pitcher than me, but he wasn't five times better."

"Why five times?"

"Because he got paid five times what I got. My ERA is 3.23 which is good. And I'm in my prime..."

"How old are you?"

"Thirty-one. I've got some good few years left to peak. I can feel it. But Jim wouldn't give up the reign."

"You've just given yourself motive."

Stark wagged his chin at me, then he lowered his head. We were now eye to eye. He took the ice cloth of his nose. It was dripping now as the ice melted. He wiped at his upper lip with a corner of unstained cloth from his right hand. There was no blood there.

"Thing is, I didn't need to kill him. I knew he was on the way out."

"How's that?"

"He was having trouble with his elbow. He'd already had one Tommy John a few years ago, and I could see that he hadn't really fully recovered. He'd come back in too strong and it was taking it's toll. I'd be surprised if he had another two years left in him."

"What's Tommy John?" I asked.

"Surgery on the elbow where they replace a tendon with another good tendon from somewhere else in the body, often from the forearm. It was named after the first pitcher who had the operation done. Worked out well for him. Thing is, Jim was impatient. He just wanted to get back to pitching as soon as he could, and these things take a long time to heal."

"How's your elbow?" I asked.

Stark put down the cloth in his right hand and massaged his left elbow.

"My elbow's just fine. I take care of it, we have great therapists here. Plus I don't use it that often. On a good game I'll maybe get an inning or two in."

"And you get five mill for that. I don't see the problem."

"The problem is I should be playing more. It's not about the money, though we could all use more, right?"

I didn't say anything to that. It was hard to talk serious financial troubles with millionaires when I was just hoping to make next month's rent.

"Well, trust me, it's not just about the money for most of us."

"Then what's it about?"

"The game, man, the game." Stark shook his head at me like I was imbecile. "I started playing baseball because I love it. I still play it because I love it and I want to play it more. There's nothing else in the world I'd sooner do. And improving stats is important too."

"So if you didn't kill him, who did?"

Stark shrugged. Then he shook his head as it pointed at the floor. Then he looked back up at me and turned his mouth upside down.

"I don't know. I just don't know. I mean we had our problems but it's not like I hated the guy. Israel told you about Gibb, I suppose."

I nodded.

"There's a guy with a temper. Man, does he have a temper. Heard he was brought up on assaulting his wife once but it was let go."

"How was it let go?"

"Word was he let her have a divorce and gave her a good chunk of money. In fact, there's a guy who probably needs more money if there ever was one."

"How so?"

"He's got four kids with her and his alimony is off the charts. At least that's what I hear anyway. I'm surprised he hasn't killed her..."

"Why's that?"

"Because he's said as much, at least to some of us. Man, he hates that ex of his. But now killing Ensor, I don't know about that."

"Then how do you know they had such a hate on for each other?"

"Because Gibb figures he should be the highest paid. And he makes good money. Second highest paid here at around six mill so I hear. Anyway, he's on his way out, but he's looking to blame everyone else. You've probably heard his batting average is hitting the shitter?"

Stark looked at me straight for a moment. I nodded at him. I was still leaning in on my elbows.

"Yeah, something about the Mendoza Line."

Stark nodded and grinned.

"What's so funny?"

"That's his nickname. Though we don't say it to his face. He'd go fucking ape shit."

"So he blames Ensor for his problems. How does the pitcher

have anything to do with a fielder's troubles?"

"Couple of reasons, at least how Gibb sees it. First of all, the other guys practice against a baseball pitching machine, but they also practice against us too. There's nothing like facing a real pitcher to hone your skills. Trouble is, Gibb keeps arguing with Ensor that Ensor's not giving him his best balls, and that really upsets Gibb."

"Well, was he?"

"Holding back, you mean?"

I nodded my head. Stark nodded back.

"Yeah, of course. It's fucking hard work pitching baseballs. It ruins you, your arms at least, but the back problems, knee problems and hip problems we have to deal with in our retirement years, it's debilitating, I'm telling you."

"I'll take your word on it."

"Really, the amount of force we throw with, the whipping of the joints. You have no idea."

Stark glanced off at the lockers. He sighed and then held his left arm out straight and rotated his fist, turning his elbow this way and that, cradling it with his right hand.

"Sure the elbow's good?"

He looked back at me. He nodded half heartedly.

"Yeah, it's fine, but I can feel it. The toll that it's already taken. Anyway, we don't send them our fastest cutters or sinkers neither do we send our deadliest curveballs and the like. We've gotta keep some stuff in the tank. We'd be ruined otherwise."

"And do most of your team mates know this?"

Stark nodded.

"Fuck yeah, it's common knowledge in baseball. I mean, you're paying a bunch of guys a lot of money to throw balls in order to beat other teams. That's the most important. It's also important to give your own guys a chance against real pitchers, but that's always secondary. Gibb wouldn't have any of it, so he starts to blame it on Ensor, and us, but Ensor the most. He's bitching that Ensor is costing him his game because he can't get really good balls off of him."

I nodded my head. I was getting schooled in baseball. It was becoming a more interesting game to me with this insider information.

"And that's it, he's blaming Ensor for his own problems."

Stark nodded.

"I suppose he's got a point. Maybe a small point but a point nonetheless."

"So you agree with him?"

Stark shook his head at me like he was trying to dissuade a mosquito from biting his earlobe.

"No, I'm not saying that at all. It's all on him. His game is shit because of his own problems. Maybe his stress, maybe his other issues. Whatever, I don't care. Even still, sometimes we'll bring in the pitchers from the Iowa Cubs, that's our farm team, our best farm team anyway, and they'll be tasked with throwing their best to our guys. But still, there's a reason these guys are in the farm. They're still maturing, still not as good as we are."

I nodded.

"But that's it," I asked.

Stark shook his head. I guess that mosquito was still trying to nibble on his ear. That invisible mosquito.

"That just started it. What really got them both on the same page of hate for each other was when earlier in this season, Gibb flubbed an easy catch."

"Tell me about that?" I asked.

"It was shortly after one of our practice sessions when Ensor was pitching to the team. Gibb came up to bat and after just three balls, he got violently upset at Ensor and ran up to the mound and pushed him telling him to throw decent balls. A couple of the guys had to come and break it up, it was definitely going to get physical."

"So what happened?"

"Ensor threw his mitt down on the mound and strode off. That was the end of his pitching that day. The rest of us had to finish it up."

"Do you think that was the right call?"

Stark frowned at me.

"Damn straight it was. I've done the same to Gibb for lesser bullshit. But Ensor was soft that way. Always trying to help the team."

"So tell me what happened at the game that Gibb screwed up?"

Stark stood up and tossed his cloths into a laundry hamper. He then went over to the sink and washed up. He came back cleaner than he'd left.

"Gibb had been playing half assed the whole game. Letting balls roll by him and making half hearted efforts to run for them. He was giving away runs. Israel had already spoken to him about it. Then in the seventh inning, we're up by one run. The other team was the Diamondbacks..."

I raised my eyes at him. I didn't know who they were. Stark sighed.

"The Arizona Diamondbacks. They're a team we should beat nine games out of ten. We're only up by one run and it's the seventh inning like I said. Gibb and Ensor have been exchanging looks all day. Arizona has men on the second and third bases. Ensor throws a ball and the batter hits it right at Gibb. I mean right at him. He has to step to one side and reach out for it to catch it. But he watches it go by him. Bam, just like that. Arizona gets two runs and by the time Gibb decides to get it, because Donovan Tinker is going for it, the batter is at third base already. We lose that game by three runs. Because that asshole decided to have a personal grudge match with Ensor."

"And by asshole you mean Gibb."

Stark nodded.

"And that's it?"

"Yeah. Ensor is fucking furious. He runs up to Gibb after the play and punches him in the face. Then they start going at it. Not for long, the rest of us come and break it up. Both of them are evicted from the game. Gibb threatens to kill him."

Stark stops then and looks at me. He shrugs slightly.

"But you know, that's said in the heat of the moment. None of us really thought."

And he stopped again and put lowered his head. He was leaning in towards me now, mirroring my elbows on knees position. He looked up again.

"Anyway, Ensor got a quarter million fine for hitting his own teammate. Never heard of before."

I stood up, and looked down at him.

"Alright then," I said. "Don't leave town."

He looked up at me and nodded, not finding the humor in the joke. I walked out and heard him walking out after me. I made my way back to the stands. I needed to speak to a man about a grudge, and I knew exactly who that was.

CHAPTER NINE

Feeling Gibb

OUTSIDE it was as sunny as when I'd left. No clouds had moved. They hung around like irascible old men at public chess tables. Or maybe that was me. Though I didn't feel particularly angry. Gibb hadn't moved either. He was hanging on the top railing just behind the catcher as if his knees were weak after taking a knock on the chin. I hadn't given him one yet. But maybe I was foreshadowing. Or perhaps I was ignorantly wishing.

A pitcher on the mound threw a lazy ball that arced towards the batter. He hit it towards a teammate further afield. They were dialing it in. Of course they were. What with the vultures circling around they were taking it ridiculously easy. I walked up to Gibb and stood looking at him with my hands in my pocket. It seemed a little cooler this close to the ground. Not with the wind. The wind was still as quiet as a deadman breathing. No, it just seemed cooler, and we weren't in the shade.

"Learning anything?" I asked.

Gibb looked out over the field and slowly shook his head. He had a fat lip that I wished I'd given him. He looked down at the ground and spat out a wad of chew. I thought that was a great idea so I lit up a cigarette and took a drag. He smelt of grapes. That was the tobacco.

"You," he said, still not looking at me.

"Me what?" I asked.

"Learn anything."

His accent made him a Southerner. I couldn't properly place it, but the gambler in me offered South Carolina. I liked it. He was still looking out over the field though he didn't seem interested in any of it. His ball cap was tight over his head. His nose was squashed up against his face and his lips were thick. The kind of lips that women would envy. His eyes were small and squinty and his complexion was dark burnt almonds. In his back pocket of his jeans I could see the outline of a can of chew.

"I'm learning tons," I said, taking a drag on my cigarette. "Like I'm learning that the Lovable Losers are gonna stay losers."

I exhaled towards him and watched him closely. He didn't move. He looked vacantly out over the field of lost dreams. He moved the chew to the other side of his lip. Then he nodded slowly.

"You're probably right."

Then he glanced over at me.

"Who are you?" he asked. "You don't look like a reporter."

"I'm a gumshoe," I said.

He looked down at my shoes.

"It's an expression," I offered.

He nodded his head and looked off again. He was built like a bull. His clothing was tight over his muscles. He was my height but had probably thirty or so pounds on me. He must have been tilting towards two hundred pounds. He was thick with it, like a good marbled steak. Not especially lean but not fat either.

"You here about Jim?"

I nodded.

"Yup. Trying to help the incompetent CPD figure out a murder. I hear you didn't like him."

"You heard right," he said.

"Tell me about that."

"Nothing to tell. I didn't like him. He was an overpaid pitcher. Simple as that. Dialed it in when we practiced together."

He didn't look at me. He looked down again and spat out more chew. At his rate he was going to need a refill soon enough. I smoked my cigarette. I looked around the stadium a while and then out at the field. Maybe I'd come and see the game if Israel came through with the tickets. It'd been years since I'd been to the ball park.

"Folks tell me you threatened to kill him."

"Yeah, I did."

One thing I could say about Gibb was that he was forthright.

"Did you?"

"Did what?"

"Kill him. You threatened to. Did you carry through with it?"

Gibb turned towards me now and crossed his arms over his chest. He tilted his head at me and looked me up and down. I'd seen that looked before. He was measuring my worth. And like most hotheads before him, he was undervaluing me.

"Yeah," I said, nodding my head. "They told me you had an anger problem."

His small eyes fired up and his nostrils flared. We were getting close to dancing. But something caught his attention up in the stadium and he looked over for a moment and then looked back at me. I glanced to where his eyes had been. I saw Stark walking towards us. I looked back at Gibb, his stance had softened but not his stare. I inhaled on my cigarette. He moved the chew back to the other side.

"You don't want to dance?" I asked.

He stared at me, not saying anything.

"Too bad," I said, "Stark wasn't feeling the music either."

Stark joined us now and subconsciously touched his nose. The bridge of his nose and his lower eyelids were starting do bruise.

"Israel says to cooperate," Stark said to Gibb.

Stark nodded at me and left again. I watched him go. He walked back up to where I'd first met him. Israel was waiting for him there, watching us.

"No, I didn't," said Gibb at last.

I looked back at him.

"Didn't what?"

"I didn't kill Ensor," he said.

He turned and rested his forearms over the railing again, looking out over the baseball field.

"But you wanted to," I said.

"Yeah, like I wanted to kill you just now. But it's not what I would've done. We had our problems but we worked them out."

"How was that?"

Gibb kept his eyes over the field, watching grown men run after small white balls.

"You probably heard about the Arizona game," he said.

"Yeah."

"Well, we duked it out on the field a bit. We both got ejected. He got a big fine. I didn't. That made me happy. End of story."

"Where you from?" I asked.

Gibb turned to look at me and his forehead was furrowed.

"Athens," he said.

"You don't look Greek to me," I said. I was being a card. He wasn't having any of it.

"Athens, Georgia," he said, turning back to the game.

"I hear you're headed towards the Mendoza Line," I said, seeing if I could reignite the fire in him.

He turned towards me and he was hot. I really thought he was gonna come at me. But he took a deep breath. Then he grinned and nodded his head.

"You're trying to bait me," he said. "That's alright. It's not gonna work."

"But you are," I continued, trying to poke the angry bear. "Your batting average is hitting the shitter and you're blaming everyone but yourself."

I took the last pull on my cigarette and dropped it on the ground. I was waiting for the punchline. I could feel it coming. It didn't come. I guess I was off my game.

"A man is not an island. Especially in a baseball team," he said.

"Except you're not looking at the one person who swings the bat," I said.

He shook his head at me like I was some sort of kidder. Then he turned to watch the other team.

"My problem is not with me. The problem is with the rest of the team. Mostly I blamed Ensor. You'll see now, my game will improve."

He spat out more chew. Grapes wafted over towards me and reminded me of my childhood, grape sodas and my first kiss. She wore grape lip gloss.

"So, you're out there in the batter's box, all by yourself. You can hit at balls because Ensor takes it easy on you in practice. Is that what I'm hearing?"

He turned to look at me and nodded.

"Yeah, that's what you're hearing."

He looked back again and moved the chew in his mouth back over to the opposite side.

"Or maybe you're too juiced up. Your muscles are getting in the way of your technique."

He didn't say anything. His nostrils flared. I could anger him easily enough but he wouldn't bite. Perhaps he'd seen what happened to Stark or perhaps he was just not in the mood.

"Do you own a gun?" I asked.

He looked over at me and then back at the field.

"I own a couple."

"Yeah," I said. "What kind?"

"A Glock 31 and a SR 1911."

"What's an SR 1911?"

"It's a Ruger. Forty-five Auto and the Glock is a three fifty-seven."

He wasn't looking at me. I was looking at him.

"And which one did you use to shoot Ensor?" I asked.

He looked over at me and shook his head.

"I told you. I didn't shoot him. Both handguns are registered and legal. I told the real cops about it too. I've had enough."

He turned and walked away. He stopped at the end of the aisle and spat the rest of his chew into the garbage. I didn't smell grapes anymore. Maybe a hint of sour ones. But that could've been my mood. This trip out here hadn't turned out to be all that helpful. First thing I needed to do was find out what kind of bullet did Ensor in. Maybe then I'd have another chat with Gibb, though he was a cool cucumber for someone who might have done a homicide.

I looked back up the stadium. Stark and Israel were just as I'd found them. Israel was talking to a boy. I pegged him as being Junior O'Riley. Israel was pointing at me. The boy was looking at me. I nodded and grinned. Then I started back up the stairs towards them.

CHAPTER TEN

Spitballing With Batboys

JUNIOR was a handsome boy. Might even call him a young man if he had manners. I hadn't figured that part out yet. He was average height. He looked me in the eye. He might yet have another growth spurt. He had dusty blond hair and a tan. His hair was thick and tousled giving him a beach bum look. He had dark green eyes and a pleasant face. I walked up the steps and he watched me the whole time. Or maybe he was looking past me at the game out on the field. That was probably it. I got to the top of the stairs and Israel started talking first.

"Anthony, this is Junior O'Riley," he said, nodding at the young man.

"I figured as much," I said, offering my hand.

Junior took it and gave it a firm shake. He'd been brought up right. He looked square in the eyes but there was nothing menacing about it. I liked this kid already.

"You know why I'm here?" I asked him.

Junior nodded.

"Yes sir," he answered, "you're helping the police find out who killed Mr. Ensor."

He was polite and respectful. The kind of kid I'd probably raise myself. Israel interrupted us.

"I'll just be down on the field with the team when you're ready to join us, Junior," said Israel.

Junior nodded at him and Israel walked off. I guessed it was time for the teams to switch out.

"Do you prefer Junior, Jim or James?" I said.

"Either of them would work sir," he said.

He stood stiffly in front of me and I wanted to put him at ease.

"James," I said, gazing at his expression as I called him by his first name. He didn't seem to mind. "The Queen of England hasn't knighted me. Please call me Anthony or Mr. Carrick."

He looked down and a grin burst on his face self-consciously, then he rubbed it off with the back of his hand.

"Okay, Mr. Carrick."

"And you're right. I am here to help the police figure out who killed Mr. Ensor. And I think you've got some great insider knowledge that'll help."

"I don't know, Mr. Carrick," he said. "I'm just the bat boy. Most of them don't pay me no attention."

"Exactly," I said. "And because of that, I bet you're like a fly on the wall. I reckon you've heard things that could probably help me."

Junior looked down again and kicked at a small pebble with his foot. He was wearing khaki cargo pants and skater sneakers with a blue tee that had a design on it I couldn't make out. He wasn't wearing a windbreaker or jacket. I thought that was brave of him. Kids nowadays, they figure they're immune to the weather. But I saw no goosebumps on his arms. He had his hands thrust deep in his front pockets. He didn't say anything to me.

"James," I said, looking at him as he looked down. He tilted his head up some to look at me. "Who's your favorite pitcher?"

He shrugged and shook his head.

"Listen, son," I said, "what we share here is just between me and you. Unless you actually saw the murder, nobody else has to know about our conversation, okay?"

He looked up quickly.

"I didn't see the murder, Mr. Carrick. I swear it."

"I believe you, James. So who's your favorite pitcher."

He grinned at me.

"Clayton Kershaw," he said.

I grinned back at him. I might not know a lot about baseball, but I knew who Clayton Kershaw was. He played for my team.

"Ha," I said, "I figured you were going to go with James Ensor."

"He's alright, but Kershaw's my favorite."

"He also plays for my team."

"You don't look rich enough to own a team," said James, grinning.

I looked at him hard for a moment. My best serious cop face. His grin fell of his mouth like a bird hitting a window.

"I, I didn't mean nothing by it, Mr. Carrick..."

I grinned at him.

"I know," I said, "I'm just having fun. Clayton plays for the LA Dodgers. That's my team. I live in LA."

James looked up at me shyly.

"I know," he said, "Mr. Kreyling told me you were from LA. So, you're like some kind of private eye, like Mike Hammer."

I nodded.

"Something like that," I said. "Though I don't take justice into my own hands. At least not when I can help it. You like hardboiled novels?"

Junior nodded.

"So how come you wanted to be a bat boy for the Cubs?"

"My father thought it would be a good idea for me. He said it would be a great honor."

"I see. You're not that much into baseball?"

Junior shook his head guiltily.

"That's alright, son," I said. "I'm not much into baseball either. I prefer being a hardboiled detective."

I smiled at him and he looked up at me and smiled back.

"I'd like to write about them one day. I just..."

He trailed off and looked back at the ground where he went to kicking invisible pebbles again. I checked. The one and only pebble he'd kicked the first time. Now he was kicking at air.

"You just what?"

He looked up at me briefly and then back down.

"I just, I just don't have time."

"Because your father wants you to be a baseball player, right?"

Junior looked up at me and nodded with eyes as sad as the copper coins on dead men's lids.

"So are you playing baseball?" I asked him.

He nodded.

"Yeah," he said, "but I'm not very good and my father keeps pushing me."

He sighed and looked off down the aisle at something. Maybe bad memories.

"I know what that's like," I said.

He glanced over at me and then back down the aisle, hands still thrust deep into empty pockets.

"My old man had me do things I didn't like for a while."

He looked back at me and smiled briefly.

"What did you do?" he asked.

"I got to like it."

He turned glum again and looked down at the gray space between us. The concrete floor as smooth as broken dreams.

"But that's not always gonna happen," I said. "You've only got another year, maybe two..."

I looked over at him for confirmation. He looked up at me.

"One year left," he said.

"Right, so you've only one more year and then you're free to do what you want."

He looked up again and smiled weakly.

"He wants me to get a baseball scholarship to a college, but it'll never happen. He says he's not going to help me with it otherwise, and college is just so expensive nowadays."

He looked down again and his dusty blond hair flopped in front of his forehead like a dog's tongue.

"Sometimes, James," I said, "you've gotta get out of the shadow in order to see the sun."

He looked and smiled more confidently this time.

"I guess. I try and write at recess when I can."

"Good for you. You've just gotta keep at it, son. It can take some time to make a name for yourself. I'm a painter. I know all about that."

He was grinning still.

"I never heard of a painter who was also a private eye."

"I never heard of a baller that's also a writer," I said.

He nodded softly.

"So maybe you can help me, James," I said. "You like to write about PIs. Let's look at this murder as if it was one of your stories."

He nodded and smiled at me.

"Who do you think would be good for it?"

"The wife," he said, though it sounded like more of a question.

"Why do you say that?"

"Well, she has the most to lose. I overheard them arguing one time about her being with another guy and he said she'd get nothing from him. That it was all in the prenup."

"I like that," I said. "Who was she sleeping around with?"

Junior looked around anxiously.

"Go on James, tell me."

"Mr. Gibb," he said, soft as a whisper from star crossed lovers.

"Vance Gibb, the left fielder for the Cubs?" I asked.

He nodded.

"So Ensor knew about them then, right?"

"Yes sir, he sure did. He was really mad. I hadn't seen him so mad in a long time. Said he was going to divorce her and she'd get nothing. It's sort of funny..."

"Go on."

"Well, I don't think Mr. Gibb was all that interested in her. I think he was just more interested in upsetting Mr. Ensor."

"I see, and what gave you that impression?"

"Just the way I saw him and Mrs. Ensor together. He seemed really disinterested in her. Nothing particular. But you know how you can tell when a girl really likes a guy but he's not that into her?"

I nodded, I'd seen that plenty of times. It was a recipe to ruin, or murder, sometimes.

"Well, that's just kind of what I saw I guess."

"So you think maybe the wife killed him so that she could get his money and set up house with Gibb?"

Junior shrugged and tossed his head to the side.

"Yeah, that's what I'd guess, Mr. Carrick. I mean if I was writing this story. Seems like she'd have the most to gain. The papers said Mr. Ensor was worth over a hundred million. But I wouldn't know about that."

"That's quite a bit more than nothing," I said. "You're being real helpful, James. Isn't this fun?"

Junior grinned at me and nodded his head.

"What other tidbits do you have? Who else did Ensor have problems with?"

"Well, Mr. Stark didn't like him much. Mr. Ensor didn't care for him either. They didn't have big arguments but I could just tell that they didn't like each other. Mr. Stark kept complaining to Mr. Kreyling that he couldn't get enough innings in to improve his score. He really wanted to play more, but Mr. Ensor was in the way, he was chasing his strikeouts and looking for that perfect game, but most people didn't think he was going to get it."

"Why is that?"

"Well, Mr. Ensor had a bad elbow. He'd had one operation already and he was always seeing the team doctor. And I know he was being referred to specialists. And I could tell he was in pain. To me, it just didn't seem like he had the same power that he used to have."

"You saw him in pain?"

Junior nodded. He looked out over the field. I turned to take a look. He was watching the Cubs get in some practice. Then Junior looked back at me.

"Yeah, sometimes I'd see him out there warming up on the mound and he'd wince. You could tell it was hard on him. I don't think he had many years left. Maybe this would have been his last.

Maybe next season. I don't see how he could have continued on."

I nodded.

"And having him out of the way would help Stark, right? He'd become the Ace?"

"That's how I understand it. But I don't see how he could have killed him. I mean he must have known that Ensor couldn't have much longer."

"That's right, but the heart wants what it wants. And Stark isn't getting any younger. He needs to be getting his time in right now if he wants to get some numbers in. I could see him needing to get Ensor out sooner than later."

Junior shrugged and looked down. I looked down there, but there wasn't anything worth looking at. I didn't get it.

"You're probably right," he said.

"What else can you tell me?" I asked.

"The doctor is doping up the whole team."

"Who knows about that?"

Junior looked up at me and smiled.

"Everybody."

"All the players?"

He nodded.

"How about Kreyling?"

He nodded again.

"The owner?"

He shrugged.

"I don't know about that. He's a successful businessman, he's not very hands-on. I've only seen a few times and that's mostly in the owner's box. I think he keeps the running of this team to Mr. Kreyling and the coaches."

I nodded. We were taking turns.

"Did anyone have a problem with taking the juice?" I asked.

"Well, Mr. Ensor spoke to the doctor about it. He thought that the steroids were making his problem worse. I don't know anything about that. He threatened the doctor that he was going to tell the MLB about the steroid abuse if he didn't get Mr. Ensor off of it."

"And how did that go?"

"I dunno, Mr. Carrick. I think it went all right. I mean the doctor was real upset. You could tell. He told Mr. Kreyling about it. Mr. Kreyling told him to get Mr. Ensor off the drugs then. But I could tell that Mr. Kreyling wasn't happy about the threat either."

"And what's the doctor's name?"

"Dr. Harry Collin."

I nodded, making a mental note of the name.

"Anything else you can think of?"

Junior shrugged and then looked around guiltily. I'd seen it before.

"Anything at all. Even if it seems small."

He shrugged again, more slowly this time and less sure of himself.

"I mean it's not a big deal, Mr. Carrick. Everybody's doing it. And I don't think it means anything," he said.

I put my hand on his shoulder and smiled at him. Thinking I might be the cool uncle he never had. Really, I was just trying to squeeze him for anything I could. He looked at me and smiled.

"Well, like I said, I don't think it's a big deal, but I know that Mr. Kreyling has a lot of money on the outcome of this series."

"How do you know that?"

"I'm pretty quiet, and they hardly ever see me it seems like. I've heard him on the phone sometimes speaking to someone."

"What does he say?"

"Well, he said that he needed them to put up the money in addition to what he'd put up. He said the outcome was gonna make them all very rich. They'd be millionaires. He said it was a fact that they'd win."

"I see, so he was putting a large sum of money on the Cubs?"

Junior nodded eagerly.

"Of course. There are only the two teams in this World Series. It's not like he'd put it on the opposition."

He grinned at that.

"Right, so this hurts him then, doesn't it? The death of Ensor doesn't help the Cubs win, does it?"

He shook his head.

"No, I guess it doesn't. My father's really upset about it. He's put some money on the Cubs too and now he says that they're as good as dead. The odds are outrageous he said. When they were coming in he said he'd make an easy ten times on his money."

"I see," I said. "Mostly because of Ensor, I guess?"

"I think so," said Junior.

"So why were you so reticent to tell me about Israel's gambling?"

"Well, I don't think he's allowed to gamble or bet on MLB games. And he was. Lots of them are, but I don't think it's legal."

I nodded. He was probably right. It would make sense. So everybody had something they were hiding, or so it seemed. I needed to get out of this place before the number of suspects rocketed into the stratosphere. I had Stark and Gibb. They were my best bets. Plus the wife. Of course the wife. I was gonna shake that tree to see what fell from its poisoned branches. And I was betting on poisoned fruit. Then again it could just as easily have been a random fan off the street come in and shot Ensor to ensure his team would win. That team being the Birds.

I didn't want to go down that road. It was a long and windy one, with steep cliffs on each side and teeth snapping monsters in the abyss. That would make a helluva case, having to find a random fan as the murderer. Could be, but I'd like to look closer at home first just to see. And that's what I was gonna do. First I had to head back to the office to see what Dykes and Jackson had been up to. And maybe share my news. Then I wanted to see a man about a woman.

CHAPTER ELEVEN
Where The Warrant Is

I walked into the CPD headquarters like they'd left the doors open and unlocked. They had. But it felt like home. Maybe like grandmother's home. A place that always felt cozy but where you had to mind your manners. Yeah, that was it. I signed out a pass and made my way up to homicide where'd I'd come from just some hours before. The day had dragged its tired corpse into the afternoon leaving the stench of manure left in dark corners never able to dry out.

Dykes and Jackson were at a couple of desks facing each other. They were busy. Or looking busy, the way office workers shuffle papers around. Jackson at least was on the phone. Dykes was tossing a baseball up in the air. He caught and put it back down and then looked at me.

"How'd it go?" he asked.

I looked over at Jackson and he nodded. I nodded back. He said something into the phone and I turned to talk to Dykes.

"You know when you're a kid," I said, "and you turn over a rotted out log you find in some field someplace that you've gone exploring."

Dykes nodded his head and squinted at me at the same time.

"And you know how all those termites, bugs, ants and spiders scurry out from under?"

I looked at him and grinned. He nodded again, still squinting.

"That's how it was."

"I don't get it," he said.

"I uncovered more dark matter having upturned that log."

"Tell me about it?"

I looked down at the baseball on his desk. It was signed by someone. I couldn't make out the signature. I thought he'd also spoken rhetorically. I was wrong.

"Seriously, tell me about it?" he asked again.

I looked over at him and smiled slowly. It was more like my lips twitching at the corners.

"Here's the short version. Gibb and Stark are still suspects. The bat boy Junior likes the wife for it. But so it seems that a lot of the players like the wife for different reasons. At least Gibb acknowledges he was screwing Ensor's wife. Don't know if he knew about it though. Both Gibb and Stark swear they didn't kill him. One or both of them is lying. Maybe neither of them. But then I'm feeling uncharitable. The Manager's putting side money on the games as are probably a lot of the players. He might end up losing a chunk of change."

"And his job if the Commissioner finds out about it," added Jackson, joining in the conversation.

I looked over at Jackson.

"You know he's making over a mill a year to manage them?" I asked.

He nodded and grinned.

"Like I've said before. Baseball is big business. He's worth it. One of the best managers out there"

I shook my head.

"So a guy that's never won a pennant is considered one of the best. That's like you're saying you're one of the best homicide detectives and you've never solved a case."

Jackson grinned at me.

"It's different in sports," he said. "You've got a team of dozens of guys and one manager. He can't be responsible for everything. It's a team sport. Sometimes a great manager just doesn't have the best environment in which to perform."

"That may be true," said Dykes, "but betting on games is a risky move. I think we've got some leverage there to shake him with."

I nodded my head. So did Jackson.

"What do you want to do?" I asked.

"I want to go shake that liar of hers," said Dykes looking at his partner. "You got that warrant."

Jackson nodded.

"We can pick it up on our way over to the lawyer's place."

"I'd also like to get some gun checks on Gibb and Stark, see if we can rule them out legally. How about we also pick up a couple of warrants for them too. Maybe they've got a three for one sale at the courthouse."

Jackson looked up at me.

"What you got that's good for them?"

"Gibb's fucking the deceased's wife, plus they exchanged knuckle sandwiches not long ago. As for Stark, he's got the most to gain from Ensor's death."

Jackson turned up his lower lip and nodded his head.

"I think we can work with that."

CHAPTER TWELVE
Crying Over Spilled Milk

DYKES and I were hanging out at a coffee shop. It was across from the law courts. Jackson was inside trying to get a couple more warrants. We'd arrived just before five and we were pushing our luck. Civil servants are known for their punctuality, in leaving on work on time. Dykes assured me that the DA Jackson knew would get us our warrants. That's why Jackson was inside and not Dykes. I asked him about that.

"She's not a fan of me," he said, sipping on a coffee.

"Obviously," I said.

"We had a thing, it didn't end well and she's holding a grudge. Likes Jackson though."

I nodded at him. Things could get complicated, then they could get sour like spilled milk left in the sun.

"Maybe Jackson has a thing with her now," I said, just filling the space between us with hot air.

"Not likely. He's a married man. Loves his wife. Besides," said Dykes, "I think she likes to do nice things for him on account of him being my partner. That way she can be seen doing her job professionally while still sticking it to me personally."

Complicated things. Always had a way of getting messy. I preferred to avoid complications if possible, except if they were in my watch. They weren't, those kinds of watches I couldn't afford.

"Sounds like it really went south," I said.

"It did, I fucked up big time. This was a couple of years ago though, long enough that I've got breathing room from it, recent enough that it still scares the shit out of me."

"You wanna tell me about it?" I asked.

Dykes looked over at the barista. He was a tall skinny lad who looked around college age. He was clean shaven with a hungry look on his face. Wolfish, if you asked me. Dykes looked back at me and shrugged. He drank some of his coffee and reached under the table with his hand. Then he brought his hand back onto the table and opened his fist and a roll of Lifesavers rolled out onto the table. It was half empty, or half full, take your pick.

"The way I see it, we need our vices. I don't trust a man who's clean as a whistle. Do you understand?"

He looked at me earnestly, his eyes peering into me searching for something. I nodded.

"I don't trust a man who hasn't looked into the dark corners of his soul."

He nodded.

"Right. The reason I'm telling you this, is I've got a sense I can trust you. Same with Jackson. And I reckon you've got vices. Any man who's trustworthy's got 'em."

I nodded again.

"What are yours?"

"Fast cars, loose women and unicorns," I said with a straight face.

He laughed at that.

"That's exactly what I mean. You see, you cover up your weaknesses with humor. It's a classic. That's what I've been learning these years in the meetings. We've got to seek a higher power in order to overcome our vices, our weaknesses. We're powerless by ourselves."

"I sometimes think that God is the doorman to the devil's lair," I said.

Dykes nodded.

"That's fair. I'm not a religious man myself, but I wouldn't quite go that far."

"That's good," I said, "I thought you were about to slide a pamphlet over to me about salvation."

Dykes smiled at me.

"Religion can be a vice, for some. I'll give you that. No, this ain't about religion, It is about salvation though. Salvation from the vices that'll bring a man to ruin."

"You tell me yours and I'll tell you mine," I said.

I took the last sip of coffee from my cup. Dykes had bought. I figured I owed him a listen, even if the last dregs were bitter.

"I think I already know yours."

"Then tell me mine and I'll tell you yours."

"Alcohol and drugs."

He wasn't far off. He stopped and looked at me for a while. Then he looked down at the Lifesavers and rolled them back and forth between us with his fingers.

"I'm not meaning to put you in a pickle," he said. "This is about me, you asked, so let me tell you. These here," he said, and he flicked the candy towards me, "are literally my life savers."

I rolled them back to him.

"You've probably noticed I like them. A lot."

I nodded.

"Well, let me get back to the beginning," he said. "About ten years I was happily married."

So were a lot of us I thought.

"I'd also just made it into homicide. Here at the CPD it's sort of the pinnacle right."

I nodded. Was in most police departments.

"And the ego gets stroked. I was one of the younger homicide detectives, thought I was all that and some. Thought I was Superman."

He paused then and drank the last of his coffee. The joint was emptying out a bit. Most folks going home.

"Then I got caught up in a bad squeeze. Started using drugs. That's my vice. Anything I could get. Turns out that led me on the path to hell. Lost almost everything. Wife got custody of the kids and took them out of state. Haven't seen them in about five years. I almost got jail if it wasn't for the DA that Jackson is sweet talking right now. She thinks I used her for a get out of jail card. Wasn't like that, I was messed up. My head wasn't on straight. Yeah, I was manipulating everyone and anyone I could. Including her, but it wasn't just about that. Not by a long shot."

He stopped for a moment and rolled the Lifesavers in his fingers. He pulled one out and popped it into his mouth. He offered me one. I was feeling social so I took it. He shrugged.

"Hard to really get you to understand just by giving it words like this. Makes it seem small and concise, a nice little package. But life ain't like that. It was a whole messy yarn that looked more like a cat had got to it in a forest. Messy. I was messed up. Could have got ten years in the joint. Imagine that. Ten years for a homicide detective. That's messed up."

I nodded.

"But here you are. The golden boy. The prodigal son."

He looked at me and smiled.

"Damn right. By the grace of something, something that I'm not quite sure I deserved. Kerri Skinner, the DA we've been talking about, she more than anyone saved my bacon. She really went to bat for me. Tirelessly worked on the Commissioner, and the Mayor, with the help of my partner, Jackson, of course, and my Captain, Lane. Somehow I got a second chance. Been sober now just over two years."

"You're a lucky man."

"I am," he said. "Had to take a leave for three months. Went out of state for treatment. The department helped pay for it. I came back a changed man. The same but different."

"That sounds more like it. I don't see people changing much."

"Right, I'm still the same, but I'm different. I see things differently now. I'm making choices everyday. Every second of every day."

"That why you come across aloof?" I asked.

He nodded.

"Probably. I'm real slow at letting my guard down now."

"And your Lifesavers?"

"Yea, they're like a talisman of sorts. This treatment center I was at, one of the things they recommended was seeking something physical that we could use to represent the change we were making. I couldn't come up with anything. Then one day at the store they had at the center I was buying a bottle of water and these things were up front by the cash register and weirdly, they jumped out at me. Lifesavers. Life savers. It was like I had an epiphany. That's how come they're here."

"So you've replaced one vice for another."

"You could say that. Nothing wrong with it. Candy's much better than drugs. It's legal and I've got a good dental plan. But they're not so much a vice as a habit now. But they're a daily reminder. How my life has been saved. I probably go through one of these rolls a day. Every time I take one out it's a reaffirmation of what I've come through. The words on these little ringed candies. Lifesavers. That's what they represent. It's always top of mind. Every hour I take one out I'm reminded. I find it comforting. Helpful."

"That's a great story," I said. "Thanks for sharing. So what's Jackson's vice then?"

Dykes shook his head at me.

"Nope. You don't get off that easy. I told you mine, now you tell me yours."

"You had it right when you guessed," I said.

"Alcohol and drugs?"

I nodded.

"Whiskey and American tobacco particularly."

"I figured you for the hard drinking, tough talking gumshoe type."

I shrugged.

"Not that you're asking, but I'd keep a tight reign on both of them. Either could easily send you into an early grave. Make you do things you'd regret."

"I wasn't asking," I said.

Dykes nodded slowly, thoughtfully.

"I wasn't either," he said. "But I needed to hear the telling."

"Both are legal, like you said. Unlikely to put me in the spot you were squeezed into."

"You'd be surprised. I'd seek out healthier options if I was you."

"I'm still waiting for that pamphlet."

Dykes shrugged.

"Yeah, alright. The timing's off, but the seeds are planted. I hope they'll blossom sooner than later."

I didn't say anything to that.

"What about Jackson?"

"Gambling," he said.

"Lane?"

"Lane's one of the cleanest cops I've known. If pushed, I'd say his weakness is bling. You've met him."

I nodded.

"And yet how does he afford it on a captain's salary."

It was a rhetorical question. Something that Dykes and Jackson and other homicide detectives probably knew the answer to. Dykes nodded at me grinning.

"You think he's a crooked cop."

"I think there's a story behind his money."

"There is," he said.

I looked at Dykes, he wasn't giving it up without cajoling.

"So, are we still sharing or are you holding out now?"

"Still sharing. Lane's father owned a business in town. Called Lane's Heating and Plumbing. He sold it some years back for several million. The old man passed away a couple of years ago and Lane's the only child. Got it all. A small fortune. He's got a good financial manager. Rumor has it he earns three to five times his cop salary from those investments. I figure his investment income is probably around half a mill a year. That'll buy you quite a bit of bling."

I nodded.

"That's good to know. I don't work with crooked cops."

The place had really emptied out now. It was coming on five thirty.

"Do you ever wonder why recovered addicts sound just like religious proselytizers?" I asked him.

He shrugged his shoulders, rolling the half empty Lifesavers candy roll back and forth between us.

"I don't know why either," I said. "Seems like both think they've found the only way to salvation. Maybe a man doesn't need saving."

Dykes looked up at me with steady eyes. He had a slight smile on his face. I couldn't tell if I liked it or wanted to smack it off his smug face.

"Everyone needs saving from themselves," he said.

"Now see, that's said like a true believer. And I don't buy it."

"What's not to buy?"

"This idea we need saving from something outside of ourselves. I've known plenty of guys don't need saving. And I've seen a handful save themselves."

Dykes cocked his head to the side and shrugged at the same time.

"Maybe," he said, "but I think most of us need help finding the light again. And I'm not talking religion with you. Like I said, I'm not a religious man. In our line of work it's hard to find religion in the gutters of human effluence. Still, I had plenty of help getting out of my own hell. Doubt I could have done it without the help of others."

Now it was my turn to shrug. And I did. This wasn't going to get us anywhere. The saved seemed to think they have the sanctimonious right answer to everyone's problems. Michael

Collins and I'd disagree. Hell, even Johnny Walker and I would see eye to eye on this one.

"I'm happy for you," I said at last, trying my best to detour around the big pile of stinking turd of righteousness I was beginning to see form between us. I needn't have worried. Jackson was my savior. Dykes nodded towards the door. I turned around to see Jackson.

"Looks like he's got a few of those pamphlets we were talking about," said Dykes.

"Took a little while to get the paperwork done," said Jackson. Then he paused for a moment before looking at his partner. "Kerri says hi."

Dykes looked at him for a moment and nodded.

"Carrick and I were just talking about that," he said.

Jackson nodded long and thoughtfully.

"Alcohol," he said. "Am I right?"

Jackson was looking at Dykes. Dykes looked at me. Then Jackson looked at me too.

"Whiskey and cigarettes," I said.

Jackson nodded and grinned. His gold tooth looking odd for his otherwise well put together business look.

"Hard to trust a man without some cracks," he said.

Nobody said anything to that. I reckon we were tired out by all the cafe philosophizing we'd done in the last half hour or so.

"Well," said I, "should we go see a man about a woman?"

Dykes nodded. He popped another Lifesaver in his mouth and offered them around. I took one. I wanted to see if this little white candy would offer any great insights into salvation. It didn't. We left the coffee shop and got back into the unmarked police car.

"It's past five thirty," said Jackson, announcing it like he was public radio. "Should we try tomorrow?"

Dykes turned and craned his head to look into the backseat where I was.

"Did you get all three search warrants."

Jackson was also turned around looking at me. He grinned his shiny gold tooth.

"Sure did. Kerri's still got a soft spot for Silent Red," he said.

I nodded.

"Works for me then. I could do some thinking in the bottom end of a bottle," I said.

"If that's what you'd like," said Dykes, getting my drift but not offering up anything to the contrary.

They drove me back to the hotel. We agreed on an eight thirty start in the morning. That gave me plenty of time for some thinking and some drinking. I walked straight to the bar and ordered a whisky. Irish whiskey. The only part I regretted was not being able to enjoy a smoke with it in the bar. Me and my vices, well, we'd have to be commiserating separately.

CHAPTER THIRTEEN
Salisbury Hill & Dale

THE night before, I'd done a lot of thinking at the bottom of a whiskey glass. But Dykes oration about salvation had been nagging at me like a rusty nail at the bottom of my shoe. I hadn't done half the drinking I'd been planning on, and the last whiskey of the night I'd adulterated with soda water.

On top of that I'd picked up some other nasty habits like drinking a glass of water before bed. Funnily, this morning I felt incredibly sprightly. I'd been up a little before seven, had a shower and shave and a hearty breakfast of steak and eggs. It was now a little before eight thirty and I was standing outside the main entrance of the hotel waiting for Crockett and Tubs, far enough away so a man could enjoy a smoke in peace without the hairy eyeballs of bingo grannies and soccer moms.

There was a younger guy having a cigarette. He felt chatty. I didn't. But I was feeling sprightly like I said. That put me in good spirits. He wore baggy jeans that were almost falling down to his ankles. His baseball cap was on backwards, the brim straight as a razor. I couldn't see which team it supported, but I coulda guessed. And I would have been wrong. He had on black skater shoes and a black T-shirt. The T-shirt had something in red on it. Might have been a word, might have been bad art. I didn't care to find out. He looked like one of those popular pop stars. He didn't look at me when he spoke. He only looked at me when I wasn't looking at him. He was short. Maybe five seven on IMDB. Likely five six in real life.

"You here for the game?" he asked me. He sucked on his cigarette like it was blocked at the other end. His veins along his neck popped out like ropes. He squinted at me with one eye as the smoke tried to lick his face.

"In a manner of speaking," I said. I looked at him.

"Yeah, I'm here for the game. Gonna be killa. The Big O's are gonna win. For sure. I've put cash money on it."

I grinned to myself. I hadn't asked him anything and I didn't realize there were different sorts of cash other than the money kind. He sucked on his cigarette again and quickly blew the smoke back out. He couldn't have been older than twenty. But when you get to my age it's sometimes hard to tell.

"I'm Nick by the way," he said.

I didn't say anything. I was looking at all the different sorts of people coming and going from the hotel. I could see him looking at me from the corner of his eyes.

"What's your name?" he asked.

I wasn't trying to be a dick. I just wasn't in the mood for chatting. But he seemed sincere.

"Mike Hammer," I said.

He nodded his head up and down like it was something he already knew.

"For reals? That's a pretty cool name," he said.

I nodded.

"Yup, for reals," I said, trying on the lingo for size.

"Never heard a name like that before," he said. "You could be a wrestler with a name like that."

You've never heard a name like that, because you've never read any good books, kid. That's what I wanted to say. Instead I said, "never wrestled."

"You heard about that murder out at the park," he said, seemingly liking the sound of his own voice. "Somebody whacked the pitcher for the Cubs. Can you believe that? I thought I was gonna win before, but this makes it a slam dunk. You know what I heard?"

The kid never stopped to give me an in. I don't think he cared for my opinion.

"I heard that it was the Mafia. That pitcher. James Ensor, he owed them a ton of money. They whacked him because he wouldn't pay up. Sounds legit to me. They do that you know. The Mafia. They won't just break your kneecaps, no way, man, now they'll just kill ya. And it don't take much neither. I heard about a guy they whacked because he stole a pack of smokes from this Mafia's guy's son. That's how serious they are, man. You don't want to fuck with them. The Mafia, people think they're no longer around. It's not true. They just got smarter. I wouldn't mess with them. No way, man. They're totally legit bad asses."

He took a moment to take another drag on his cigarette like it was still a straw that had something stuck at the other end.

"Thanks for the tip," I said. Inside I was laughing the hardest I'd laughed since coming to Chicago.

"No worries, man. I can tell with a name like that. Mark Hammer?"

"Mike Hammer," I said.

"Yeah, Mike Hammer. Cool name by the way. With a name like that I bet you don't get many guys messing with you. Still, I'd be sure to stay away from the Mafia. They're bad news. My girlfriend said she heard that they even control some of the cops around here. That's why crime is so bad here. I'm from Baltimore, and I can tell you that Baltimore is a way cooler place than Chicago. And I don't mean cold. No way, man, we just have better government. No Mafia there. But still, I wouldn't bet against them coming to Baltimore. It's a popping place. They'd do good business there. But we have good cops. At least most of them. Though this one time my buddy got pulled over for jaywalking and the cops took him down, man. They gave it to him pretty hard. I told him he shoulda sued the city for cop brutality. He got a scuffed cheek and he bit his lip when they took him down. It was brutal. Some cops, man, they're assholes, just on huge ego trips."

I could see the unmarked police car drive into the main entrance. Thank God for small mercies. Nick's verbal diarrhea was pushing my blood pressure through the roof. I couldn't tell if he was bored or just lonely. I went to put my cigarette out in the trash can with a sand filled cigarette dispenser on the top.

"I gotta get going, Nick. Good talking to you," I said.

"Oh yeah, no sweat man. Geez, is that your ride. Fuck, you're a cop. Listen," he said. "I didn't mean anything by that. You know, most cops are good. But sometimes you get a bad apple, right? I'm not saying you're a bad apple, shit, man, I even like the Mafia okay. They've never given me any grief..."

I walked up to the car as they pulled right up to the curb. I got into the back and closed the door. I didn't look back. For all I could tell Nick was still verbally vomiting verbosity all over the place.

"Thank you, Jesus," I said.

"You making friends I see," Dykes.

"Jesus, you have no idea. Nick there just couldn't stop talking ever since I gave him the time of day."

"Probably just lonely," said Jackson.

"Get this," I said. "He asked me my name. I said Mike Hammer. Figures it'll make a great wrestler name. What the fuck?"

Jackson laughed and slapped his knee.

"Damn, I like that. No shit. He had no clue who Mike Hammer was?"

I shook my head.

"Not a friggin' idea."

I could see Dykes look at me from the rearview mirror.

"Still, would be a good wrestler name," he said.

"Sure would be, but if you're going to make up wrestler names you've got to take your favorite James Bond movie and then add to that the name of the street you grew up on," said Jackson.

He got no takers from the rest of us.

"Okay," he said. "I'll go first. My favorite Bond movie is Moonraker. I grew up on Fifth Street. So my wrestler name is Moonraker Fifth. But you can play with it right, so I'd probably go with Moonraker the Fifth."

Jackson was having fun all by himself, so it seemed. He turned around and looked at me.

"What about you."

I was feeling sprightly like I'd said, so I decided to play along.

"Skyfall Lightning," I said, just pulling out the first James Bond movie I remembered and coming up with a word that sounded good with it.

"Really? Man, that's an awesome wrestler name," said Jackson. "You really grew up on Lightning Street?"

I shook my head.

"Nah, it was Lightning Lane," I said, lying through my teeth.

Jackson nodded, impressed with the yarn I'd just spun. He turned towards Dykes.

"Okay, Dykes," he said. "Your turn."

Dykes didn't say anything for a minute.

"Well?" asked Jackson.

"I'm thinking," said Dykes.

We continued driving for a few moments. I spent the time looking out the window.

"Dr. No Frost," said Dykes.

"I dig it," said Jackson. "Moonraker the Fifth, Dr. No Frost and Skyfall Lightning. Those are some winning wrestler names."

"I still like Mike Hammer the best," I said.

"Was that Frost Street you grew up on or something else?" asked Jackson.

"Frost Place," said Dykes.

Jackson nodded and we rode in silence for a while. The sky was patchy with smears of gray and just the slightest hints of blue. Looked like it could rain but it wasn't.

"We're headed to that lawyer first?" I asked. "Salisbury?"

Jackson nodded, and then he turned round to look at me.

"You gonna love this one," he said.

He pulled the warrant from his inside jacket pocket and looked at it again.

"Salisbury, Hill and Dale," he said.

"You're shitting me," I said.

Jackson shook his head.

"I wouldn't pull your leg about something this serious."

He was grinning his white and gold toothy grin.

"Unbelievable," I said. "You can't make up this shit."

"I know, right?"

We drove in silence for a while further. It didn't take long to get to the office building. One of those generic modern looking office towers with the blue glass all up the sides. The kind of place that might have looked impressive twenty years ago, now they're everywhere. If you saw one in a picture you'd have no idea which city it was from.

Dykes pulled up front and parked the car. We all got out and walked into the lobby. We didn't need to look at the addresses, we knew where we were going. Twenty-fifth floor. Salisbury, Hill & Dale was at 2508. They likely took up two or more floors was my guess.

We got to the reception desk and Dykes talked to the receptionist. She was hired for her looks. I could tell that right off the bat. She was a young twenty-something baby doll with long curly blonde hair that crashed onto her shoulders like every teenage boys wet dream. She was clueless. And that was to our benefit.

"I'm Detective Dykes, that's Detective Jackson CPD Homicide." He flashed her his badge. "Can you tell me where Frederic Salisbury is?"

"Um, he's in a meeting if you'd just like to take a seat," she said as if she hadn't heard a word we said.

"I'll find him," I said as I walked past the three of them. She went to pick up the phone, fumbling a bit. "Tell him Peter Gabriel sent us."

She looked at me with a slack mouth part open looking for flies. She didn't get it. But it gave her something to think about. Dykes and Jackson joined me. I entered the main hallway and reckoned

145

that he'd be in one of the corners. I had to guess as to left or right. I noticed he was a righty when he came down to the station so I went right. Bingo, at the end of the hall was his office.

His name was on the wall just to the right of the door. Real walls enclosed his office and the door was a solid wooden one. We walked in like it was our own. It was a huge office that seemed almost the size of my apartment back in Santa Monica. A large wooden table sat back away from the door with a plush and comfy cushioned black leather chair behind it. There was a fancy rug on the floor, between the desk and the small conference table where Salisbury sat with two other men. I assumed them to be Hill and Dale.

Even with two large tables in this office, it was several strides for us to reach them from the office's door. Salisbury had on the same round glasses. He was just as well dressed as before and his hair just as dyed. He wore a bad looking suit. It was well tailored and no doubt expensive but it looked like something that was more at home in the seventies than the tens. Might it have been called salmon? I don't know my colors that well, I'm not a fashion designer, but it looked like Pepto-Bismol had puked up on cream.

He stood up and his eyebrows arched. He was visibly upset. I got that.

"What is the meaning of this? I'm in a very important meeting."

"Not as important as meeting with us," I said. I looked at the other two. "Hill and Dale?" I said, grinning from ear to ear.

"I'm David Hill," said the shorter and fatter of the two. He was also older than Hill and Salisbury.

"Then you must be Dale," I said, looking at the slimmer but still fat middle aged man in a dark blue suit. He nodded.

"Gareth Dale," he said. "What is this intrusion about?"

"It's about Salisbury's client, Celia Ensor," I said.

I stepped aside and let Jackson come on in for the home run. He offered the warrant to Salisbury. Salisbury took it.

"This is a warrant for any records you have related to Celia Ensor," he said.

"This is highly improper," he said. "I'll have this cancelled in ten minutes."

"Ten minutes is about all the time we need to make a mess of this place," said Dykes.

"You wouldn't dare," said Salisbury, looking worried.

Hill and Dale left the office, most likely to call on a favor from another judge. I wasn't sure a warrant like this was legal for privileged information, but Jackson had convinced someone to issue it and that was good enough for me.

"Salisbury, Hill and Dale," I said, trying to deflect the conversation. "You couldn't have gone with "Dale, Salisbury and Hill?"

I looked at Salisbury with a straight face. He looked back at me unamused, the warrant still in his hand.

"It sounded better," he said. "In any event Solsbury Hill is spelled very differently. So you aren't being all that clever."

"Sounds the same," I said, "and it gave me a very good chuckle."

"Me too," said Jackson. "So are we going to exchange witticisms or are you going to help us."

"Why should I make your jobs easier?" asked Salisbury.

"Because if you're not inclined to," said Dykes,"we're going to start rummaging through the offices here and your files. Who knows what other secrets we might come up against."

Salisbury looked at the paper in his hand. Such power with words. He didn't say anything for a moment.

"Fine," he said. "What do you want to know?"

He sat down at the table and we joined him.

"We want to hear about Celia," said Dykes. "You can start telling us about any will or prenups."

Salisbury sighed like the last gasp of a balloon.

"I was James Ensor's attorney first. I've become hers since his death as you can imagine, because of the documents that James had me sign. Well, and I suppose the documents she witnessed."

"That's what we'd like to hear about," said Dykes.

"Do you really want to open up this can of worms?" he asked.

"The egg has already been scrambled," said Dykes, swapping metaphors with Salisbury.

Salisbury nodded and pushed his glasses up his nose. Dykes popped a Lifesaver in his mouth. It was likely the first roll of the day. Only a couple seemed to be missing. He didn't offer us any.

"I specialize in sports contract law. At our firm we like to offer full service law and we have on hand other lawyers specializing in family law, entertainment law, as well as criminal law. We tend to over deliver for our clients and it keeps them happy."

"And you rich," I said.

Salisbury looked at me. He didn't say anything, but I heard every word behind his mouth.

"Carrying on," he said, "I first got Mr. Ensor about five years ago when his contract was up for renewal. He wasn't happy with his previous legal representative. I made him very happy."

"And how happy was that?" I asked.

"What are you insinuating, Mr. Carrick?" asked Salisbury, remembering my name which was very good of him.

"How much did he get?"

"You know that already."

"I mean specifically."

"I don't know specifically. I'd have to look at my records. He gets twenty-five million a year for five years. There was a three million dollar signing bonus the first year. Our firm takes ten percent of all income as well as deducting business expenses. Not to mention the endorsements Mr. Ensor has received which have been worth several million in most years."

"So, it'd be fair to say he got more than thirty million a year in his pocket?"

Salisbury nodded. I bit my tongue. This was a racket if I'd ever heard of one. Legal or not.

"And before you, what had he received?" I asked.

"Three million a year."

I nodded my head.

"So we make our clients very happy. That's why they're happy to give us such a large percentage of their income. We always increase salaries."

"What about this year's negotiations?" asked Jackson. "We heard they weren't going too well."

Salisbury nodded.

"They're going to be tougher. Mr. Ensor wasn't playing as well as he had in previous years."

"Were you signed on to negotiate his upcoming contract?" asked Jackson.

"We were negotiating that," said Salisbury.

"So your whale was swimming away from you probably," I said.

"I believe he was negotiating with us on good terms," said Salisbury.

"But you're not sure he was going to sign with you for another term," I said. I could see the worry and doubt etched all over his face.

"I didn't say that," said Salisbury.

"You didn't have to," I said.

"Look," said Salisbury, looking at me, "you can't get blood from a stone."

"And yet Ensor was trying to get more than he'd received in the previous five years. Some were saying he'd get, maybe, twice as much."

I looked at Jackson. Jackson nodded at me in agreement.

"Yes, that might have been the case at the beginning of the season, but this season has not been quite that good compared to the last few," said Salisbury.

"So you're saying you weren't going to get him more?" asked Jackson.

"I'm not saying that. I'm saying it was going to be harder. The Cubs were willing to renew at the same rate if he won the Championship."

"And if he didn't?" asked Dykes.

"I prefer not to dwell on pessimistic outlooks."

"Humor us, Fred," I said.

Salisbury looked up at me with disdain plain as dog shit on a putting green.

"From my understanding, they wouldn't renew for anything more than ten a year."

"And as an agent that goes above and beyond for their client, you were shopping around for a team, right?" asked Jackson.

Salisbury nodded.

"Absolutely. My desire is to get the most for all of our clients. It's a win-win. Unfortunately, nobody was going to pay more than his current rate, and that was only if he had a championship under his belt."

"And why was that?" I asked. "I mean a guy with a World Series ring has gotta be hotter than a fried egg at an all-you-can-eat buffet."

Salisbury smiled at that.

"Well yes, I suppose he would be." Then he paused for a moment. "If he were ten years younger and hadn't had any Tommy Johns. Unfortunately for Ensor, he was both peaking in age and in ability. Plus all the scouts talk and it was apparent that this season he was on the downswing. He might have pulled off a win but next season wasn't looking good for him."

"So with your biggest client walking away you've got a lot of money to lose," I said, always trying to stir the pot.

"I'm not sure what you're trying to insinuate," said Salisbury.

"I'm just saying. If you could get him for another five years at the same salary that's an easy two, three or more million in your pocket. Per year."

"That's correct, Mr. Carrick. You've missed your calling as a mathematician. Ensor might have been our most valuable client but he's hardly the only one. We have over two dozen sports clients bringing in over ten million in fees to this office."

"Exactly, you've made my point. Ensor was likely worth thirty percent of your take."

"Are you suggesting that we had him killed because he might have walked to a new agent?"

"I'm not suggesting anything, but since you are, did you?" I asked.

Salisbury wasn't getting as riled up as I'd hoped. He pushed his glasses back up his nose. They didn't seem to be sliding down, but what did I know.

"I don't see how you can make any reasonable case for us having him murdered. It's a preposterous and insulting idea. If he were to leave, which was only a small possibility, having him murdered does nothing for us. We lose out on the money regardless. And like I said, we do not depend on any one client for the ongoing survival of our business."

"So you say." I couldn't help but to keep poking the bear.

Salisbury looked up at me like an impatient parent at their wits' end from countless sleepless nights with a colicky baby. That's me, just crying and whining endlessly.

"Besides which, Mr. Carrick," said Salisbury, "I have an alibi."

"Is that right?" I said. "You thought of everything."

He didn't take the bait, didn't even go for a nibble.

"I was at home with my wife and kids."

Dykes decided to end this sparring. I was tiring of it anyway.

"I understand that," said Dykes. "You didn't murder Ensor. Doesn't make sense you would anyway. You've got nothing to gain from it regardless of whether he would have stayed with you or not."

"Exactly, Detective," replied Salisbury.

"But," said Dykes, getting to the thrust of his comment, "I think you might know more than you're willing to let on."

"How do you come to that?"

"I think you have more information than you've been sharing with us."

"Of course I do," said Salisbury, getting annoyed with Dykes this time. "It's called client privilege and like I said earlier I'm happy to give you further information if you ask the right questions, but I'm not going to offer anyone up on a silver platter. That's your job. I will however say that I believe my client is innocent of this crime."

"Your client being Celia Ensor?" asked Dykes.

Salisbury nodded.

"We didn't suggest she was guilty," said Dykes.

Salisbury shook his head slowly. We were clearly irritating him but he wasn't getting upset with us. He was a man very much in control of his emotions.

"You might as well have said it. Your questions last time were pointed and insinuating as they are now. If you don't want to get to the point, perhaps I will make that call to a friend of mine who will have this warrant nulled in minutes."

"I have a question," said Jackson, getting into the fun. "Was there a prenup between Ensor and his wife?"

Salisbury moved his gaze over to Jackson and nodded.

"Of course there was, it would be reckless of me not to have suggested one to my client."

"So at the beginning of your relationship with Ensor he was unmarried?" asked Jackson.

"That's right. Five years ago he was single. Happily single I should say."

"And when did he get married?"

"Not sure off the top of my head. I'd say a couple of years ago or so."

"And you advised him to have a prenup with his soon-to-be bride, Celia?" asked Jackson.

"That's right and he agreed. He was bringing in a lot of money. I saw no point of him losing half of it to a greedy gold digger."

"That seems like a harsh thing to say about Celia Ensor," said Dykes.

Salisbury looked over towards Dykes.

"Not really, Detective. I didn't know Celia at the time, but I know my clients and the sorts of women that go after them. It's just a fact that eighty percent, and I'm being kind, of the women who seek out relationships with these super stars are gold digging. Now, they might not be looking for a quick smash and grab but they're eager to get on the gravy train. You might not understand that as you've not experienced the problems that come with great wealth."

"I have," I said. "My wife turned into a gold digger after we'd been married some time."

Salisbury looked at me.

"Perhaps you didn't choose well at the beginning. My wife and I have been together many years. We were married shortly after I got out of law school and didn't have two pennies to rub together."

I didn't say anything to that.

"So Ensor agreed to a prenup and I imagine that Celia signed on?" asked Jackson.

Salisbury nodded.

"You assume correctly, Detective," said Salisbury. "We pride ourselves in airtight prenups but we can't get all our clients to use them. Sadly, that often ends up to their detriment."

"Tell me about that," said Dykes.

"Well, I'd say that those of our clients who have prenups, their divorce rate is roughly fifty percent. And they lose less of their assets. Those without prenups generally lose half of everything and their divorce rates are around eighty percent."

Dykes nodded his head with an upturned mouth.

"And how much are the prenup divorcees losing?"

"That depends on the client. Sometimes they're willing to offer more depending on how much they love their fiancees. Generally it's between twenty and fifty percent of their incomes during the time they've been married. Fifty percent is rare, but usually the minimum payout is a couple of million for our bigger clients."

"And what's been the largest loss to one of your clients who didn't have prenup?" asked Dykes.

"North of fifty million."

Jackson whistled.

"Ensor was a smart man to have taken your advice," said Dykes.

Salisbury nodded.

"But it might have also put a target on his back."

"How so, Detective?" asked Salisbury.

"Well, now that he's dead, who gets the entire estate?"

"His wife of course. There is some for his parents as well. But his wife will get around ninety percent of it."

"And that ninety percent will be how much?" asked Dykes.

"Probably over a hundred million."

Jackson whistled again, I raised my eyebrow. But nobody saw nor cared. Salisbury looked over at Jackson.

"Ensor did well with his investments," said Salisbury.

"And yet Celia Ensor's not happy with their financial advisor."

Salisbury shrugged.

"I recommended Dennis to James when he was first a client. He was happy with him."

"This is Dennis Blaney?" asked Dykes, referring to his notes.

Salisbury nodded.

"You have to understand, if you want the best results you very often have to pay for them. Dennis offers the best results that's why we recommend him and that's also why most of our clients are happy with him."

"But not the wives," said Jackson.

Salisbury shrugged again and pushed up his glasses.

"I can't speak for all the wives. The wives are generally not our clients. Celia has become our client by default if you will. She's not particularly satisfied and once this estate has been transferred to her she can do what she wants with the money. But Dennis is upstanding, I'd bet my reputation on it."

"But he takes a large chunk of the money he invests," said Jackson.

Salisbury shook his head slowly like he was trying to explain something to his elderly forgetful mother.

"No, Detective, he doesn't. If you recall our previous discussions at your offices Celia told you how much he takes. Five percent management fee and twenty-five percent performance. That is, he only takes twenty-five percent of any profits he makes. Something Celia didn't tell you was that he only takes that twenty-five percent on the amount he's beaten the S&P 500 by."

"Still," I said, tagging off of Jackson, "Celia seemed pretty confident with her numbers. Seems she keeps a close eye on the Ensor money."

"It would seem that way. So what?" Salisbury asked.

"Well, it doesn't make the murder look less like her responsibility," I said.

Salisbury shook his head and looked at me.

"Wives often like to be part of the financial decisions. I know my wife does, doesn't make her guilty of murder."

"Getting back to motive," said Dykes. "Celia gets north of a hundred million now he's dead. How much would she have gotten had Ensor divorced her?"

Salisbury thought about it for a moment.

"I can't say for certain, the formula is in the prenup, but I believe in Ensor's case it was twelve and a half percent per year they were married. His made a little over thirty million the past couple of years, if they were married two years, just for arguments sake, then she'd get roughly seven or eight million."

"And what if she cheated on him?" I asked.

Salisbury looked at me.

"Then she gets one million and she'd need to consider herself lucky. There is an infidelity clause in the prenup."

I looked at Salisbury. He was a man who didn't miss much, and I'm sure he knew about Celia's wandering eye.

"And you knew about that, didn't you?" I asked.

"Knew about what?"

"Knew she was sleeping around. Specifically with Vance Gibb."

Salisbury nodded.

"And you didn't think to mention that to us?" asked Dykes.

"That's right, Detective. I told you I wouldn't help you out. Detective work is your domain. You have to ask the right questions if you want the right answers."

Now Dykes was shaking his head.

"So instead of getting seven or eight, Celia would be lucky to get one million," I said, "if Ensor was going to seek divorce. Was he going to seek divorce?"

Salisbury grinned at me. It seemed almost genuine.

"Now you're asking the right questions," he said. "Yes, he had come to me a few weeks back asking me to ready the papers to seek divorce based on infidelity."

"And did he have proof?" I asked.

Again Salisbury nodded and smiled.

"Yes. I'll give you a hand, he had hired a private investigator."

"Whose name is?"

"Robert Skeef."

"And you still don't think your client is guilty of murdering her husband?" I asked.

He looked at me and nodded.

"That's right, Mr. Carrick, I don't believe she's guilty of the crime. But then what do I know? Sure looks like she has motive. But I don't see her getting her hands dirty."

"Does she own a handgun?" I asked.

Salisbury shrugged.

"I don't know. You'd have to ask her that," he said. "In any event, unless you can pin this on her, she's getting the estate."

"And you didn't think of hiring a PI to investigate her, what with her vested interests in his death?" asked Dykes.

"Nope," said Salisbury. "That's not my domain. Sometimes innocent people commit heinous crimes. Sometimes the guilty are as innocent as baby lambs."

"Sounds like you have some knowledge of criminal minds," said Dykes.

"Just my observations about human nature. I've had clients that seem as pure as the driven snow and yet they're beating their wives, screwing around with hookers and snorting coke. Then, on the other hand, I've had highly disagreeable clients. Assholes really, and they're guilty of nothing other than rubbing people the long way. Perhaps like your friend Mr. Carrick here, though I can't vouch for that."

Salisbury didn't look at me. He pushed up his glasses again. After a long pause Salisbury spoke again.

"If there's nothing else, I'd like to get back to work," he said.

Dykes looked at Jackson and Jackson passed the gaze on over to me.

"We could dance around the floor with Fred here and still not get anywhere in the next couple of hours," I said. "Our time is probably better spent following up with others."

Jackson nodded. He folded up his notebook and put it away. Dykes flipped his closed. He looked at Salisbury.

"There's a lot you're not telling us," he said.

Salisbury smiled feebly at him but didn't say anything for a while.

"You've got to ask the right questions," he said.

"No shit, Sherlock," I said.

I was already standing. Jackson got up and waited for Dykes to stand. After a some time Dykes stood up too. He stared at Salisbury for a moment.

"We'll likely be back," he said.

"I'm sure of it," replied Salisbury.

"One last thing," I said.

Salisbury's smile almost fell of his face.

"Yes, Mr. Carrick," he said exasperated.

"I get the impression that you act as Ensor's agent."

"Yes, you could say that."

"And yet he had an agent already. Sunny MacKsay," I said.

"What about it?"

"Well, who really was Ensor's agent?"

"We were," he said. "Sunny was a hanger-on. He'd been Ensor's first agent, but when he moved over to us we took over."

"And Sunny was left out in the cold?"

"No, not really. Ensor was generous with his friends and he considered Sunny a friend. He made sure Sunny got a finder's fee. We had to give him one million each year from Ensor's take."

"So you were down a further million each year," I said.

Salisbury shook his head.

"No, Mr. Carrick, it came from Ensor's portion, not ours."

"How did Sunny feel about that?"

"He was upset that Ensor wasn't using him anymore, but that was a long time ago. I imagine he was happy with one million a year for not having to work for it. Anything else?" asked Salisbury visibly weary at this point.

I turned to go but paused for a moment and then turned back scratching my head. I'd seen some Columbo reruns lately.

"At our first meeting, Celia said she'd heard her husband arguing with Sunny about something. Do you know anything about that?"

Salisbury shook his head.

"No I don't."

"Was Ensor going back to Sunny as his agent?"

I looked at Salisbury, seeking any tells that might give away more than his mouth was saying. I didn't find anything.

"I have no idea," said Salisbury, "like I said, I felt he was negotiating with us in good faith, but he could have been speaking with Sunny as well. Nothing to stop him."

Salisbury stared at me for a while. I looked him in the eyes. There was nothing else I needed for the time being.

"Well?" he asked.

"That's it," I said.

Nobody offered their hands to shake. We all turned and walked out of the office and out into the hallway and waited for the elevators.

"There's something more to this than Salisbury's letting on," said Dykes.

"That's for certain," said Jackson. "Slippery snake like him. No wonder I don't like lawyers."

"I liked him," I said, standing with my hands in my pocket and watching the red numbers above the elevator count higher. Jackson and Dykes turned to look at me. Jackson wore a furrowed brow. I

160

looked at him.

"He gave us everything we need. I think a visit to Dennis and Bobby might be all we need to close this up."

"If you say so," said Dykes.

I looked at him and smiled just as the elevator beeped and opened up its gaping maw to swallow us in.

"I say so," I said, full of smug confidence that might have been as clear as false hubris. But I had a feeling we were getting places.

Jackson stepped into the paneled box. Dykes followed him and I entered last. Dykes fished out his Lifesavers and offered them around as the door closed. We all took one. I was feeling minty, but I was thinking we might have been the three stooges instead.

"Then let's go and see a man about some money," said Dykes.

I grinned and nodded my head.

"Works for me," said Jackson.

CHAPTER FOURTEEN
Blue Ocean LLC

NOT far from where Salisbury, Hill and Dale were located was another blue faced windowed building. Slightly different front entrance, but if you'd blindfolded me and taken it off in the lobby I coulda sworn we hadn't left the building where we'd had the generous chat with Salisbury.

This tower of technological triumph wasn't as tall as Salisbury's but just as opulent, especially the thirty first floor. That's where we were headed. Blue Ocean LLC. It reminded me of Santa Monica, of home. I missed the ocean, the tang of salty air nuzzled into my nose by the ocean breeze.

Blue Ocean LLC was a hedge fund for the rich and famous. Actually, it was for the rich. If you were famous but not rich, it wasn't for you. At least this is what I was led to believe. Not in such pedestrian language mind you. No sir, Blue Ocean was nothing if not consummately professional.

They took up the whole thirty-first floor. The elevators opened up into a cavernous and opulent reception area. It smelled of old wood and fine leather. Perhaps that was the smell of old money. Coulda been new money too. It smelled rich. I already felt uncomfortable and nobody had said a word to me.

On either side of the elevators were large leather sofas, soft as clouds or so I imagined. There were lazy boys too and large, thin TV screens on each side, angled off the wall slightly so that nobody should have to crane their neck to watch Bloomberg and other such financial news channels. Each side of the waiting area had it's own espresso machine. I walked up to it. It must have been a ten thousand dollar machine. There was plaque just above it that read:

"Thirsty? Just request your beverage of choice from reception."

There was also a cooler with an assortment of soft drinks, waters, juices and the likes. Next to the espresso machine were baskets filled with perfect looking fruit, bags of nuts, chips and the like. I walked back over towards the receptionist where Dykes and Jackson were about to talk to her. I noticed there was nobody in the waiting area.

Her desk was large and modern and with real wooden top. I fancied calling it teak or mahogany but truth be told I hadn't a clue. All I knew was that the wood looked heavy and it was dark. Dark like burnt almonds. She was a pretty blonde woman with her hair in a bun behind her head and librarian glasses. She looked like every teenage boys dream of the naughty school teacher. But she was all business with us. She wore a white blouse, blue blazer and blue skirt. She wore a name tag that had her first name on it. Vivienne. Jackson went first, smiling like he'd brought home the prize.

"Vivienne," said Jackson. "I'm Detective Jeramie Jackson and this is my partner Detective Bradley Dykes and that's Anthony Carrick. We're with Chicago Police Homicide. We're here to see Dennis Blaney."

She nodded and picked up the phone.

"You have three homicide detectives here to see you," she said.

She nodded again and then put down the phone.

"Please follow me," she said.

We followed her into a larger and more opulent space behind two large dark wooden doors that were off to the left of her desk. They were mirrored on the opposite side as well. These doors opened easily for such surprisingly heavy and tall doors, there was probably a mechanism that enabled that. The doors stood from floor to ceiling which I put about ten feet high. At least.

We followed her left towards the corner of the floor. We passed a couple of conference rooms with dark wooden doors and frosted glass windows that walled them off from the hallway. We passed offices with dark doors of the same wood and similarly frosted glass walls with a slim rectangular strip of clear glass just by the door to give you a small look into the interior.

At the end of the hallway she knocked on a door that stood floor to ceiling. I could see by the clear glass strip our man Dennis Blaney inside behind his desk. He stood up and I heard him say, "Enter."

Vivienne opened up the door and we walked in after her.

"These are the homicide detectives that are here to see you, Mr. Blaney," she said.

She waved her hand towards each of us in turn, palm up.

"This is Detective Jeramie Jackson, Detective Bradley Dykes and Detective Anthony Carrick."

"Mister," I said.

"Sorry?"

"Don't be."

Dennis had come around and shook each of our hands in turn. He was a middle aged man in his late forties at about six feet in height. He had a good grip and he was dressed impeccably. A blood red pocket square matched his tie against a pale blue shirt under a navy blue suit that fit him perfectly. His dark brown hair was styled and perfectly in place, likely with the help of product though it didn't look wet. He had a square face and at the right angle some women might find him handsome. He had silver or platinum cufflinks that matched his tie bar. It looked to me like he did some manscaping on his eyebrows.

His smile was warm and genuine and he smelled great. An expensive cologne that was bright, citrusy but with musky undertones. It was not oppressive. His shoes were shiny and clean and black. He looked like he took good care of himself, as though life had been good to him. He was thick teetering on the seesaw of fatness. He seemed superficially pleasant but I wasn't going to let him babysit Aibhilin.

"Can I get you detectives anything to drink?" he asked.

Dykes and Jackson declined. I was inclined to try one of their fancy coffees I'd seen earlier.

"A coffee would be terrific," I said.

Blaney smiled and nodded at me.

"How do you like it?" he asked.

"Two sugars and cream," I said.

Blaney nodded at Vivienne and she left us. He waved towards the glass window of his expansive office. There was a couch and two large leather chairs. They looked to be of the same design as those found in the waiting room. They looked new. Dykes and Jackson took the couch. Blaney and I had a chair each. They were comfortable. They didn't look like they reclined but I liked one for my apartment in front of the TV. We all had a view outside of downtown Chicago. A mix of high rises, older buildings and dotted green spaces like squares of mowed lawn.

"How may I help you detectives?" he asked.

"Just mister," I said.

He looked at me with a quizzical look.

"Carrick is from LA, he's a private investigator," said Jackson.

Blaney nodded.

"I see. How can I help you three gentlemen?" he asked again.

"I imagine you know why we're here?" I said.

He nodded again and put on a grave and serious face. I preferred the smiling, collegial mask he'd worn earlier.

"Yes, I imagine it must be about James Ensor. Terrible and so random."

"Very seldom random," I said.

He looked at me again.

"You know who did it?"

"Not yet," I said.

There was a knock at the door and behind it Vivienne entered carrying a coffee in a dark blue mug. It had the logo and the name of Blue Ocean LLC on it with the tagline. The logo was a curling wave in a circle and the tagline was "More Profits, Less Turbulence." I took the coffee and thanked her. I took a sip, it was perfect. Just how I liked it. Good coffee.

"Anything else?" she asked.

"No thank you, Vivienne, that'll be all," he said, smiling at her as she left. He turned back and looked at the two detectives.

"So how can I help you?"

"We'd like to know about Ensor's financial situation. Any insights you can give us about his personal issues related to money or otherwise," said Dykes.

Dykes fished out another Lifesaver and popped it in his mouth.

He put the roll away and opened up his notebook. Jackson had his notebook already open, pen in hand. I had my coffee in my hand and my charm in my pocket in case it was needed.

"Well, I can tell you that James was a friend and he'd been with us just under five years," said Blaney, preferring to use the deceased's first name.

"Now I understand that you only take clients with a minimum of twenty-five million to invest?" I asked.

Blaney turned to me and smiled. He smiled like a politician who had practiced every morning in front of the mirror.

"That's correct."

"And yet, I doubt that James Ensor would have had that sort of money when you first met him," I said.

The smile wouldn't slip of his face. It was making me tired just looking at it.

"You're right, Mr. Carrick," he said. "When James was introduced to my firm he only had a couple of million to start with. But we make exceptions for some of our preferred clients."

"High profile clients then, like actors and sports stars," I said.

He nodded. I sipped my coffee.

"That's right, high profile clients give UHNW individuals more confidence in our services. You know what UHNW means?"

I nodded.

"Celia was very eager to school us in the lingo," I said.

Blaney nodded.

"Ultra high net worth individuals are our bread and butter but folks with that sort of money are a, rare and b, not quick to trust just anyone with that sort of wealth. Having a roster of professional sportsmen and women as well as actors and the like helps imbue confidence in our services."

"Is Salisbury a client?" I asked.

"Of course," said Blaney, still smiling like the wax statue of himself.

"I'd be hard pressed to believe he has the minimum to invest with you," I said.

"And you'd be right. Like I said, we do make exceptions. Fred is extremely valuable to my firm with his referrals. More than that, we go back a long way and I consider him a friend and colleague."

I considered Blaney a politician. He was as smooth and slippery as an oiled baby.

"Everyone speaks highly of your services and your results," said Dykes.

Blaney nodded and turned to look at Dykes with that smile of his.

"We do aim to achieve above market returns. In fact, our own income is performance based. We only make money if our clients make money."

"Well now, that's not entirely true," I said.

"What do you mean?"

"Celia mentions that you take a flat management fee," I said.

"Quite correct. Five percent is our management fee to cover expenses. It is expensive to manage a lot of money and outperform the market consistently."

"But," said Dykes, getting back into the discussion, "Celia did not seem quite as happy as you'd think she should with the returns you're able to produce."

Still smiling Blaney said, "I'm quite aware of that, Detective. And she's free to take the money now that it is hers and to do what she likes with it, which is probably to fritter it away."

"The two of you seem to have a mutual disrespect," said Dykes.

"If I can speak freely and confidentially," said Blaney looking at Dykes and Jackson.

Dykes nodded.

"I often don't care for the wives of my clients and I'll tell you exactly why. In fact, Celia is the poster girl for this dislike. The only thing she has going for her is her looks. She has no education. She's uneducated and backwards in many ways. She's your classic gold digger, as most of them are. All she knows is what she hears from her peers and I use the term peers loosely. She'd be what we'd call in the vernacular white trash, though she pretends not to be."

"That's quite an opinion," said Dykes.

"It's my honest and confidential opinion. Never liked her from the beginning, it was a good thing that Fred had James do up a prenup."

"So you don't think your fees are unreasonable?" asked Jackson.

Blaney looked over at Jackson and smiled again.

"Not at all, Detective. They might seem high to you, but they are commensurate with our peers. More than that we are one of the top three performing hedge funds in North America. Over the past ten years we've attained returns of twenty-three percent on average annually. We take twenty-five percent if our returns for the year are above the market rate. So, for example, last year the S&P returned fifteen percent which was a good year for the market, we managed thirty-three percent. Our clients made on their money almost twenty percent. That's a good return."

"Celia said she made," and Dykes flipped through his notebook, "uh, twenty-four point seventy-five percent."

Dykes looked back up at Blaney. Blaney continued to smile and nodded at Dykes.

"Quite right, Detective. But that doesn't take into account our management fee which is then deducted on top of that. Five percent is our management fee."

"Which is where Celia had her problem with you," said Jackson.

Blaney chuckled. This seemed almost unrehearsed and natural.

"Yes, yes she did," he said, looking at Jackson. "She's continually tried to barter with me as if we're some sort of bazaar in Iran. Our fees are not negotiable. If clients aren't happy I counsel them to look elsewhere."

"And did you counsel Celia Ensor to do just that?" asked Dykes.

"Certainly not, Detective, Celia was not my client. James was."

"Well, how did she go about trying to negotiate your fees?" asked Jackson.

I sipped on my coffee and thought of Emily on the beach in a bathing suit. It must have been the Blue Ocean logo. Outside there were no beaches and no Emilys in bathing suits. Just little upright ants crawling all over the Chicago asphalt thinking how important their lives were. From this vantage point it looked more farcical than anything.

"Like I said before, Detective," said Blaney looking over at Jackson with that practiced smile on his face, "the wives love to be involved in these meetings. On more than one occasion at these meetings Celia has voiced her concern over the management fee. Nothing comes of it of course as James is quickly able to steer the conversation back on course."

"How often do you meet with your clients?" I asked.

"As often as they like. We are here to serve them. Usually we'll set up meetings quarterly to go over the results and to discuss where we're going in the future. The least often we see our clients is once a year. I prefer not to leave them without any contact from us longer than that."

"Because you're worried they'll be stolen by others?" I asked.

The smile broadened into a grin. I was quickly becoming a connoisseur of smarmy smiles and facial ticks. I was also quickly realizing that the English language didn't have enough words for the repertoire of facial expressions that masqueraded as smiles on Blaney's face. That made me think of all those hundreds of words the Inuit have for snow. Or so I'm led to believe.

"No, Mr. Carrick," said Blaney, unperturbed, "I am not worried they'll move. You must have heard of Newton's Laws of Motion?"

I nodded. I had heard of them. Remembering them was something else. Thankfully, Blaney was about to school me in physics.

"Newton's First Law of Motion is also known as the Law of Inertia. Basically what it means is that an object at rest, or an object moving, will stay at rest, or keep moving, so long as no other force is applied to it."

"Sounds swell," I said.

"Okay, Mr. Carrick, I'll humor you. What I'm trying to say is that applying a force to either a stationery object or a moving object requires a lot more energy than leaving them be. This is the case in my business. I don't have to be the best, but so long as I'm performing adequately my clients are reticent to change anything."

I nodded.

"I get it," I said. "So you're sort of like the Jedi of Inertia. The force is strong with you."

Blaney let out a forced laugh.

"Not exactly."

"Getting back on track," said Dykes. "What is the value of the deceased's investments with Blue Ocean?"

"If you'll give me a moment I can tell you exactly how much?"

said Blaney, starting to get up.

"Just a ballpark figure will do," said Dykes.

"North of one hundred million."

"Perhaps I should put my money with you," I said. "I like your returns a lot better than the eight percent I'm getting on my mutual funds."

I was lying through my teeth. I didn't have any mutual funds. I didn't think I had money under my mattress either, but there were some quarters jangling in my pocket and that gave me comfort. Blaney looked at me.

"Mutual funds are a very good way for the average investor to safely earn market returns," he said.

"But I want above market returns. I want north of one hundred million," I said.

Blaney smiled and nodded.

"Don't we all, Mr. Carrick. Don't we all."

"Can you tell us anything interesting about Mr. Ensor's personal life?" asked Dykes.

Blaney looked back over at Dykes and then looked back down at the table in thought.

"Uh, usually our conversations revolve around investments and other financial matters. I prefer not to get involved in my client's personal matters."

I drank the last of my coffee. I was sorry to see it go. I put the mug back down on the coffee table. Blaney looked at it. Then he looked at me.

"Would you like some more Mr. Carrick?" he asked.

I shook my head.

"But certainly sometimes, some clients will give you an inkling into their lives," said Dykes.

Blaney looked back at him and nodded.

"A few weeks ago James came to me asking about making sure that Celia couldn't access his money."

Dykes nodded.

"The thing is, Celia couldn't access the accounts, not without his signature. The most we'll allow is a combined account where both spouses need to sign off on any withdraws. Oftentimes it's just our client who has full control of their account."

Dykes nodded.

"And Mr. Ensor wanted to change this?"

Blaney nodded again.

"He did, he wanted the account to revert to single account holder privilege."

"And did you do that?"

"Of course, Detective, we are here to serve our clients. Since it was his account originally and he authorized her to be a cosigner it was easy enough just to revert it back to a single authorized holder."

"Did he give you any idea as to why he wanted it this way?" asked Dykes.

"As you probably know he didn't trust her. Not that I blamed him. He said she was being unfaithful. I asked him if he was certain. He said he was. He insisted that I put a note on his file that nobody was to access his account without his authorization and in the event of his death to freeze the account until the manner of his death had been determined."

Dykes nodded and added scribbles to his notebook.

"I see, and did you do that?"

Blaney nodded.

"I did. But I thought it odd that he would mention his death.

Seemed a little macabre to me."

"Did you mention that to him?" I asked, getting back into the dialogue.

"I did, Mr. Carrick. I asked him if he was concerned for his safety. He didn't exactly say he was, he just wanted to be sure that things would be taken care of in the event of his, well you know, death."

"But he didn't give any indication of who or why he felt threatened?" I asked.

"That's right he didn't. I did tell him that if he feared for his safety that he should telephone the police. He shrugged it off. Said it was nothing and that he was probably being a little paranoid. Still, I fear I should have been a little more pointed with him in that regard all things now considered."

"Nothing you could have done," I said. "Unless you knew something about why he was feeling threatened."

Blaney shook his head.

"Absolutely not, I would have said something then. I mean come on, he's a big enough fellow, surely his wife wasn't about to kill him?"

Blaney looked at me incredulously. I didn't say anything for a moment.

"You know about that story in the bible about Goliath?" I asked.

He nodded.

"Of course."

"There you go. Even a mouse can kill an elephant with a gun, Mr. Blaney," I said.

He shrugged and look down at the table where my blue coffee mug stood empty on the dark wooden surface. Perfect and polished. Much like the facade of these lives.

"I suppose so. I just can't accept that. Celia might be a bit uncouth, but a killer I doubt she is."

"You'd be surprised who could kill given the right circumstances and the right motive," I said.

He looked at me.

"You really think she killed him?"

"I didn't say that," I said. "But she hasn't been excluded yet. You must know that with his death she stands to inherit everything? This north of one hundred million you spoke of earlier."

"Yes I do know that, Mr. Carrick. Except in the event of divorce..."

Blaney trailed off and looked back down. This time further down at the expensive rug that was under the coffee table. It was the only splash of color in the office save for a Kandinsky that I figured was original and worth an easy few million itself. Blaney shook his head slowly.

"Terrible thing to have to think about," he said. "That she would have killed him for money."

"It's often the only motive that's needed," I said.

Blaney sat deep in thought. None of us said anything for a while. I looked up at the painting by Kandinsky. It was a brightly colored blocky painted cityscape with two figures in the foreground. I liked it, but then again I understood art.

"Do you know who she was having an affair with?" I asked.

Blaney took his eyes away from the floor and put them back on my face.

"No, I didn't get into that much detail with James."

"Was it one or several men?"

"I don't know. I assumed just one. Do you think it could have been more than one?"

"We're just looking to pursue leads," I said. "One we know of for sure, but you never know where the rabbit hole leads."

Dykes closed his notebook. He looked over at Jackson. Jackson did the same.

"Well, I think that's all we need," Dykes said, standing up.

Jackson stood up and I stayed seated. Jackson reached into his jacket pocket and pulled out the warrant. He handed the warrant to Blaney.

"What's this?" Blaney asked.

"It's a warrant for records," said Jackson. "You've been very helpful but you'll probably want this for your records, as we do require copies of Mr. Ensor's account transactions for the last year."

Blaney nodded.

"Of course," he said. Then he opened up the warrant and read it. He headed over to his computer and tapped away for a few moments. On the side of his desk was a printer. It started up not long after and spat out a couple of pages. I walked over to the window and looked outside. It was sunny and looked warm. It wasn't that warm though. The Windy City earned its name honestly. The streets were rather barren, only the odd pedestrian walking along the sidewalks, dragging their secrets behind them like petulant shadows.

Blaney picked up the pages from the printer and handed them over to Jackson.

"Not much activity over the past year, Detective," he said. "We encourage our clients not to invest with money they might need for five or more years. Their returns will be hurt if they keep cashing in."

Jackson nodded and we moved towards the door. I stopped by

the Kandinsky. It was not large. Most people don't realize how small many of the great paintings are. Take the Mona Lisa for example, it's but a sketch in size. Thirty inches by twenty inches. This Kandinsky was smaller than that, almost half the size. I put it as eighteen by twelve. Blaney stopped next to me and admired his own painting.

"You like it, Mr. Carrick?" he asked, turning to me and smiling.

I nodded.

"Do you know who it's by?"

There seemed to be a small overtone of gloat in his voice. He was about to school me again. I wasn't about to let that happen. I turned to him and smiled.

"Vasily Kandinsky," I said. "This was painted in nineteen oh eight during his Impressionism period. If memory serves it's called 'Businessmen in Antwerp'."

I grinned at him. He smiled back at me. A slightly hollow and perhaps sad smile.

"You know your art," he said.

"Some of it," I said. "Must be worth a small fortune."

"It is," he said. "I had it evaluated earlier this year for insurance purposes. Its current value is six million."

I nodded.

"And yet you keep it out in the open like this," I said, nodding at the painting.

"What is art for if not to be enjoyed? And what is insurance for if not to allow art to be enjoyed?"

He had a point.

"What's your interest in art?" he asked, turning and looking at me.

"I'm a painter," I said, looking back at him. "A really lovely specimen."

"Do you sell?"

"Sometimes," I said. "You can view some of my current work at Triangle Gallery in Beverly Hills. Online as well. It won't cost you six million either."

"This Kandinsky didn't cost me that much. I got it some years ago for one point five."

I nodded and moved towards Dykes and Jackson.

"Thank you for your time, Mr. Blaney," said Dykes.

Blaney had joined us and we all shook hands.

"I'll look you up," Blaney said to me as we shook hands. "Perhaps there'll be a sale in it for you."

"That would be terrific. It might be to your taste."

We left and found our own way back to the main reception area and to the lobby where Jackson pushed the button for the elevator.

"Off to see Skeef?" I asked.

"Not yet," said Dykes. "While you were discussing paintings I got a call from Lane. He wants us to head back to the headquarters and fill him in."

CHAPTER FIFTEEN

The Fast Lane

IT wasn't even lunch time but I was getting hungry. We were back at headquarters by about eleven thirty. Up on the same floor I'd been a few times along the exterior wall were offices and boardrooms. You know all that. What you don't know is that one of those offices was Lane's and I was led straight to it like a stray dog.

The office wasn't very big, maybe the size of a regular bedroom. But unlike a bedroom it was filled with expensive furniture, not the bureaucratic offcuts that you'll often find in homicide offices. This was nice stuff. I felt like I was in a smaller version of Blue Ocean's offices.

Lane got off the phone as we came in and he walked round his desk to greet us. He shook my hand and patted me on the shoulder. His smile was easy and large, much like his stature, and his eyes were still sleepy. It gave the impression that he might be a dull bulb, but that was hardly the case. He wore a charcoal gray suit with red socks, red pocket square and red tie. He looked like a model, but for a magazine like Big and Tall or Humble Man's Riches.

He was also wearing the Saint Jude medallion pinned to his suit. This one was gold though. And his watch was gold too. Another

Rolex. Between his two watches I knew about he almost wore my entire salary on his wrist. He led us to the sofa stuffed in the corner of his office. Dykes and Jackson sat down, I remained standing. There was a chair if I wanted it. I didn't. Lane sat on the corner of his desk, he turned towards his desk and reached for something. It was a toothpick. He stuck it in is mouth. Dykes popped a Lifesaver in his, not offering anyone.

"I hear you looked into my old man's plumbing company," Lane said to me. I nodded.

"Seems I misjudged you," I said.

He grinned at me and nodded. His hands were comfortably together in his lap.

"No offense," he said. "There're bad cops around, but my team is clean."

"I know that now," I said. "Who told you?"

Lane nodded over at Jackson. I looked over at him. Jackson shrugged.

"I didn't just take his word for it," I said. "I called Lane's Heating and Plumbing to verify."

Lane nodded.

"Good, that's good. I like it. That's why we've got you onboard," he said.

"So," I said. "You invest with Blue Ocean?"

Lane laughed loudly and tossed his head up.

"No, I take care of my own investments. Besides, I don't have that much. Way less than twenty-five mill."

"How come you still work on the job?" I asked.

He looked at me with those sleepy eyes that looked sharper than knives.

"I'm trying to clean up this city. I like what I do, and I'm personally invested in bringing bad guys to justice."

"You should tell him," said Dykes.

Lane looked over at Dykes, shrugged and then looked back at me.

"When I was thirteen my younger brother was killed in a hit and run. Never found the guy who did it. That's what got me into policing."

I nodded, that was a bum break.

"You know," he said, still looking at me, "I've got another nickname for you. Irish is fine and all, but I think your initials work even better. AC."

"And how's that?" I asked.

"'Cos you're cold as ice, you're a cool operator. I can tell that now."

Jackson nodded.

"Yeah, that's a good one," he said.

I turned to look over at him.

"And seeing as how we're just spitballing, what're their nicknames."

Lane looked over at Dykes and nodded in his direction.

"Dykes over there is Red, and Jackson is Goldie. When they're together it's Red and Gold or RG."

I nodded, they were okay.

"I had him as Silent Red."

Lane looked back at Dykes and nodded.

"I like it," he said.

"Was Silent Red the Viking," said Jackson. He then looked at me. "You never gave me one."

"Baller," I said.

"How's that?" asked Lane.

"He keeps telling me how he's not really a fan, yet he knows more about the game than anyone I know."

Jackson grinned and shrugged.

"What can I say?" he said.

"You know baller's usually used in the context of basketball," said Lane.

I shrugged.

"I like it better for baseball," I said. "Besides, Jackson here tells me it was used for baseball at one time."

"That so?" asked Lane. Jackson nodded.

"Why are we here, Captain?" asked Dykes getting to the brass tacks.

Lane looked up at him and smiled. The toothpick a sharp point in his direction.

"It's been what, almost five days," he said, "since the murder."

"Not even three days," I added helpfully. "Three days tonight around eight."

Lane looked back at me, and his smile wasn't so friendly this time.

"Feels like five days," Lane said, "with the heat I'm taking. I just got off the phone with the Mayor's office. Earlier today the Chief was breathing down my neck. They want this wrapped up."

"They want it wrapped up or they want it swept under the rug?" I asked.

Lane didn't say anything to that.

"Look," I said. "Three days is not long. This homicide is a dog's breakfast. The more we pull at the corner the more it unravels. We've got suspects up to our eyeballs."

"That so?" asked Lane. "And how long does it usually take to wrap up a murder where you're from?"

"I reckon up to a week is not a bad time frame."

"And the longest?"

"Well, the longest that I've been involved with was a cold case. Probably twenty-five years give or take."

"We don't have twenty-five years," said Lane.

"Neither do I."

"The World Series is starting tomorrow," said Lane, reminding us of the obvious. "It would be nice to have something to give them by then."

Lane looked at Dykes and Jackson.

"Where you at?"

"Following leads," said Dykes. "Just got back from Salisbury's, the vic's lawyer and now his wife's. Also just got back from Blue Ocean where the vic had his money."

"Fill me in," said lane, pinching the toothpick between thumb and forefinger and transferring it to the other side of his mouth.

"Lawyer was a bit of a dick like they can be, until we served him with a warrant..."

"A warrant, seriously?" asked Lane.

Dykes nodded.

"Ms. Skinner was kind enough to get one through for us," offered Jackson hopefully.

"And you're both hoping to get fired?" asked Lane.

"Aw, come on, Captain, it's a legit warrant," said Jackson.

"That might come under review," said Lane.

"Anyway," said Dykes continuing, "it helped us get some info on the vic and his wife."

"Like what?"

"Like the fact that the vic was looking to get divorced. That makes her a prime suspect. She was screwing around on the vic with at least one other person. Carrick here found out it was Gibb, the left fielder. Anyway, might be others. Point being, the prenup was buttoned down tight. She only gets one mill if the vic divorced her for infidelity which he was going to do."

"And how was he going to prove it?" asked Lane.

"That's the thing. He hired a PI. We're gonna speak to him next."

"One million is not chump change. What's she missing out on?" asked Lane.

"North of one hundred million," said Jackson.

Lane whistled.

"Now we're talking real money. Have you got a warrant for the vic's home yet, see if she left the gun there?" asked Lane.

"That's coming next," said Dykes.

"Should've come first," said Lane, showing no signs of real frustration.

"Well, we haven't heard back from the Coroner yet on the type of weapon used."

"Was a Ruger SR9 according to ballistics," said Lane. "Heard from them this morning too. Been a long day for me already."

"Captain," said Dykes, "FSD swabbed her hands the same night the vic was murdered for GSR. Nothing found, that's why we've been reticent to head on over too quick. Besides, Carrick here figures that we don't want to push her too hard or she might clam up. If we reel her in slowly she might let something slip."

I said no such thing to him. In any event I was leaning on her pretty hard in the boardroom the other day. Lane looked over at me.

"That true?" he asked.

"Something like that," I said, giving Dykes a hairy eyeball. He just grinned at me.

"You guys are making slow progress. Like fat Santa trying to get down the chimney. I need something by tomorrow, something more concrete," said Lane.

"We've got lots of leads," I said. "We're pulling at strings, but soon enough they'll come apart and we'll see which one is tied to the murder."

"Help me with that," said Lane.

"Well," I said, "there's the wife, Celia. She looks good for it. No GSR apparently, which I've just found out. Still, she could have been wearing gloves, changed clothes, showered. Any number of reasons there was no GSR on her and she still could have pulled the trigger. We'll figure that out. Or maybe she's an accessory. There's also Gibb, owns a couple of guns."

I looked at Jackson and Dykes. I'd hoped they'd looked into these sorts of things while I was out at the field talking with the team. Jackson nodded.

"He told us the same. We verified his handguns. He has two registered like he told us. A Glock 31 which shoots 357s and a Ruger SR 1911 which is a 45 auto."

"So those couldn't have been used," I offered.

"And did you swab him?" asked Lane.

Jackson nodded.

"Clean."

Lane looked over at me.

"Seems we're getting somewhere," he said.

I shook my head.

"Any criminal worth his gunpowder is gonna wash well after using a firearm or he's gonna use gloves of some sort."

"And were gloves found in the search of Wrigley Field?" asked

Lane, turning to his detectives.

Dykes shook his head.

"Nope," he said, "but then again, we didn't find the murder weapon either."

"Alright," said Lane, "so maybe no gloves were used."

"In any event," I said, "not sure if you guys are up to snuff on your GSR but I wouldn't hinge my case on it. It's easily defeatable, easily washed off, easy to cross contaminate. Just hanging around the three of you and headquarters here I probably have GSR on me."

"It would still give you clowns something to go on," said Lane, chomping on his toothpick. I wondered if it was spearmint flavored.

"I've got plenty to go on," I said.

"Help me understand," said Lane.

"There are a lot of people who might have had a reason to kill Ensor," I said. "We've got the ex-wife. We've got the guy she was screwing around with."

"Who's that?" interjected Lane.

"Gibb, the left fielder," I said. "They got into it too a while back on the field. It was at the Diamondbacks game. Gibb flubbed a catch on purpose so the thinking goes. Ensor was enraged. Ran over to him and they duked it out. Gibb tells me they were both ejected with Ensor getting a big fine. Then there's Stark, the next best pitcher. He doesn't think he's getting enough action. He had issues with Ensor too. Works out well for him that Ensor's out of it. He's gonna get the glory now."

Lane looked back at his detectives.

"Was he swabbed?"

Jackson nodded.

"Clean. He doesn't have any weapons either, at least not registered ones. And that goes with what he told us."

Lane nodded his head towards the floor.

"We got into it at the stadium," I said. Lane looked up at me with a furrowed brow.

"What do you mean you got into it?"

"Well, he wasn't very chatty at first. Said some things that hurt my feelings. Pushed me around a little so I pushed him back."

"And when you say pushed, you mean you actually pushed him?" asked Lane, holding on to the toothpick as he chewed at it.

"Well yes, that's exactly what I mean. It might have been a hard push. It might have been with my fist, and it might have been on his nose. But nothing's broken that can't be fixed."

I grinned at Lane but he wasn't having any of it.

"You broke his goddamn nose?"

Lane raised his voice that time. I was still grinning, but I could see my charm wasn't winning him over.

"No, no. I didn't break his nose. Everything's fine, we had a great chat after that. Told me about Gibb's financial problems. Seems the guy owes a lot of alimony to his ex for the four kids. But I don't know that's enough for him to have killed Ensor. Even if he did threaten to kill him."

"And Stark told you all of this?" asked Lane.

I nodded.

"We had a great chat."

"That's not how we do things around here, Anthony," said Lane, sounding very official in his capacity as Captain of homicide. "And I doubt it's how you do things out west."

"You're right. I prefer cuddles by the fire and long walks on moonlit beaches. Listen Lane, it's not a problem. I guarantee it.

189

Stark's not gonna make an issue of it. He was hotheaded and tried to push me around. I had to cool him down."

Jackson and Dykes hadn't heard about this. Jackson was grinning at me. It might have been admiration or he might have been happy to see me raked over the coals by Lane. I chose the first option. Lane looked at me silently for a while, his eyes on mine.

"Alright, but this can't be the default option," he said.

"Never is," I answered.

He nodded.

"Is that it?" he said.

"Sure isn't. I'm just getting started," I replied. "Then there's the manager Kreyling. The bat boy tells me he's putting money on the games. That's a no no. He could get fired for that."

"I assume he's putting money on his own team," said Lane.

"I assume that too, but I don't know for sure. We need to look into it. If not, then he's benefiting from the murder too. And he might be squeezed, might have a gambling problem. Lastly the bat boy, Junior O'Riley tells me the team doctor's doping up the whole team. Ensor isn't happy about it. Wants to get off the juice as he thinks it's making his problem worse. Threatens to take it to the MLB Commish. Anyway, apparently the doc was gonna be taking him off the juice, so I'm not sure that's a strong lead, but might be something to look into if we can't find anything else."

Lane shook his head.

"This is a goddamn dog's breakfast. I used to like baseball. Back in the simpler times."

"Like when they had the color line to put it euphemistically," I said, pushing my luck.

Jackson couldn't believe what I'd just said. I could see him shaking his head slowly from side to side. Dykes was grinning, probably from embarrassment for me.

"Are you always such an asshole, Anthony?" asked Lane, though he didn't seem as upset as he might've been. That meant he took it with the spirit it had been sent.

"Listen," I said, "I've never been a fan of baseball. I like to watch it sometimes to pass the time, but there's been problems with it for decades. Started with the color line. You know all about that, probably better than me. Now we have all this other bullshit. We've got a corrupted league, doping, shady dealings. It reminds of what's wrong with this country."

The view from my high horse was wide and expansive. I could see all the way to the wall just past Dykes head.

"And what exactly is wrong with this country?" asked Lane.

"The same thing that's wrong with baseball," I said. "The idolization of money, of stars. It's supposed to be a team sport. Teams take care of each other. Then how come we've got a handful of stars on each team making the big money. It's not natural and fair. You've gotta be doped up to make it. You've got a whole business machine here working not to make a sport about fair play and honest competition but about how to make billionaires richer. How to squeeze every last nickel out of the hardworking American and how to make the stars richer too. It's rigged like the rest of this country. That's the problem with it."

Dykes gave me a little clap. Seemed sincere, but I couldn't be sure. Jackson grinned at me.

"I like it," said Jackson. "Didn't take you for the philosopher."

Lane looked at me for a while before smiling big and broad like his shoulders.

"You might be an asshole, but I like you," he said. "You may be right, but right now, I've got ninety-nine problems and cleaning up baseball isn't one of them. Can we get back to the task at hand?"

I didn't say anything. I'd probably already said too much. But the reason I got on the job in the first place was to try and make a difference. Try to make this place a little more just and fair. Sounds like I was the sucker.

"We've gotta go see this PI. I think there might be something there. If not, we'll lean on the ex again. If that comes up empty, then we've gotta dig into Gibb or Stark, Kreyling or the doc. One of these wack-a-moles has got to be good for it," I said.

Lane looked from me to Jackson and Dykes. Dykes and Jackson nodded at him.

"I like it," said Dykes. "Feels like we're close. One of these suspects has got to be good for it. Personally, I think the wife's involved somehow. I mean isn't that the way it usually is, Captain? Those closest and those with the most to gain are usually the ones committing the crimes."

Lane nodded.

"Yeah, probably eight, nine times out of ten. But you haven't brought me anything concrete yet. You've got to shake some trees. You've gotta bring me something I can take back to the Mayor."

Dykes nodded.

"Look," said Lane, turning back to me. "You might be right and all with your analogy of baseball and the problems with America. And right now I'm feeling the heat from that massive billion dollar business we call the MLB. They want answers and we've got to give it to them. And if not for them, don't you want to just get down to brass tacks and just find justice for the deceased, even if he was a highly paid sports star?"

"I sure do, Lane," I said. "That's what I signed up for."

"Then get me something, for god's sake. Tomorrow would be

nice. This murder is hanging over the World Series like a drunk evil stepmother at wedding. The sooner we get this done the better off everyone will be."

Dykes and Jackson got up.

"We're on it, Captain," said Jackson.

"Good," said Lane.

"Anything else?" asked Dykes.

Lane stood and shook his head, the toothpick seemed shorter than when he'd first put it in his mouth. Maybe it was his fiber supplement. He seemed pretty anal. Maybe constipation was his problem.

"I'm not trying to bust your balls," said Lane. "But the shit's gonna roll down hill, you know that."

Dykes and Jackson nodded. We all left the Captain's office and walked towards the elevator.

"I thought that pep talk went very well," I said.

Jackson laughed.

"Easy for you to say," said Dykes, "you get to leave at the end of all of this."

"But until then," I said. "I remain your ever humble servant."

I grinned at them. I got a wry smile out of Dykes. He pulled out an almost empty roll of Lifesavers and popped one in his mouth. He offered them around. What I needed was a smoke. What I got was a little white mint.

CHAPTER SIXTEEN

Skeef Surveilance Systems

THERE'S a place in most cities where the good rubs shoulders with the bad. It's not a firm line. Nothing like that. Just a slow rolling over into harder times. Sort of like when you're at a bar chatting to a woman who starts to look better the more drinks you have. All cities I've visited have that woman. Only it's sorta backwards, where the pretty woman turns into a witch real slow. Chicago's like that. And in case some of you Chicagoans are feeling bent out of shape it happens everywhere. My lovely LA is a classic example. Take a lazy ride up Van Nuys sometime and you'll see what I mean. That lovely model of a lady starts off fine in Sherman Oaks, starts getting a little unruly around Van Nuys before slapping on some lipstick around Panorama City and Arleta, but she's drinking hard, until she gets rolled up wet and ragged in Pacoima. But it happens real slow, like I told you.

I was getting the same vibe in Chicago. The thing is this lady was so blitzed you could walk a few blocks and end up in a place like Hyde Park where she was looking like a classy hooker looking for her first John and then some streets down you're in Back of the Yards where's she's taken a beating and giving head for nickels.

This I'm seeing with my own eyes and what Jackson is telling me as we're heading down to a place called Armour Square in the South Side. It's squashed up against slightly better neighborhoods like a bum curled up against a warm vent.

You've seen places like this. The grass is never green, fact is, it's hard to tell the grass from the dirt. The strip malls that seemed like a good idea in the fifties are now run down and in need of some paint. It was in one of these places that Dykes pulled in and parked the car in front of a panel of pane glass. Above an entrance was a plastic sign like they have in these places. The name of the business, all of the businesses using all the space above their front for their name. This one was in red lettering. Slightly cursive. Might've looked good in the seventies. Not so much anymore. Skeef Surveillance Systems is what it read.

We got out of the car and I looked around. There wasn't a lot going on. There was a halal butcher a couple of doors down, a Hispanic grocer and a lawyer. The lawyer's business was his own name. Deshawn Johnstone JD. I coulda used a smoke about now, but I had a feeling Silent Red and Baller were itching to catch a break on this case.

"Why'd a guy like Ensor hire a bum like this," I said aloud.

"That's a good question," said Dykes. "Let's go and find out."

I followed the two of them into the office. The front was a large reception area. It smelled like cigarettes and whiskey. I thought of my apartment. Only this smell was stale. The carpet was old, thin and beige. Beige was not a good color for carpets in places like this. Stains were all over the place such that it looked mottled. There were cheap reception chairs lined up against the wall. They had thin gray cushioned bottoms and backs. I took a look at a few of them and decided to stand.

A generic, cheap reception desk stood back against a thin, cheap wall with a door off to the one side. This door led into the back. Probably where Skeef had his office. We walked up to the receptionist. She was a middle-aged woman, wide and wrinkled and white. I wanted to say something nice about her. But I couldn't find anything. She didn't look like there'd been better days behind her. She was the type of woman I figured had never seen better days.

Leaning up against the front of her desk which was rib height we could see onto her side. An ashtray was filled with dead butts. A fresh one had grown a long gray nose, the smoke rising in a still, straight stream towards the ceiling. Unperturbed, undisturbed. She looked up at us, over reading glasses as she typed on a computer that was probably seven years old.

She had the jowls of a bulldog and thin gray eyebrows that could've been transplanted from a man. Her hair was calico, but mostly dark gray roots, with a bad tint job that was something like the color of rust on the fenders of my LeSabre. Her hair hung in a pony tail down her back. Her glasses pinched the bottom of her nose and a loose, cheap beady chain mimicked her jowls and hung from her glasses round her neck. She had some makeup on, but it didn't hide her ashen complexion. Her lips were bright red, thin, wrinkled with a smoker's pucker. She didn't smile.

"What can I do you gentleman for?" she asked.

She looked down at her cigarette, picked it up and tapped the ash off before taking a long suck on it. She blew the smoke up towards the ceiling. I followed it. There was a thick cloud of smoke like pregnant udders clinging to the dropped ceiling panels which were stained and mottled like the floor.

"Detective Dykes and Detective Jackson. Homicide," said Dykes.

"We want to speak with Robert Skeef."

She nodded as if this was a routine call. She picked up the phone.

"Bobby, you've got visitors," she said. She nodded for no apparent reason. "Yeah, it's them police from homicide."

She hung up the phone and looked at Dykes.

"He'll be right out," she said. "Yous can wait over there."

She was already looking down at her computer terminal. I figured she meant the chairs when she said 'over there'. I stood where I was. Dykes and Jackson walked off and stood facing the window by the chairs, looking out into the parking lot. I was enjoying the only fresh smell in here which was her burning cigarette.

I picked up a trifold pamphlet in a cheap plastic display. This one was photocopied and therefore grayscale. I looked at her.

"What's your name, darling?" I asked.

She looked up at me like I'd insulted her cat.

"Dolores," she said, looking back at the computer.

"Dolores," I said, "you got anymore of these pamphlets in color?"

I figured they had them in color, or at least they were supposed to be in color. She didn't look at me.

"Supposed to be here last week. Printer come up with some excuse why's they're late. I can mail one to you if you like?"

I shook my head.

"Nah, this one'll be just fine," I said. "Skeef quite busy these days?"

Still wouldn't look at me. She shrugged though as she pecked away at her keyboard.

"Some days busier than others," she said.

"Today being others," I said, grinning at her for my own benefit. She still wasn't looking at me. She didn't say anything to that, so I tried something different. "What's the bread and butter of your business?"

"Cheatin' spouses," she said. "Eight or nine times outta ten it's cheatin' spouses."

I looked at the pamphlet. The top third of the front page just had Skeef Surveillance Systems on it. The next third had what was supposed to be a corporate quote but it was way to generic to be trademarked.

"Have a cheating spouse? Call Skeef. Need to find a missing relative? Call Skeef. Have any sort of beef? Call Skeef. We find anything you need with greater speed than the other guy. Cheaper too!"

Inside I groaned. But who was I to judge, I didn't even have an office. The last third of the front page showed who I presumed to be Skeef and a client with thumbs up. Inside was more of the same. Though the inside pictures seemed to be more like staged royalty free photos you'd buy online. There were also three client testimonials that weren't very convincing. Testimonials from first name, last initial that could have been made up. The back page was blank except for the middle fold which had the contact information for Skeef Surveillance Systems.

I put the pamphlet back. It was the last one after all, and I wouldn't be needing his services. I went to join Dykes and Jackson when I heard the door open. We all turned to see who was coming out. Must have been Skeef, at least I recognized him from his pamphlet.

A guy of average height came out. He had several days worth of stubble on his face. A round face that was youthful with fat. I put him in his mid thirties. He had small eyes that seemed a little too close to his nose. He was balding but chose the combover. Some guys. What can I say, a toupee would've been better. His hair was graying. The corner of his mouth had a little mustard stain. Must have caught him at lunch. There was a small stain on his shirt, just over the pocket. It was a white striped shirt that was now off gray. It had blue stripes down it. He wore a black tie that was loose around his neck and shouted polyester. Probably like this gray slacks. He wore brown tasseled loafers that needed replacing.

He was hairy. His forearms were thick with hair under his rolled up sleeves which were rolled haphazardly just below his elbows. He wore a gaudy, chunky gold chain around his right wrist. I was gonna go with gold plated. On his left wrist was a bulky Rolex. I'd bet my last bottle of whiskey it was a knockoff. On his right ring finger was a large gold champion ring. Probably from high school. His belly burst at the buttons on his shirt and rode over his trousers like a huge boil. He was friendly though, I gave him that. He walked right over to us with a big friendly smile on his face.

"Detectives," he said, his warmth was contagious. "What can I do yous for?"

Seemed like this little office had its own accent. Skeef reached out his hand. He went for the tallest of us first. That'd be Dykes. They shook hands.

"Detective Dykes," he said, and then looked off to Jackson. "Detective Jackson and that's Anthony Carrick."

Skeef shook hands with all of us.

"You Robert Skeef?" asked Dykes.

"Yes sir, Bobby. My friends call me Bobby," he said.

"Can we talk privately, Bobby?" asked Dykes.

"Yes sir," he said, nodding his head and still smiling. "Let's go into my office."

He turned and walked back from where he came. Just before he entered through the door he turned and spoke with Dolores.

"Dol, can you hold my calls until these here detectives have left?"

Dolores nodded at the computer screen. We followed him into the back of a thin but long office he rented. We passed a small bathroom that needed a clean from the looks of it. There were a couple of other rooms before the big one at the back. Those rooms were closed. On the door to his office was his name.

Inside the office I smelt mustard and cigar tobacco. Smelt sweet like Black and Milds Wine. I was right, I saw a couple of untipped butts in an ashtray on his desk. Also on his desk was an inch left of a 7-Eleven hotdog in its tray. Another empty tray was in the wastepaper basket on the right side of his desk. A Big Gulp was on the desk next the hotdog and a brown bag with a clear window on it held an uneaten donut.

Skeef walked round to his side of the desk and sat down. In front of him on our side were a couple of chairs, the same kind as from the reception area. I took a look. These ones were cleaner. Dykes and Jackson sat down. Dykes popped a Lifesaver in his mouth, offered all of us. All of us declined, including Skeef.

"I'm just finishing my lunch. Yous don't mind?"

It wasn't really a question. He popped the last bite of hotdog into his mouth and washed it down with a long drink from his Big Gulp. Then he took a white napkin and wiped his mouth and tossed that and the hotdog tray into the basket. He picked up his packet of Black and Milds and put one in his mouth. I took this as an invitation and put a cigarette in mine. He lit a match, fired up his cigarillo and offered the match to me. I leaned in for the spark. He turned around and opened a window behind him about a foot.

It opened up to the back alley.

"Sorry about the mess," he said. "AC's on the fritz. Called the guy but you know how these monkeys get things done. Amiright?'

He smiled at us and took a puff from his cigarillo.

"So what can I do yous for?"

"We're here about Ensor," said Dykes.

Skeef shook his head slowly and sadly.

"Man, I can't believe it. Who'd wanna kill him?" he asked, looking at the three of us.

"That's what we'd like to know. Mr. Frederic Salisbury tells us that you were helping Ensor out with something."

Skeef sucked on his cigarillo and blew smoke up to the ceiling, chasing it with o-rings.

"Yup. Jimmy wanted me to tail his wife. Thought summin' was up with hers. He was right."

"What was she up to?" asked Dykes.

I sucked on my cigarette and leaned in to tap its ash into his ashtray. I didn't see any others. Skeef pushed it towards me. It was now towards the end of the desk. That was nice of him. I appreciated the consideration.

"He reckoned she was screwing around on him. And he was right. She was giving it to this nig..."

Skeef realized Jackson was with us. He cleared his throat.

"I meant to say she was screwing this African American team mate of his. Guy's name is Gibb."

Skeef didn't look at Jackson. Jackson was looking at him. I looked at Jackson and then I wanted to clean Skeef's clock. But we needed some information from him. Fuck it. I stuck the cigarette in my mouth and walked round the side of the desk and clocked him on the beak. He bounced back against his cheap leather chair, his cigarillo fell out of his hand. I grabbed him by his tie and pulled him in real close.

"What the fuck were you gonna say?" I asked.

My blood was boiling. Maybe I was tired and cranky. Most likely I was sick and tired of the racists in this country. Blood started trickling from his nose. His eyes were wide, watery and scared. He held up both his hands in submission. Smoke from my cigarette was curling into my left eye. I squinted it half shut.

"Geez man, I..I..I'm sorry," he said.

"You owe your apology to the detective you insulted, you piece of white shit."

Skeef looked over at Jackson.

"I'm sorry," he said. "I didn't means nothing by it."

Jackson nodded. I slowly released my grip on him. He put his left shoulder to his nose and dabbed the blood off with his shirt. He leaned down and picked up his cigarillo. I didn't look at anybody. I didn't want to deal with Dykes being pissed off or pleased. Made no difference to me. I was in a mood. And the white trash needed taking out. Besides, I figured it might have loosened Skeef up a bit. He might be more talkative now. Skeef licked the top of his lip where blood was trickling down. He stuck his cigarillo into his mouth and pulled on a drawer on the side of his desk. He pulled out a couple of tissues and dabbed at his nose. He didn't look at me.

"You got any pictures from your surveillance?" asked Dykes, after giving Skeef a few moments to collect himself. Skeef nodded, looking down at the clump of red and white tissues in his hand. He tenderly put the tissues to his nose again. The blood was slowly staring to clot. Despite what it looked like, I hadn't hit him hard enough to break his nose. As if reading my mind.

"Shit, man, I thinks its busted," he said.

"I didn't hit you hard enough," I said, my voice clotted with anger and hatred. He still didn't look at me. He put the tissues into the trash can and pulled out a couple more. Then he got up and walked over to his right where two stacks of metal filing cabinets sat against the wall. He shuffled through some files and then pulled out a blue folder. He put it on his desk and sat down behind it. He opened it up. There were a bunch of photos. He took a stack of them and rifled through them. Then he pushed them towards the end of the table towards Dykes. I had seen them when he shuffled through them from my vantage point.

Dykes looked at them. There were half a dozen or so he'd shown us. Pics of Gibb and Celia by a nice house. Probably Gibb's but I couldn't be sure. There were three pics of Gibb and Celia outside. Kissing, hugging and holding hands. The next three were the interesting ones. You could see the two of them through a window in an upstairs room of the house. Both of them were naked in the first one. The second shot showed her on her knees giving him head. The third shot had her facing the camera with Gibb giving it to her from behind. There was no doubt what was going on.

"You took these with a telephoto?" asked Dykes, looking up at Skeef. Skeef dabbed at his nose. Not much new blood was leaking out. He sucked on his cigarillo and still didn't look at me or Jackson. The two of us didn't feel much like talking to him so that was on Dykes.

"Yes sir, I musta been a couple hundred feet away in my car."

"And you showed these to Ensor?"

"Yes sir. He was real pissed off. Said he was gonna kill her. But I reckon that was just the anger talking. He wasn't like that. Asked me to hold onta them. Said he was gonna divorce her and that he needed them for the lawyer."

"And did you speak to the lawyer?" asked Dykes.

"No sir. Jimmy said he was gonna do that."

"Did he?"

"I dunno. I thinks so, but he never told me for real. I just guessed."

"Where was this taken?" asked Dykes.

"At Gibb's place in Forest Glen."

"How long did you tail her for?"

"Just a coupla weeks. I got lots of stuff on her in that time," said Skeef, dabbing at the crusting blood on his upper lip. He took a sip on his Big Gulp. Then he took a drag on his cigarillo. I tapped ash out into the ashtray.

"Did you see her with anyone else?" asked Dykes.

"Yes sir, there was this other guy."

"Did you catch them in intimate settings like this?"

"No sir, but I gots pictures of them two."

Skeef got up and went back to the filing cabinet. He pulled out another blue folder and put it on this desk. He sat down in front of it and put his cigarillo in his mouth. He opened it up. The insides were the same as the first folder. A scattering of photos and a sheet of paper on the inside with times and places and such.

Skeef looked over the photos and handed four of them to Dykes.

"These all of them?"

"No sir, I just prints out the best ones. I've got a whole memory card here. Probably a few dozen I reckon of both sets."

At the bottom of the folder on both inside sides was a sleeve. In the first one, Skeef pulled out a small manila envelope. There was a hard, square item inside. He pulled it out and showed it to us. It was a memory card. Sixty-four gigabytes. He put it back in the envelope and put the envelope back in the sleeve. Dykes looked at the photos and shared them Jackson. I'd seen them from my vantage point close to Skeef's desk.

They were good photos in that you could see the people in them clearly. Also taken from a distance with a telephoto. It was of Celia with a long, scraggly haired Jesus-looking guy. If Jesus had the look of a heroin addict who hadn't eaten in a few weeks or shaved for that long. He had stubble on his face and his hair looked greasy or wet. It was slightly curly and hung to his shoulders. He was gaunt-looking with beady, crazy eyes and a hooked nose. They were sitting at a coffee shop by a window. Two drinks were on the table. One of the photos had Jesus addict looking at the photographer, at least that was the impression. The other three were similar shots but not giving such clean lines of sight. The best shot of Celia was a three quarter profile pic. She didn't look happy.

"Who is this guy?" asked Dykes.

Skeef shrugged.

"I dunno. I followed him for a while to this motel not far from here in Pullman. He's a rough looking character, but theys were never intimate."

"What were they doing together?"

Skeef shrugged again.

"I dunno. Never heard what they talked about. But she gave him some money. Quite a lot of money. I took pictures of it but I hadn't developed them yet. A big envelope probably an inch thick. He seemed pretty agitated. She looked scared though."

"You just have them meeting this one time?"

Skeef nodded and finished up his cigarillo and squashed it out into the ashtray. I did the same with my cigarette. He still didn't look at me.

"Yes sir, just this one time. Like I said, I followed him to this motel. A real rundown place. Called Nite Owl Motel in Pullman likes I said. I took this all to Jimmy and he said he'd handle it from there."

"When was this?"

"Last Friday," said Skeef, looking at his notes in the folder. "This meeting here at that coffee shop was on Friday morning. I followed this guy to the motel that afternoon and went to see Jimmy in the evening."

"Was he driving?"

"Yes sir, was an old Crown Vic. Bad shape it was. Had a whole bunch of primer all over it, round the wheel wells and such. Otherwise it was maroon and probably a ninety-two model."

"Did you go back to the motel to tail him some more?"

"No sir, Jimmy said that was all he wanted. I gave him copies of the photos I took and he paid me and said that's all he needed. Said he'd take it from here."

"You happen to get the guy's name?"

"No sir."

"You didn't head into the motel to ask?"

"Geez, no sir, I never did think of that."

Skeef sucked on his Big Gulp like he'd just come out of the Sahara. He still didn't look at me.

"I don't like the look of those photos," I said, looking at Dykes. "Something's going on here. She's paying this guy off for something."

Jackson looked up at me.

"You thinking murder for hire?" he asked.

Skeef looked up at us.

"I don't reckon she'd do anything like that," he said.

We ignored him. I tilted my head to one side and then shrugged.

"Maybe, but I'm not sold on it. She didn't seem like a woman who'd just hired a guy to murder her husband when we interviewed her."

Jackson nodded.

"Looks like we've got someone we need to talk to."

Dykes returned three of the photos to Skeef. Skeef looked at the last one still in Dykes hand like he was longing for it.

"We'll hold onto this one," said Dykes.

Skeef nodded.

"Ok," he said. "I can print more."

"Tell me something," I said, looking at Skeef still trying to figure out his relationship with the deceased. "Why'd Ensor hire a bum like you."

Skeef was over getting angry at me. He looked at me with distaste in his eyes.

"Me and Jimmy, we's go ways back. I've known Jimmy ever since we were on the high school football team back in Lexington, South Carolina. Jimmy's a loyal friend. Something you don't unnerstand."

It was his best attempt at a barb. I just left it.

"So that's your high school ring?" I asked, nodding at the championship ring. He looked at me again and nodded.

"State champions we were. Jimmy played baseball and football. He was real good athlete."

I nodded.

"You never got to the NFL then?"

He looked away and shook his head.

"Didn't pick me. But Jimmy always remembered his friends. He helped me set up my business here after I finished my criminology course."

I nodded. Skeef didn't look at me.

"You getting any money from his will?"

Skeef shrugged.

"Dunno," he said. "I never did kill 'im if that's what you're suggesting."

"You have a gun?"

Skeef nodded.

"In my drawer here," he said, looking at the drawer where his tissues were.

"What type?"

"Beretta Px4 Storm with forty Smith and Wessons."

"Show me," I said.

Skeef opened up the drawer and slowly pulled out his gun which was in a clip on holster. He left it in the holster and passed it over to me. I had a look at it. It was as he said. I slid it back.

"Registered?"

He looked up at me with a sulky face.

"Of course."

"Any others?"

He shook his head.

"If you're lying," I said. "Detective Jackson is gonna be back like a ton of bricks."

Skeef looked over at Jackson and then back at me.

"I ain't lying."

I nodded. I then looked over at Dykes and Jackson.

"Alright," said Dykes, standing up. "You've been helpful. If we need anything else we'll see you soon."

Skeef nodded but didn't say anything. We walked out and I could feel Skeef's eyes burning a hole in the back of my head. Outside by the car, Jackson turned towards me.

"You didn't have to do that," he said. "I could've handled it myself."

I nodded and looked over his shoulder at a shawarma joint.

"Guess I was just in a pissy mood," I said. "I'm hangry, so that probably didn't help. Besides, nothing pisses me off more than racist assholes taking cheap shots."

Jackson grinned at me.

"Still, shit man, did you see his face after you popped him?"

I nodded and grinned.

"That was worth the price of admission," he said.

Dykes was smiling off to the side, enjoying our conversation. He popped a Lifesaver in his mouth.

"Must be nice not to be encumbered by a badge," he said.

I looked at him.

"It helps," I said. "Though a badge never stopped me from straightening out ignorance."

"Good to know," said Dykes, "because we've been on our best behavior trying to figure you out."

"And now we understand each other, right?" I asked.

Dykes nodded and turned to open his door.

"Listen," I said, "I am seriously hangry. Can you smell that meat? I just wanna grab a quick bite."

Dykes turned and looked at the shawarma place. He nodded his head.

"Yeah, I could put something down."

"Damn right," said Jackson.

We walked over to Shicago Shawarma. It was a stand up restaurant, with a counter to order from and a tall thin counter up against the window to eat at without seats. But the shawarma was one of the best I'd had in my life. That, or I was just really, really hangry.

CHAPTER SEVENTEEN
Nite Owl Motel

PULLMAN was one of those communities that had let middle age beat him down. He'd grown a paunch, sat on his porch, unshaven, hair scraggly, drinking beer and wagging his fingers at the kids walking home from school. But something had been happening to him in the last decade or so. Seems he was working out, eating his veggies and shaving. Hell, he was even wearing nicer clothes, not new, but new for him, and he was wearing cologne. Might be cheap drugstore cologne, but still, I reckon nobody would have recognized him from the man he was twenty years ago. Old age had given him a new lease on life.

I was expecting Pullman to be a ramshackle place full of hoodlums and gangsters on every corner. That wasn't the case. It was a community of hard working folk coming together to reinvigorate their place in the greater Chicago area. Sure, its age was showing. Sidewalks were cracked, infrastructure needed some work, but folks' homes were their pride and joy. You could see them spending real money on them to bring them back into the twenty-first century.

We'd taken a detour off of South Cottage Grove Avenue and

driven past Hotel Florence. Dykes had explained to me that this hotel was as old as the hills. Built by George Pullman, famous for the Pullman train sleeping car, he named it after his daughter. It was the only place in Pullman, which he'd also designed as the first planned community in America, which offered liquor. Pullman was a dry town back in his day. We're talking the early eighteen eighties.

It was a fine looking hotel but no longer available for sleepovers. The Illinois Historic Preservation Agency owns it now and uses it for tours and special functions.

That was our only brief stop. We carried on towards the Nite Owl Motel. It was barely inside Pullman as I understood it, and you can tell. This is where old man Pullman after a long day's work loosened his belt and let his smaller paunch stick out under his wife beater. We were on East 115th Street not far from the Bishop Ford Freeway. This was a mixed area of town. Some commercial, industrial and run down motels.

Nite Owl Motel was probably from the fifties. It was a two story strip style motel with blue trim that needed a new coat of paint. As we drove up into the driveway, the office was on our left and the two floors of the motel sprawled out to the right. The sign was on a tall white pole. The sign itself was oblong and blue with similar lettering to Skeef's only it was in white. You couldn't tell if there was vacancy because the vacancy light wasn't on in the bright sun, but we figured a place like this always had a room to rent. Dykes pulled us up right out front the office. There were three cars in the parking slots right up against the rooms. Old beaters of American sort. Nothing newer than ten years.

We all got out. The sun was bright and watery, the sky pale blue in contrast to the Dodger blue of the motel's trim. It wasn't cold, but I was grateful to be wearing my windbreaker. It was my hat that I missed. I followed Dykes and Jackson into the office. It smelt of stale cigarettes and eggs. I couldn't figure out the eggs until we moseyed up to the front desk and I saw a paper plate that once had a couple of fried eggs on it just off to the side of the man behind the counter.

He was a guy in his thirties with stubble and a natural tan. He wore a polyester mesh baseball cap with a logo of an engine on the front and a name I didn't recognize. He wore two round black nuts as earrings. At least that's what they looked like to me. I coulda stuck my finger through them. He had two metal horns sticking out each nostril about a half an inch. I figured that was another sort of piercing. Around his neck was a black leather string with a crystal ring hanging from it over his camo green T-shirt. Both his arms had full sleeves. Nothing literal, mostly some sort of tribal art without color. His pants were black cargo, combat pants, similar to the kinds that SWAT and others might wear. His left front pocket showed a clip that was attached to a knife inside his pocket. He was skinny but looked tall. He was reading a tattoo magazine. He looked up at us and I could see the walls go up.

His eyes were clear and intelligent. I wasn't expecting that. He reminded me of a crafty, intelligent weasel for some reason. Maybe I was about to find out. Dykes opened up his jacket with this right hand to show his badge.

"Detective Dykes, homicide," he said.

I watched the guy behind the counter. He didn't say anything. He put his magazine down and pushed himself away from the counter a bit.

"What's your name?"

"Barry," he said, and I called bullshit on that. Dykes wasn't buying it either.

"What's your real name, Barry?" he asked.

'Barry' cocked his head up towards the ceiling in defiance.

"I ain't done nothing," he said. "I don't have to tell you my name."

Dykes stood there for a moment looking at him. I wanted a go.

"You're eating breakfast food for lunch," I said. "Where I come from that's a felony."

I wasn't playing with him either. I was itching for some action. 'Barry' stood up and leaned over his side of the counter towards me. He was a tall drink of vinegar alright. Probably taller than Dykes.

"And where's that from, old man?" he asked. "Bumfuck, Missouri."

It was the opening I'd hoped for. Firstly, I wasn't that old. Forties is the new twenties so they tell me. And secondly, I'd never heard of this place called Bumfuck. 'Barry' was sneering at me as he leaned in. I wasn't sure where he got off being such a smart ass in front of three men, two of whom were carrying handguns. Leaning in was perhaps his biggest mistake though. I grabbed him round the back of the neck really quickly and brought his head down onto the higher part of the counter that was on our side.

It wasn't that hard. He was off balance, like I said, that was his error. I also caught him by surprise. The edge of the counter caught the bridge of his nose. As his face bounced off I knew he was gonna need stitches. I wasn't hangry anymore, but I was still pissy. I couldn't figure out why. Maybe it was the wind in Chicago. Wind always wrecked a half decent day, and Chicago had been windy since I'd arrived. It was probably that goddamn whistling wind in my ear the whole time.

The noise of his face bouncing off the counter was a louder crack than I was expecting. He pulled back and instinctively reached for his face with his hands. Blood didn't start coming out of the cut on the bridge of his nose right away.

"What the fuck," he said, "you've busted my nose."

I hadn't busted any noses yet in my trip to Chicago. I hadn't planned on it either, but this put me in a spot. We were likely gonna have to call an ambulance for this douchebag to get his nose stitched up. That was gonna take some explaining.

"Your nose isn't broken, Barry," I said. "But if you don't give me your real name I'm leaning towards breaking it for you."

He looked at me through watery eyes. That happens when you get smacked on the nose hard. Can't be helped. I didn't consider him a wuss for it.

"Dorian Bronitt," he said.

"That wasn't too hard now, was it?" I asked.

Dykes tapped me on the shoulder. I turned around to look at him. He nodded at the far corner. The three of us walked over to the bank of windows close to the entrance door. To our right were a couple of wooden, cushioned chairs and a table between them with news magazines.

"You've put us in a spot here, Anthony," said Dykes. "Dorian's nose is going to need stitches you realize?"

I nodded.

"Yeah, sorry about that. I'm just in a pissy mood. Didn't mean to ring his bell that loudly."

"Listen, I get you're not a cop, but still, you're with us and it's not gonna look good if Lane hears about this."

I nodded again and looked outside at the traffic going by. Jackson tapped Dykes on the shoulder.

"I can probably take care of that," he said. "I bet there's a first aid kit here. A bit of butterfly tape and some gauze and it'll heal better than with stitches anyway."

Dykes looked over at Jackson and sighed. He nodded slowly, reached for a mint and popped it in his mouth. He didn't offer us any.

"Okay," he said.

We walked back to the counter where Dorian was swabbing at his nose with a clump of tissues and trying to open up a red first aid kit.

"Let me help you with that," said Jackson, helpfully.

Dorian nodded at him. Jackson went through the swiveling door to the side of the counter over to Dorian's side and opened up the first aid kit and found what he was looking for.

"I'm gonna complain to IAD," said Dorian.

"Won't help you," said Jackson, looking at the nose. "He's not a cop. I'm going to dab it pretty firmly here to clean up the blood. Then I'm going to tape it shut and put some gauze over it, okay."

Dorian took his clump of tissues away from his nose. Jackson cleaned away the wound with an alcohol swab and then dabbed at it with some tissues. He then taped it shut and covered it with a small piece of gauze and taped that over the wound.

"Then I'm gonna sue the bastard," said Dorian.

Jackson turned round and looked at us. He was sitting on the waist high side of the counter, next to Dorian.

"That's not gonna help either," he said. "What I recall was you tripping over your chair as you got up to greet us when we came in and you banged yourself pretty good on the edge of the counter here. Good thing I was a medic in Fallujah."

Dorian looked over at Dykes. Dykes nodded at him, unwrapping some more of his Lifesaver tube.

"Yup, sounds about right to me," said Dykes.

"Assholes," said Dorian under his breath.

Dykes walked up to the counter and I joined him. Dykes offered a mint towards Dorian. Dorian took one. He offered one to Jackson and then to me. We both accepted. I decided to step back and let the police do some questioning, now that I'd warmed the man up for them.

"Listen," said Dykes. "We're here to ask some questions. We're not interested in you. But if you're gonna be a dick I can always make a call and see if there are any outstanding warrants on you."

Dorian shrugged, which probably meant he was clean. That also explained his bravado.

"Alternatively," said Dykes, "the book of law is a thick book, and I bet if I look hard enough I can find something to take you downtown for. I bet your boss would like that. What do you think, Jackson?"

Jackson came back round to our side. He looked at Dorian.

"Yeah, that book of law. Sure is thick. Lots of nuance and interpretation there too. I bet that knife in his pocket is probably not legal. Maybe the blade's too long. I dunno, but I sure do believe we could find something."

Dorian looked at them uneasily.

"Jesus," he said. "Alright, what the fuck do you want?"

"Tell me how this place works," said Dykes. "You do hourlies?"

Dorian shook his head.

"Nah man, we're not a place like that."

Dykes looked around.

"Shit, well excuse me for not mistaking this place for a five star Sheraton."

Dorian smiled a little at that. He was sitting back in his chair. It was a cheap office chair with a back that tilted. He touched the edges of the gauze tenderly. It was taped pretty good. Jackson knew what he was doing.

"Take some Tylenol and you'll be alright," said Jackson. "Though your eyes will swell a little and bruise."

Dorian nodded and put his hands back on his thighs.

"So how does this place work?" asked Dykes.

"Minimum is one night. We have deals for weekly and monthly. We have the cheapest rates in the city, so we attract a certain clientele."

"What are your rates?" asked Dykes.

Dorian didn't have to look at any notes.

"Twenty-nine ninety-five a night. One ninety-nine ninety-five a week and seven ninety-nine ninety-five a month."

"How many on monthly right now?" asked Dykes.

"Nobody. Monthly's not that popular on account that we take their ID if they want monthly. For nightly and weekly we take the cash up front and a deposit if they don't want to leave a credit card."

"How much is that?"

"Hundred bucks deposit in case of incidentals. Sometimes we get the wrong sort here who makes a mess."

"Sometimes?" asked Dykes ironically.

"Poor folk aren't always criminals," he said. I nodded to that. "If somebody looks high or wasted we won't rent to them."

Dykes nodded, then he turned to Jackson.

"I forgot the photo in the car."

Jackson nodded and walked out. He returned a few moments later with a manila envelope in his hand.

"So you don't keep tabs on who's renting?"

Dorian shook his head.

"Nah man, not usually."

Dykes leaned in towards Dorian, putting his elbows on the counter.

"So you're telling me that you have no idea who rents a room from night to night unless they're monthlies. Am I hearing you correctly?"

Dorian looked down and around at his workspace. The plate of eaten eggs was still there. We'd passed a Denny's close to this joint. I figured that's where he'd gotten them. Dorian looked back up at Dykes.

"Nah man, we don't ask for ID unless they want to pay with credit. Most folks don't want to pay with credit. We're discreet like that." He paused for a moment. "But I take down the license plates of the cars they drive in on, you know, just in case we have an incident and need to go after them. It happened before so that's why I do it."

Dykes nodded and looked over at Jackson. Jackson grinned.

"That's smart thinking, Dorian," Jackson said.

Jackson took the photo of skinny, scraggly Jesus from inside the folder and put it on the counter facing Dorian. Dorian leaned in and looked at it.

"You seen this man recently?" asked Dykes, pushing his finger onto the man's face.

Dorian looked up and nodded.

"Yeah man, he was a weekly for a couple of weeks. Just left today. Drove a Crown Vic maroon in color."

Dykes nodded. I liked where this was going.

"I don't suppose you got his name?"

Dorian shook his head.

"Nah, but he didn't cause any problems."

"But you got his license plate right?" asked Dykes.

"Yeah, but I threw it out, I don't keep it forever. Like I said, we try and offer some privacy here. We did a walkthrough not long ago. Everything was in order. I gave him his hundred back and he went on his way."

"So you just threw it out?" asked Dykes.

Dorian nodded.

"Well, in that case, why don't you look for it?"

Dorian reached under his side of the desk and pulled out a black plastic open faced wastebasket. He rifled through it. It was filled with papers, some cigarette butts and ash, bottles and old wrappers of food. He found what he was looking for. It was piece of paper about four by six inches that looked like it'd been torn off a spiral notebook. It was crumpled up and stained, still damp in parts. Dorian straightened it out and put it up on the counter by the photo.

It had the date. Monday the twelfth of October. That was Columbus Day. The time was next to it at three thirty-seven pm. This was underlined. Underneath was the room number. One oh two. Under this was the guys description. Five ten, one fifty, scraggly hair brown, unshaven, maroon Crown Vic nineties, Indiana plate 042HGG. Jackson jotted this info down on the back of the manila envelope.

"Did he give you a name?" asked Dykes.

Dorian smiled at Dykes and looked at him. He tapped his fingers on his knees.

"I try to be social," said Dorian. "Sometimes just getting the license plate isn't all that helpful. We've had more than one asshat come here with a rental or worse, a stolen vehicle."

"And I thought you said poor folk aren't criminals," I said. I couldn't help myself. He looked over at me with anger hot in his eyes.

"I said not all poor folk are criminals."

He looked back at Dykes.

"But you know, the kind of rates we offer, the privacy, that attracts a certain person."

Dykes nodded.

"You don't suspect him for that murder of James Ensor do you?" asked Dorian. He was smarter than he looked. I had picked up on that earlier. Dykes smiled at him again, he was no longer leaning on the counter. Dykes was standing straight and tall.

"We're following leads. Can't be sure who's involved yet or not. It's not like in the movies."

Dorian nodded.

"You were telling me how social you like to be."

"Right," said Dorian. "I like to ask folks a bunch of questions and see where they're at. It's sorta like a background check."

Dykes was nodding.

"I get where you're coming from. How about we get down to brass tacks."

"Okay man, shit, you don't have to be such a dick. I'm trying to help you out here."

Dykes didn't say anything. Jackson had walked over to the glass door we had walked in from. He was looking outside towards the motel's rooms. A black sedan with tinted windows drove in and parked in front of one of the rooms towards the far end. A hispanic man got out wearing a bandana and a carrying a brown paper bag that probably had a quart of beer in it. He walked towards the stairs on the far side of the motel and took them up to the second floor. He opened a door to a room on that level that was unlocked and walked in. He was oblivious to us.

"I asked that dude his name, where he was from, what he was in town for, that sort of thing."

"Yeah, I'm surprised you aren't that busy considering the championship starting tomorrow," I said.

Dorian shrugged.

"We're steady most of the time, things like that don't affect us much. Our customers have more immediate concerns than watching overpaid athletes."

I nodded and took a step back to let Dykes get where he was going.

"So?" asked Dykes.

"So he tells me his name was Jonathan Frakes..."

Dorian grinned at that. I got it. I looked at Dykes. He stared at Dorian not getting it. He shrugged his shoulders.

"So you figure that wasn't his real name?" asked Dykes.

Dorian was still grinning.

"No man, geez, Jonathan Frakes? Number One?"

Dykes stood and stared at him.

"Frakes played Commander Ryker on Star Trek, The Next Generation. He's an actor," I offered, trying to be helpful.

Dorian looked at me grinning. He nodded his head and offered me his fist. I gave it a bump. I guess we were Trekkie pals now. Dykes looked at us.

"Really?" he asked, shaking his head like a disappointed father. I grinned at him.

"So anyways, I told him I was LeVar Burton."

Dorian stopped and looked over at me. I nodded.

"LeVar Burton," I said, getting cut off.

"Is an actor on the same show," said Dykes, showing slight frustration as he turned to me.

"Yeah," continued Dorian, "but he's a black dude man, he played the blind Geordi La Forge on The Next Generation. See, I'm not black or blind. This guy got it. This 'Jonathan Frakes'."

Dorian was grinning. I offered him another fist bump and he took it. Nodding his head vigorously as we bro fisted.

"Alright," said Dykes, "can we finish with the Star Trek Convention and get to it."

"Well, he's obviously a Trekkie man. He knows his Star Trek stuff," said Dorian.

"That's not helpful," said Dykes.

"Okay, maybe this will be more your style," said Dorian. "I asked him where he's from. He told me Indiana. I said, oh yeah, I've been to Indiana, whereabouts? He told me it was a small place I wouldn't have heard of but he wouldn't give me any deets about it."

"Deets?" asked Dykes.

"Details, man, details."

Dykes nodded.

"And what did you make of that?"

"I figured that was the truth. I knew he was from Indiana after I took down his plates so that much was true. Maybe he is from a small town there."

"What else?"

"I asked him why he was in town. Was he here for the game? He said no he wasn't, he was here to look up an old friend. But he wasn't real chatty. Couldn't get anything else out of him after that. He got frustrated, just wanted me to show him his room."

"Did he request a particular one?"

"Nah, but one of the first things he asked was if he could pay cash. He wanted to know that right off the bat."

"Did he say how long he'd be staying?" asked Dykes.

"Nah, I asked, but he said he wasn't sure, maybe a week or two. He paid a week upfront with the deposit and then he paid for another week this past Monday."

"So he got change back this morning?"

Dorian nodded, and looked down at a ledger on the table in front of him. He flipped back a couple of pages. The ledger appeared to be based on room numbers. He drew his finger down the page.

"Uh huh, yeah, so that first week he used up, the second week he didn't. But because he didn't use the second week up I deducted three day rates off the weekly and then gave him the change. Two ten back. One ten for the refund from the weekly and then the hundred back for the deposit."

"Anything else?"

"Nah, I thanked him for his patronage and asked if we might be seeing him again soon. Said it's always nice to have folks from outta town. He said he didn't think so. But he seemed a little agitated. He was in a rush to get going. Even told me to keep the deposit and not bother with the walkthrough, but I told him it wouldn't take long. But he bailed as soon as we got done. No pleasantries as he left."

Dykes nodded.

"Anything else you can tell me about him?"

"He signed the forms with his left hand, and he was married," said Dorian, "but when I asked him about the wife and kids he didn't say anything. Just ignored me. Obviously, his wife wasn't with him. Didn't see any kids either. But his wedding ring was odd."

"How so?"

"Had this big red gemstone in the middle at the top of the gold ring. It sat out about an eighth of an inch. Really crappy looking thing if you ask me."

"Can you draw it?" I asked him.

Dorian nodded and sketched on a piece of paper from a spiral notebook that was off to the one side of the counter. He tore off the page and handed it to me. I looked at it. Reminded me a bit of Green Lantern's ring. Or at least how I imagined it way back in the day. The ring was a thicker gold wedding ring with a gemstone seated in the middle at the top covering the width of the band.

"How wide you figure that band was?" I asked.

"Just how I drew it man," he said.

"So around a quarter of an inch?"

I looked at Dorian, he nodded at me.

"Any markings, tattoo on him that stood out?" asked Dykes.

Dorian looked back at Dykes.

"Yeah, looked like he might have done some time. He had two spiders tattooed. One on each hand by the thumb."

Dorian squeezed the V fleshy part of his left thumb with this right thumb and index finger where it attaches to the hand.

"They were small, maybe half an inch and blurry, not good tattoos that's why I figure he was in jail," offered Dorian.

Dykes nodded. Jackson was taking notes. I was thinking about meeting this Jonathan Frakes character. Maybe I'd introduce myself as Jean-Luc Picard, or maybe Q. Hadn't decided yet. Although if we were using the real actors' names I'd probably be Patrick Stewart or John de Lancie.

"We'd like to take a look at the room he was in," said Dykes.

"Sure thing, man," said Dorian. "I'll just have to get the key and lock up the shop here."

Dorian stood up and turned around where he opened up a metal box that looked like an electrical box but was filled with room keys. Two for each room. One oh two had both keys side by side. Dorian took one off the hook and closed up the box and locked it again with the key he'd used to open it. He turned around and locked the cash register which was to his left.

"You keep two keys for each room?" I asked.

"Yeah," he said. "Had a problem before where we only had one key. This was before my time and some asshole lost the key. We had to call in a locksmith to open up the room. Since then we keep two and if one goes missing we get another done. It's cheaper that way. Still bill it back to the customer though. We have a master set that the cleaner uses, but that's kept locked up in the utility room."

"And has that happened often?" I asked.

"A few times since I've been here."

"And how long is that?"

"Couple of years."

"So you've got rogue keys out there that can open up some of your rooms and your customers are none the wiser for it?" I asked.

Dorian looked at me for a moment.

"Yeah, I guess you could say that. Never thought of it like that. But, I mean, the keys only have a tag with the room number on them, not the motel's name."

He showed me the example in the one he was carrying.

"That's very comforting," I said, ironically.

"Come on man, there's always someone on duty here in the office twenty-four seven. And we've never had a problem."

"Let's go," said Dykes, holding his arm out to encourage Dorian and the rest of us to leave.

We all followed Dorian out of the office. He closed the metal framed glass door behind us and locked it. Before he did so, he put a sign on the door from inside that had a clock on it with moveable hands that said he'd be back in fifteen minutes. If that, I figured.

The motel was shaped like a hockey stick. The blade end was the office and we followed it up towards the shaft. Along the way we passed an ice room with a couple of vending machines in it, a laundry room and another closed room with a push button locked door handle on it. That was probably for employees. Where the shaft started from the blade was one oh one. The next one on the main level was one oh two. A maid was just leaving as we got there. Dykes stopped her.

"You just starting or finishing?" he asked.

She looked at Dorian and he nodded at her.

"Just finishing," she said in a huff.

"Did he leave any garbage behind?"

"Only what's in my cart," she said. She pointed to the far end where a large black plastic bag was stretched over the cart. The front part held toiletry supplies and cleaning supplies. Dykes looked in. There was a bottle of whiskey and a couple of cans of beer, some used tissues, an empty bag of potato chips and a chocolate bar wrapper. Dykes helped himself to a couple of latex gloves in a box on the top of the cart. The maid gave him a hard stare that he ignored. Dorian caught it.

"It's okay, Isabella," he said. "These are homicide detectives. They're investigating the James Ensor murder."

Isabella looked over at him and nodded. That satisfied her. Dykes pulled out the whiskey bottle and the cans of beer. He looked at Isabella, she was wearing a set of latex gloves too.

"You touch these with your hands?" he asked.

"Yes."

"Without the gloves on?"

"No sir, I always have my gloves on when I'm cleaning a room. Sometimes there's liquids in the rooms that we're not sure the source of."

I understood exactly what she meant.

"What about one oh one? Is this the first room you've cleaned today?"

Isabella nodded.

"Yes sir, that one," and she pointed to one oh one, "was not rented last night."

She held up a clipboard that had the room numbers and check marks next to the ones that needed cleaning. One oh one had an X next to it, not a check mark.

"So no one else has touched this garbage before you?"

"Nobody who works here," she said.

Dykes nodded.

"You guys go in, I'm going to take this back to the car and meet you inside."

"Thank you, Isabella," said Dorian. "Are you finished with this one?" She nodded. "Okay, you can carry on."

Isabella took her cart a couple of doors down and opened up one oh four.

"You always try to keep a room between renters?" I asked.

"We do if it's possible," said Dorian. "It helps keep things quieter for our customers."

Dorian walked into the room and Jackson and I followed him. The room was one large square. There was a queen-sized bed in the middle with two bedside tables with lamps on either side. Each one had a lamp and an ashtray on it. The decor seemed late seventies and cheap particle board. The headboard was just a piece of veneered particle board. The bed had a slight sag in the middle. The mattress was probably a couple of decades overdue for replacing.

The smell was musty with an undertone of brewery and smoke. Like a sloppy drunks bar at closing time. Opposite the bed was a cabinet that held about a twenty-eight or so inch cathode tube TV. It was probably fifteen years old or more. Next to the cabinet was a small desk and a chair. Everything was cheap, but that's what this place got you.

The curtains were a beige, hard to tell if that was their natural color or they were just dirty. Similar to the thin carpet on the floor. The window overlooked the parking lot. The room was old and in need of a designer, but everything seemed to be working. The paint was not peeling, the popcorn ceiling wasn't stained with watermarks. It seemed like good value for your money.

"What's your usual customer like?" I asked.

Dorian stood and looked at me as Jackson looked around.

"We don't have a specific type," he said, "but we try and keep the criminal element away. We kick out people that are making a lot of noise or doing drugs. We turn a blind eye to traveling salesmen who bring hookers round so long as there's no problem. We get a lot of homeless folks looking for shelter in the winter. They'll often come in pairs and spend a night or two when it's real cold. We've had single mothers with their kids escaping what I assume are abusive husbands. On more than one occasion we've had to call the cops when the assholes come looking for their wives."

I nodded.

"And you work the day shift?"

"Yeah, you could say I'm the defacto manager for the guy who owns this place. He's had it over thirty years. We have three other guys who do the other shifts."

Dorian looked over at me steadily with keen eyes.

"Look, we try and offer something for the working people here that they can't find anywhere else. Like I said, I try and run a good business and keep that bad element out. We're mostly successful. If I came at you hard today it's because that's how I've gotta be with some of my customers."

I smiled at him and nodded. I patted him on the shoulder. He sure was tall and probably intimidating to a lot of folk.

"I get it," I said. "Just looks like you've got caught up in something you couldn't have known about."

"So you think this 'Jonathan Frakes' guy might have been involved in the murder?"

I shrugged.

"Don't know yet, but this is where it's taking us. But you need to keep this to yourself until someone's been arrested. You understand?"

I looked at him hard and steady. He nodded.

"Yeah, for sure, man."

Dykes came back into the room and joined us.

"Anything of note?" he asked.

I shrugged at him.

"Haven't been looking. Dorian and I have been talking. I wouldn't think so though, this place just got cleaned remember, and unless he left anything behind..."

Dykes nodded and walked around the room. Jackson had gone into the bathroom. I didn't join them, I walked back outside. I'd seen enough dingy motels like this in my life to know what the bathroom looked like. Shower, tub, sink, shitter and mirror. Nothing to it. Cracked tile around the shower maybe, maybe on the floor too. Who knew. What I did know was that this place wasn't gonna help us. 'Frakes' was in the wind, and if we wanted to catch him we needed to be on the lookout for him. But we had nothing on him other than he was seen with the vic's wife.

I pulled out a cigarette and stuck the filter end in my mouth. I walked up to Isabella's cart and found a stack of match booklets. The Nite Owl Motel logo was on the front of them. I helped myself to a pack and used it to light my smoke. I had to turn around and hug the wall of the motel and cup my cigarette for the damn wind.

It was fresh outside. The air was clear, my mind wasn't. I took a long drag and looked around. I was facing the main road, it was getting busy. I'd figure it for after three. I wondered what time 'Frakes' had left. I wandered what his rush had been and why he was here. I figured he was somehow connected to Celia and putting the squeeze on her for something. Why else would she be giving him an envelope of cash the weekend before her husband was murdered. Still didn't like him for the murder though. But you never know. I didn't know enough about him.

Dykes, Jackson and Bronitt came out of the room. Bronitt closed the door behind them. I looked over at them.

"Nothing?" I asked.

"Nothing," repeated Jackson.

"Pretty clean for a cheap motel," said Dykes, almost impressed.

Dorian smiled.

"We try to keep it that way," he said. "Anything else I can help you guys with?"

Dykes shook his head.

"I've got a question," I said. Dorian looked at me.

"Yeah?"

"You said earlier that 'Frakes' left earlier today. What time was that?"

"I can tell you back at the office the exact time," said Dorian, "I've got it on the papers he signed."

"Not necessary," I said, "give me your best estimate."

"Shortly after noon," he said.

I nodded.

"Good, thanks," I said.

I sucked on my cigarette and we watched the tall man walk back towards the office.

"What about checking out those papers for his signature?" suggested Jackson. "Maybe he slipped up and used his real signature."

"Not sure how that'll help us," I said. "We've got his license plate."

"What if the car was stolen?" asked Jackson.

I shook my head slowly.

"Nah, I don't think so. The guy's up to something. At the very least he was blackmailing the vic's wife for some reason. I don't see him holding onto a hot car from Indiana for a couple of weeks. If he was smart he'd have curbed it and picked up a local one."

Jackson nodded.

"Besides, we've got his fingerprints," I added.

"Maybe," said Dykes. "Or maybe he cleaned them off."

"Maybe," I said. "And maybe Chicago's not really the Windy City after all."

Jackson grinned.

"It was just an idea."

"Well," I said, before taking another drag, "we could always grab those papers for fingerprinting if you wanted. But I don't see the signature helping us."

Jackson shrugged and put his notebook back in his pocket. He was a keen detective. He'd probably been jotting notes about how the motel room looked. Dykes looked back over at the car.

"What I'd like to do is get back to headquarters and run the plate and get these bottles printed," he said.

I nodded. He looked back at me.

"You want to come with?"

"I'd sooner head back to the hotel. It's got to be five o'clock somewhere."

Jackson grinned.

"Alright," said Dykes as he walked back towards the car with Jackson and I in tow.

"But come and get me if anything transpires," I said.

Dykes nodded, but he was looking towards the car.

CHAPTER EIGHTEEN

Champs Bullpen

I was eating salted peanuts. I couldn't help myself, and they were making me thirsty. To solve that problem I was drinking a beer. I'd had a whiskey earlier. But then I got into the peanuts. Whiskey was no longer cutting it. Beer was washing the salt away.

I was in the hotel the CPD was graciously putting me up at. More specifically I was at Champs' Bullpen, the only bar inside. It was busier than a urinal at half time. I was squashed up at the bar minding my own business. It was noisy and rowdy with fans of mostly the Chicago Cubs. At least that's what I was making out. It was a little after four thirty when I noticed I'd missed a call on my phone. I looked at the number. It wasn't one I recognized but it was local. The only local people who knew my number were the cops.

I listened to the message. Dykes was telling me to get myself ready, he was coming to pick me up. There had been a major development in the case. I liked the sound of that. He said he'd be at the hotel in about fifteen minutes. I looked at my phone. That was about ten minutes ago. I had half a beer to finish. I drank it quick like it was evidence that needed hiding. I put a Jackson on the bar counter, drawing the bartender's attention. I didn't trust the young schmucks in here not to steal it. He nodded.

I headed out, putting on my trench coat and my hat. I turned up the collar and walked out into the dying day. It was bright enough to see, but the sun was low on the horizon like the watery eye of a rheumy old man. I'd taken the beer too quick. It wanted to come back up but I held it down. A belch helped, and I tasted the peanuts. I took a cigarette out of my pack and walked off to the side to take a smoke. I didn't have long. But a man never needs long for a smoke break.

The parking lot out front of the hotel was busy, but most folks were inside partying or out on the city getting ready for the game tomorrow. I liked the idea of breaking this case tonight. Maybe the Chief or Lane could make a camera appearance and let the public know it'd been solved with the help of a PI from LA. That last part wasn't gonna happen. Still, a guy's gotta dream.

I had been thinking about the case. There was something oddly suspicious about 'Frakes' being here just around the time of the murder and heading out so quickly today. Could be related. Could be coincidence. But I'd seen a guy marry his sister coincidentally. At the very least, 'Frakes' was taking money from a married woman whose husband was now dead. That wasn't cool any way you looked at it. I wanted to talk to Celia. She obviously knew more than she was letting on. As these thoughts trickled through my mind like light rain against a window pane, Dykes and Jackson pulled up. They were happy to see me waiting outside. I was happy to see them. It was getting cold.

I squashed my cigarette underfoot and got into the back seat. I could smell mint and I could see Dykes was chewing on one.

"We gonna crack this thing wide open tonight?" I asked.

"Could be," said Dykes.

He was driving and took off just as I closed the door. He was clearly in a hurry.

"Where we headed?"

Jackson turned around to address me.

"We're heading to Ensor's place. The old lady's been murdered."

"Celia?"

Jackson nodded.

"Shit," I said. "Didn't see that one coming."

"None of us did," said Jackson. "Best we saw, she might have been in on it."

I nodded somberly and looked out the window as Dykes sped along. He was speeding with lights and sirens.

"Where is their place?" I asked.

"North Howe Street in Lincoln Park," said Jackson. "One of the most expensive neighborhoods in Chicago."

"Of course it is," I replied. "How far?"

"'Bout ten minutes," said Dykes, keeping his eyes on the road.

"Tell me what you got?" I asked. "Did you run the license plate? Check the fingerprints?"

Jackson still craned his neck round to see me. I'd scooted over to sit behind Dykes to make it easier on him.

"Yeah, both the license plate and the fingerprints came back to the same guy. The guy we have the picture of, this 'Jonathan Frakes' is actually Forest Gilder."

I nodded. I felt like making a smart ass comment about the forest and trees. But I decided against it. This was no time for levity.

"What do we know about him?"

"Not much. Done some time, petty stuff. Robbery and assault. Most recently there was a domestic charge against him. He's a small-time asshole but hasn't had anything outside of Indiana."

"I wonder why he's here then?"

"Maybe he's a Cubby fan," offered Jackson jokingly.

I grinned at that.

"With that domestic, confirms he's married then."

Jackson nodded.

"What's the wife's name?"

Jackson didn't have to look at his notes.

"She went by Corinne Gilder, family name was Van Buren."

I nodded.

"And I suppose she's waiting at home with the kids while her husband comes out to catch a game."

"Most likely, didn't look into it. But you know how it is. Battered women most often don't leave. So yeah, she's probably home. Not sure about the kids, there was nothing about kids in the domestic report."

"How bad did he beat her? Did you see the photos?"

Jackson shook his head.

"We've asked for that stuff to be faxed over. Probably come in tomorrow. Not really important though."

I shrugged. I didn't see how it was related to the task at hand.

"So this asshole has probably headed back to Indiana. What do we know about this murder?"

"Not much," said Jackson. "It was called in just before four. Girl Scout with her father was selling cookies in the area. The driveway gate was open so they walked up to the front door. Door was open. They rang the bell but got no answer. Father's a doctor who lives in the neighborhood and thought it was odd. So he goes in, calling out to see if anyone's in distress. Just off the main entrance way in the lounge is Celia, messed up. The place is a mess. Daughter saw some of it and she's real shook up, as you can imagine."

I looked out the window. We were heading into tony town. The roads were in great shape. The trees were tall and mature and lined the streets. The houses were large and two and three stories of what looked like sandstone. Didn't take long for Dykes to pull into the driveway of a modern looking sandstone house that was two stories tall. Angular lines with small windows that faced the road. Tall, seven or eight feet black wrought iron fence bordered the property with fleur-de-lys finials. There were a couple of marked cop cars in the expansive driveway, an unmarked vehicle, crime scenes van and the coroner's van.

In front of us was a four car garage. To the right was the house. We all got out and closed the doors. We walked up to the front door and Dykes greeted the uniform as we passed. The interior was cavernous. A main foyer opened up in front of us. A ways in and to the left was a grand staircase heading to the second floor. Opposite this staircase was a large living room. This is where the mess was.

Lane was standing in the room looking down at the body. Celia's body was lying in the middle of what would have been a glass coffee table. Broken glass was all around her. The coffee table's frame was black metal. Looked like she might have hit her head against the far side. Her legs were propped up over the metal frame at our end. We had to walk past a large white sofa to see her. Against the wall was a built-in cabinet with a large TV. A couple of large white recliners were on either side of the sofa, angled inwards towards the coffee table. All the furniture seemed to be leather.

Off to our left as we faced the TV was a large bank of windows that looked out onto a large and still green yard. Tall trees lined the far side of the garden eliminating any view of the neighbor's house. Most of the mess seemed limited to this area of the lounge. There had been two people here. One obviously was Celia. The other, well, we didn't know who that was. But a mug of coffee, half empty, was on a side table between the far recliner and the couch. Celia's head was at that end of the larger coffee table. Bits of broken mug were dotted on the thicker white carpet that was under the coffee table Celia had fallen through. The mug's pieces were dark blue. The same color as the unbroken mug on the smaller side table not far from where her head now was.

The carpet looked shaggy. White was never a good color for furniture or carpeting. It took to stains easily. Just looking at a ketchup bottle would cause a red stain on a white carpet it seemed. There was a brown stain off to our left as we looked down at the body from the feet. This was close to where most of the broken pieces of mug were. I figured it was coffee. I walked around the back side of the sofa again towards the far recliner. The blue coffee mug which was half empty was a pale brown from cream.

I looked around the rest of the room. It was immaculate. Paintings dotted the walls. All original and probably worth several hundred thousands of dollars if not more. They were newer artists, up and coming but I didn't know many of them by name. It wasn't important. What it did tell me was that this was not a robbery or home invasion. I walked towards Dykes and Jackson. They were squatting down by Celia's head. A crime scenes investigator was lifting Celia's head up carefully and showing everyone the large gash on the back of her head and the dark red pool of still wet blood on the white carpet.

Dykes and Jackson got up and looked at a man in a lab coat. I took him for the coroner.

"So you're calling it death by blunt force trauma?" asked Dykes.

The older gentleman with round glasses nodded.

"Yup. Appears she was either thrown or fell into this coffee table and hit her head on that hard edge there."

He pointed at the coffee table's black metal frame.

"I'm going to suggest she was hit hard and the force of that threw her down with enough force to kill her as her head hit the corner. You'll notice the cut on her right cheek, and the slight bruising. That's where she was hit."

I knelt down and looked at the cut on her cheek. It was about an inch and a half long. Someone had hit her with anger and force. I stood up again.

"Can you tell us more about that cut?" I asked the coroner. He looked at me with a raised eyebrow. Dykes nodded and pointed his thumb at me while looking at the coroner.

"He's with us," said Dykes. "Anthony Carrick, this is Dr. Markowitz."

I nodded at the doctor and he nodded back.

"I'd say from the force of that strike that the victim was hit by a man. A left-handed man."

"Why is that?"

"Because I think her zygomatic bone on the malar surface is possibly broken."

"Her cheekbone," I said.

Markowitz nodded.

"Yes, her cheekbone has possibly been broken. I'm not sure many women would be capable of that."

"And the cut?"

"Clearly from some sort of ring, most likely on the middle or ring finger."

"And such a ring would likely have a protruding gem to it, like an engagement ring?" I asked.

"Something like that," said Markowitz, "though I doubt it was an engagement ring on account of the perpetrator most likely being a man."

I nodded and looked at Dykes.

"I think we need to get Gilder found."

Dykes nodded.

"You think he did this?"

"I think it's looking very likely. We know he knew her. There is no sign of a break in nor of burglary. Bronitt mentioned him being a lefty, and that ring of his could have done this. Plus, I'm betting we'll find his prints and DNA on that coffee mug over there."

Dykes looked behind him towards the coffee mug.

"And I think we have the murderer of Ensor too," I said.

Lane grinned at us.

"I've already put word out to be on the lookout for Forest Gilder and his maroon Crown Vic. I spoke to the primary on the scene. Said this is the only area where there's been any disturbance in the house," said Lane.

I nodded and looked around the room.

"Who was that?" I asked.

"Kingston," said Lane, looking over at a uniform who was looking out the window. Kingston turned and hurried towards us.

He looked eight years old.

"Mr. Carrick here might have some questions for you," said Lane.

"Yes sir," Kingston said, nodding at the Captain.

Then he turned to look at me. He was a thin young man about my height. His hair was shaved close to his scalp and he was handsome. His uniform was clean and pressed, from his sky blue shirt, black jacket to his black pants. He was green around the ears though the rest of him was the color of city roasted coffee beans.

"How long you been on the job?" I asked.

"Six months, sir," he said.

"First homicide?"

He nodded.

"You'll get used to it," I offered, trying to be helpful.

"Yes sir," he said with a queazy smile.

"Captain tells me you were first on the scene?"

"Yes sir."

"Tell me what happened," I said.

Dykes, Lane, Jackson and I were standing around facing the young officer. His training had prepared him well. He was articulate and professional.

"I was on patrol when I got the call. I got here within three minutes and entered the house. The front door was open and I declared my presence as a police officer. I came over to the lounge area here, first. I noticed the victim as she is now. I took a pulse but found nothing. I ascertained her to be deceased. I called for backup and for an ambulance just to be certain. Then I cleared the rest of the house and returned here just as backup and the paramedics arrived."

I nodded.

"And nowhere else in the house was there any sign of a struggle or burglary?" I asked.

"That's correct sir, no signs of struggle and it doesn't appear that anything was stolen."

"Any signs of force entry?"

"No sir, as I mentioned, the door was open. No windows have been broken and I noticed no marks by the front door's dead bolt and lock."

I nodded. Lane looked at me. I nodded at him.

"Thank you, Kingston, that's all."

"Yes sir," said the young officer. He disappeared back towards the back of the room.

"You think this Gilder did it?" asked Lane.

Jackson nodded.

"We got his picture from the PI earlier today. We showed it to the guy at the motel and he recognized Gilder as the man in the picture. Said his name was 'Jonathan Frakes'. Left the motel this afternoon around noon."

"We know he knew Celia, as the PI, Skeef, had pictures of the two of them meeting. From the images we saw, she passed him a thick envelope, most likely filled with cash," offered Dykes.

"And do we know their relationship?" asked Lane.

"No sir, not yet. We know Gilder is a small town douchebag out of Indiana, but there's nothing on him from any other state. Not sure why he was up here."

"You need to figure that piece out," said Lane.

"I've got some thoughts on it," I said.

Lane looked up at me, his hands were still on his hips, flaring his suit open.

"I'm all ears," he said.

"I think this Gilder is likely good for both murders."

"How do you figure that?"

"Well, he's been at the motel for almost two weeks, so he's been around since before Ensor's murder. In fact, Skeef tells us that Gilder met with Celia on Friday morning. Last Friday. Skeef followed him to the motel and told his buddy who had hired him, Ensor, about it. Ensor said he was gonna handle it. Skeef said Celia gave Gilder quite a bit of money."

"So he was somehow trying to blackmail her," said Lane. "Doesn't get us to the murder."

"I think it will when we get more info. I think they're a pair of grifters."

Dykes shook his head.

"I dunno about that," he said. "She was married to the deceased for a couple of years, right?"

Jackson nodded.

"That's a long time to wait," he said.

"Maybe," I countered. "Could be she was meeting him monthly to hand him these bills. Could be they were in for the long game, taking their time."

"Okay, then why kill him?" asked Lane.

"Well, here's how I think that went. She starts to get a roving eye, as petty criminals without morals will. She married Ensor right, for the score, not because she loves him. So she finds a side hustle with this Gibb fella. Ensor finds out and he's gonna divorce her, poof there goes their big score. She comes clean with Gilder and he decides to murder the man so that Celia still ends up getting the money. The lawyers tell us that in the event of divorce for cause, she gets next to nothing. So with Ensor dead she now gets it all."

Lane smiled at me.

"I like the line of thought, but then why go kill the golden goose here," said Lane, turning to look at the deceased still on the floor in the middle of the coffee table. I shrugged.

"Could be a bunch of reasons. Most likely one being, there's no honor amongst thieves and grifters. Maybe she tries to put the squeeze on him, because she knows he killed Ensor. So she tries to use that as leverage. He gets pissed off and in a moment of anger, strikes her and things go bad. I don't think he meant to kill her. Just bad luck."

"I like it," offered Jackson. "I mean, it makes a lot of sense to me."

I looked at him and smiled.

"Yeah, I think you'll like it more once we figure out the relationship between the two of them. That's the missing piece. We need to tie these two together," I said.

"Alright," said Lane. "Sounds good to me. I want everyone on the lookout for this Gilder."

"My inkling is he's left Chicago heading back to Indiana," I said.

Lane nodded.

"Agreed," he said. "I've already got the State Police onboard. All major highways out of Illinois are being monitored."

Dr. Markowitz butted into our conversation.

"You mind if we take the body?" he asked, looking at Lane.

"My people finished with it?" he asked the coroner.

Markowitz nodded. Lane nodded back. A couple of his men put the body onto a stretcher that had an open body bag on it. They zipped her into it and rolled her out with Markowitz following. I looked around. There was nothing much left here we needed. Lane's crime scenes people were bagging the bits of glass and broken mug on the carpet. Another one was dusting for prints on the half empty mug on the other side table before bagging it.

"I guess we'll wait and see who picks him up," said Dykes. "Everyone's got his picture right?"

Lane nodded.

"Yeah, his driver's photo has been released. He won't get out of Illinois even if he's taken a different car, which I'm betting against."

"Your people know he's armed and dangerous?" I asked.

Lane nodded.

248

"We're treating him as such."

"Good. He's a desperate man now. Nothing much to lose, I don't think, especially if he doesn't have kids," I said.

I turned around and noticed that Jackson was on his phone. He was nodding at something the other side was telling him.

"We don't know if he has kids, right? I'd guess he doesn't"

I looked at Dykes and he shrugged.

"Jackson's just checking in to see if any of that information has come through."

I nodded. Lane had turned around and was talking to his crime scenes investigators.

"Captain," I said.

Lane turned around to look at me.

"They know to be looking for a Ruger SR9, right?"

"They sure do, we know how to do basic police work here, AC," he said, grinning at me.

I grinned back.

"This guy's killed two people. It'll be nothing for him to take out a couple of cops," I said. "I'd sooner not see that happen."

"As would I."

Jackson rejoined us. He had hung up his phone and he was looking eager.

"I just got off the phone with Indiana State Police. They've sent us next of kin info including photo. Gilder has no kids. I asked him to describe the wife. Said she was thirty, five feet eight with blonde hair. Doesn't give us much, but he said the wife left a couple of years ago. Gilder put in a missing persons but they never found her."

"Maybe we just did," I said.

"You mean to say, Celia Ensor is actually Corinne Gilder?" asked

Dykes, shaking his head.

"Why not," I said. "It would explain everything."

"I don't see how," said Dykes. "Why didn't she just divorce the asshole and make a fresh start with Ensor."

"Probably because she was trying to get a fresh start. Didn't want him to be able to contact her. Divorce is one of those things that piss people off and give them access to each other," I said.

Dykes shrugged. Jackson nodded slowly, thinking about what I'd said.

"We should head on back to headquarters and see if we have anything they've sent over," said Jackson.

"I think that's a good idea," said Lane. "I'd like to be able to find this guy tonight and put the city's mind at rest before the game starts tomorrow."

Dykes nodded. He started to leave and Jackson and I followed him. I felt optimistic. Primarily because this murder of Celia was spur of the moment. That meant that Gilder wasn't thinking straight. He was on the run and stressed out. That would give us a greater chance of catching him.

The more I thought about Gilder and Celia the more I thought she was perhaps an innocent pawn squeezed by an abusive husband. This was now my working theory, rather than the two of them being a pair of grifters working together.

CHAPTER NINETEEN

Long Lonely Highways

WE'D gotten back to headquarters by six after stopping to pick up some Chinese pork, fried rice and noodles. That's what Jackson had wanted and Dykes and I were on board. We'd taken it back to the office and ate it at their desks. Jackson had received an email from the Indiana State police who had forwarded the Muncie police report on the Gilder domestic. It showed Corinne Gilder's bashed up face. Not the worst domestic I'd seen but he'd still managed to split her lip and give her a black eye. More importantly, it was obviously a photograph of the woman we knew as Celia Ensor.

This was confirmed by the driver's license database picture that Jackson pulled up. That has a more flattering photograph of Corinne Gilder, which was not saying much. Our victim, Celia Ensor, was the one and same Corinne Gilder still married to the suspect Forest Gilder who we were pursuing.

"You're right, AC," said Jackson, grinning to me over a box of Chinese food.

"About what?" I asked him, stuffing salty noodles into my mouth with chopsticks.

"About Gilder," he said. "Celia, or Corinne, is his old lady. Makes this whole thing fucked up."

I shook my head and swallowed the food before speaking.

"No, not really," I said. "Makes it clear as mud."

Jackson nodded.

"At first I figured them for a couple of grifters, but now knowing the two of them are married, I see her as another victim."

"But how did you suspect the relationship between the two?" asked Jackson.

"Human nature," I said. "Next to evidence, that's the most damning aspect in most crimes I've discovered."

"I don't get it."

"Ever since we met Celia yesterday, I figured she was involved somehow."

"Hindsight is an easy twenty-twenty," said Jackson, grinning at me.

I looked at him and smiled back.

"True, but let me tell you what I mean. I've been around a lot of different folks in my time. I can tell the difference between old money and new money. And I can tell the difference between crisp Benjamins and tarnished nickels."

"Man," said Jackson, smiling wide, "you talk in riddles."

"James Ensor is new money. Crisp Benjamins. Celia Ensor is a tarnished nickel looking for new money. She's blue collar, maybe even trailer trash. No disrespect, just never had the opportunities to do any better. But she tried. Her way of getting out of the bleached ghetto was to find new money. And she did with James, right? But at the same time she hadn't found out how to move within those circles yet. She's like Cinderella at five minutes to midnight. You know she's not a real princess yet even though she looks like one."

Jackson put more food in his mouth. Dykes had finished what he'd wanted to eat and he was sucking on a Lifesaver.

"I can see that," he said. "But that's a reach to use that to put the two of them together."

"I don't think so. It's just using deductive reasoning, my dear Watson," I said to Dykes.

I'd had enough Chinese food. I pushed my takeout box towards the edge of the desk and took a long drink from a can of coke. I would've preferred a beer, but Red and Gold were still on the job. It'd have to wait until I got to the hotel. Dykes shrugged at my argument, playing with the Lifesaver in his mouth.

"We knew she was involved somehow. Most times in cases like this it's got something to do with people close to the victim. We just needed motive and evidence. We found the motive. She makes bank with Ensor dead especially in light of him divorcing her and leaving her with next to nothing. Relatively speaking that is."

Dykes didn't say anything, he continued to look at me.

"We followed the trail and found Gilder. Now we have the relationship between the two. Before that he seemed like a stray thread on his wife beater. Now we know better. You've just gotta be open to possibilities."

Jackson stuffed another mouthful of food into his maw. He pushed his box away and sipped on some Sprite.

"I liked Gibb for it originally," he said. "You know the guy had a temper, he was banging Ensor's wife. Looked like that could have turned out to be a neat and tidy little package."

I nodded.

"I would have rested easy with that too. If that's the way it would have gone. Or even Stark, the pitcher that's gonna get all the glory now."

Dykes looked at the two of us as if we were playing a tennis match.

"I'd have put money on Gibb and Celia being in it together. I figured her for a gold digger. Turns out she was, but not the murdering kind."

"Yup," I said. "Just an attractive woman caught up between a rock and a hard place."

On the desks that Dykes and Jackson shared stood a police radio that Jackson had borrowed from the local state police. We'd been listening to it in the background as we ate our dinner. Not much was going on. Mostly routine traffic stops. But the state troopers had been notified of Gilder and we were hoping to catch some action about that. It had been a long wait. It was coming on eight pm before we got any news.

"Dispatch, this is Unit 22," said the male voice over the radio.

"Dispatch here, go ahead Unit 22," said the female voice.

"Can you give me more information on that 0110 out of Chicago, suspect's name Gilder, Forest."

Dykes, Jackson and I turned towards the radio and craned our necks. Jackson turned up the volume.

"Suspect last seen driving a ninety-two maroon Crown Victoria with Indiana license plate zero four two hotel golf golf. Suspect is considered armed and dangerous and might be fleeing a murder."

"Copy that dispatch. I am in pursuit of said vehicle. A maroon Crown Victoria with Indiana plates zero four two hotel golf golf. Unit 22 requesting backup."

"Any units in district ten available to backup Unit 22?" said the female dispatch voice.

"Unit 33 two minutes out," said another male voice.

"Unit 17 on my way."

"Unit 25 two minutes out."

"Where are they?" I asked.

Jackson looked up at me and put his index finger to his lips.

"They'll say any minute now," he said.

"Unit 22, I'm traveling Eastbound on I74 about five miles out from Danville."

"Unit 33, copy that Unit 22. I see you on my GPS."

"Unit 22, driver is the single occupant in the vehicle. Obeying speed limits. I'm going to attempt to pull him over before we get too close to Danville and populated areas."

I figured that Gilder probably wasn't aware of his tail. It was dark and maybe the state trooper had only pulled onto I74 recently.

"Unit 33, I'm right behind you Unit 22."

"Unit 22, copy that Unit 33."

"Unit 25, not if I get there first Unit 33."

"Dispatch to units involved in the traffic stop on I74. Caution is advised. Suspect considered armed and dangerous."

"Unit 22, copy that. Lights on. Suspect is slowing and pulling over."

Silence was on the air for a few moments.

"Unit 25, at scene."

"Dispatch, copy that Unit 25."

"Unit 33, at scene."

"Dispatch, copy that Unit 33."

"Unit 22, suspect has pulled over and stopped. Will attempt extraction."

There was more silence on the air. I wasn't expecting to hear the next few minutes until Gilder was in custody. Then the state trooper's would likely come back on air.

"Unit 17, arriving on scene."

"Dispatch, copy that Unit 17."

"Unit 17, we're approaching the vehicle."

More silence. This was the nerve wracking part. I was hoping for a peaceful arrest. But you never knew with a guy like Gilder with two recent murders under his belt. Worst case he was going to end up dead and we'd never know why he did it or what he was trying to accomplish. Best case, he'd be in our custody with a couple or three hours.

The three of us stared at the scanner as if we were watching TV and could actually see what was going on. Time marched on like a line of soldier ants along a sticky path of spilled cola. It was achingly slow. I was desperately hoping for a quiet unobtrusive arrest. But you never knew in cases like this. A fleeing fugitive with a loaded gun was a fifty-fifty event. I'd never make a bet like this in Vegas. Depended on whether Gilder fancied living or if he was at the end of his rope. I was hoping a narcissistic asshole like him would choose the living fork.

"Are we feeling confident on a living Gilder at the end of this?" I asked, looking from Jackson to Dykes.

Dykes unrolled more paper from his tube of mints. He offered them around. I took one. It was something to do. Jackson declined and sipped on more Sprite. Dykes shrugged.

"I'm hopeful," he said, popping a mint into his mouth. "Or maybe I'm just hoping we'll get some one on one time with him to figure out why he did this."

"I think we already know why," I said.

"Sure, it's a viable motive, I'd like to get confirmation though."

Jackson nodded. He had taken his eyes off of the scanner and was looking at us.

"Gun to head," he said, grinning, "if I had to make a call, I'd say this asshole is gonna want to live."

"Gun to head, hey?" I said, grinning back at him. "That might be happening right now to our perp.

Jackson nodded.

"We can hope," he said.

I was trying hard not to start chewing on my mint. I kept rolling it on my tongue, eager to ride it out. But the waiting was driving me nuts. I could use a cigarette, a whiskey and a slap on the face from a beautiful woman. What I had was a mint and silence and dread. We all waited. Jackson sipped Sprite. He fiddled with the volume dial. The seconds dragged on into minutes which seemed stuck in a month of murders.

"Unit 22, Gilder is in custody. We have located the Ruger SR9."

Jackson pumped his fist.

"Yeah!" he shouted.

Dykes and I grinned, letting out air like an old boxer sucker punched in the gut.

"Dispatch, copy that."

"Unit 22, I'm driving him back to Chicago. Lane on the air?"

"Lane here, Unit 22," said Lane's baritone.

"Where do you want the package dropped off, Captain?"

"Bring him downtown to headquarters. Detectives Dykes and Jackson will take him from you."

"Unit 22, copy that Captain."

The rest of the chatter coming from the scanner now seemed unimportant and irrelevant. Units 33 and 17 had signed off and headed back out on patrol. Unit 25 was following 22 back up to Chicago with our package.

"Well, we've got about two and a half hours to kill before Gilder gets here," said Dykes. "Time to review the file."

Jackson nodded. He opened up his notebook and Dykes got onto the computer and opened up the hardcopy file.

"I'll be with you guys in a minute. Need to grab some fresh air."

They nodded and I left, making sure to take my visitor pass with me.

Outside it was a dark night, and for the first time since getting here, the wind was as still as a whisper. Trees dotted the front of headquarters and lights from cement planters and pylons lit the sidewalk with a smokey yellow. I was glad to be closing this up. I'd be making fifteen hundred bucks for three days work. That was enough.

This was a case that hadn't gone how I'd expected. From a bag of lucky surprise suspects that turned up empty to a battered woman looking for a white knight, what we got was that root of human evil, jealousy and his bastard son anger, and the two of them had committed a couple of murders. I sucked on my cigarette and blew rings out into the night air. It was hard not to be cynical about this. It was hard not be cynical about any murder. The fickle finger of humanity's stunted maturity stirring the boiling cauldron of our dark sides.

I watched folks pass me by oblivious to this dark underbelly until they got caught in its mouth. Men in business suits heading home. Young kids out partying before the World Series started. And a lone gumshoe trying to clean the shit from the sole of his shoes. And I couldn't help but keep stepping in it.

CHAPTER TWENTY

The Daily Grind

IN the police locker rooms of the basement at headquarters where they kept the gym was a dark room. It had 4 beds in it with plastic sheeting and woolen blankets that you wouldn't let your dog sleep on. It was something though. Better than nothing. Meant for officers who had come off shift and needed a few hours shut-eye before having to appear in court. It served its purpose.

Jackson had told me about it. It was either try to take a couple of hours shut-eye or find a local watering hole. And I was still technically on the job. So I went for shut-eye. Jackson had taken me down to show me the room. It was just a room with four walls and a door and these four single beds with firm mattresses, the kind you might find in an insane asylum. Each bed was tucked up into one of the corners of the room. I chose the one furthest from the door as you entered on your left. I also put the pillow up against the far wall.

I shut the door and had to feel my way back to the bed. It was pitch black. A black that I hadn't experienced in a long time. The kind of black that even with your eyes adjusted they couldn't drink in any light. The only light was sixteen red numbers and eight blinking dots from the four clock radios on a small side table by each bed. I set the alarm for ten thirty. Nobody else was in here with me. I'd find it hard to sleep if there was.

LAPD headquarters had a similar set up that I'd used on occasion. After I'd set up the alarm which I'd done with the door open, I fiddled with the dial to find a jazz station. The one that I came to first was WDCB somewhere around ninety on the FM dial. It was the closest to jazz I found. The DJ was Nick Spitzer and the show I was listening to was American Routes. Some jazz, blues and the like.

I took off my shoes, closed the door and fumbled back to the radio and bed I'd chosen. I turned the volume real low and looked at the time. It was eight thirty-seven. The last thing I heard was Count Basie's "I Ain't Mad At You." That seemed apropos.

Ten thirty woke me from a bad dream like an angry fishmonger yelling down at the docks. The yelling beep of the alarm clock hit me like a sledge hammer to the back of the throat. It took a few blaring beeps to wake me up. I'd incorporated it into my dream. Last thing I remembered was grabbing Gilder by the throat and hitting him in the face over and over. He was grinning like a bloody Joker and each time I hit him he made this weird sound, which I realized was the alarm beeping until I woke up.

I pushed a bunch of buttons until the damn thing shut off. I sat on the edge of the bed and put my feet awkwardly onto my shoes. It hurt, so I placed them back on the thin, firm carpet. Took me a moment to figure out I was awake. I felt like a drunk man brought back to life from an alcoholic blackout. I felt like shit. I hadn't been drinking but still I felt worse than when I'd laid down.

I tried to remember where the door was. I walked towards where I thought it was with my hands held out like a zombie. As I got closer to it I could vaguely see it from the dim bloody red glow of the radios closest to it. I fumbled for the door knob and opened it. The light jumped into the room like a sucker punch to the face. I walked back to the bed, sat back down and put my shoes on. I walked out and found the sinks. I splashed cold water on myself and started to feel like a human being.

There was a phone on the side of the wall close to the exit. I picked it up and dialed Jackson. He'd given me his cell number. He picked up quickly. I asked if our package had arrived. He said no. Said Trooper Harvey Rampton had an ETA of about eleven on the nose. I thanked him and hung up. I had time for a smoke and a coffee. I walked out of the locker rooms and up to the main floor and headed outside, my visitor pass around my neck like a schmuck. I took it off and put it in my pocket. I took out a cigarette and lit it. There was a woman outside to my left having a smoke. I moved over to my right. I was still in no mood for chit chat.

She looked over at me. I could see her from the corner of my eye. She gave me the up and down and then tossed her head back like I was some sort of bum. I was trying not to encourage conversation. I didn't know her and I didn't want to. Across the road was a local coffee shop. It was called 'The Daily Grind'. That was my kinda coffee shop. I walked towards it. I looked both ways for traffic and sauntered across the road like a pimp looking for his girl.

It was dimly lit inside. I liked that too. There were just a handful of people inside. I looked at the business hours by the front door. They were only open till ten on Thursday night. But now it was coming on quarter to eleven and they were still open. I took a couple of big, quick drags on my smoke then tossed it on the ground and stepped on its neck until its lights went out. I exhaled the ghosts of cigarettes past and walked into The Daily Grind. Two things smell the best to me. Cigarettes and coffee beans. I'd put whiskey in there too, but whiskey is nuanced. It punches you in the gut but tickles your nose. You have to get up close to it like a flower.

A bald guy behind the counter greeted to me. He looked like Mr. Clean. He was big and muscled in a black tee. He had an earring in each ear. He would've looked more at home in a gym than a coffee shop. But he was friendly.

"Three coffees... large," I said.

He looked me up and down.

"You look like a heavy weight," he said, grinning.

I looked him up and down with a furrowed brow. I'd never punched heavyweight. Middleweight was my style.

"What kind of roast do you want? We have heavyweight or lightweight. Dark or light."

I got it.

"Heavyweight it is. By the way, I need a tray and a carafe of cream."

He nodded.

"Seven buckaroos," he said. He was a chipper lad for a slow Thursday night.

I handed him Hamilton.

He wanted to hand me back three Washingtons, I declined. He was happy with that. He turned around to pour three coffees. He placed them in sleeves and topped them with lids and those stupid green stoppers like I'm a geriatric who can't hold a coffee cup without bouncing it around like juggling balls. He poured cream into a small cup and capped it with a lid and a green stopper. He slid them over to me.

"So you working late on a case?" he asked.

He seemed like a good kid, so I threw him a bone.

"Yeah," I said, "that Ensor murder."

He shook his head.

"That sucks man, I was sure hoping for a Cubs win, now I'm not so sure."

"Me neither."

"Still, a guy can dream, right?"

Dreams are like bubbles, I thought, just looking for a prick to pop them. Instead I said something like, "Sure thing."

"So do you know who did it?"

I nodded.

"Can't say yet. It'll be on the morning news though. Stay tuned. What's the time?"

He looked at his register.

"Ten to."

"What time you close?"

"Midnight while the World Series is on."

I nodded and picked up the tray of coffees. I raised it at him. He nodded at me and I walked out the coffee shop. The woman across the road at headquarters had disappeared. I had to get my game face on. I was in a mood to bust this nut wide open. I wanted answers, and I had a feeling I was gonna get them.

CHAPTER TWENTY-ONE
The Answer To Everything

DYKES and Jackson were grateful for the coffee. Between the three of us we used up all the cream, but not all the packets of sugar I'd smuggled out of The Daily Grind. Jackson and Dykes liked their coffee. I liked any dark, hot liquid that posed as coffee at eleven at night on the ass end of a homicide investigation.

"Rampton should be here any minute," said Jackson.

"We're gonna take him to room oh forty-two," said Dykes.

I smiled broadly. I took a long sip of my coffee, as long as it could be without burning my tongue.

"That's terrific, we'll get the answers to everything."

I grinned at them. They both looked at me quizzically.

"Well, hopefully we'll get the answers we need to wrap up this case," said Dykes.

"You don't get it, do you?" I asked.

"Get what?" asked Dykes, trying his coffee.

"The answers to everything in room oh forty-two."

He shrugged his shoulders and cocked his head to one side pinching his lips together as if to say whatever.

"Never mind, obviously haven't read *The Hitchhiker's Guide to the*

Galaxy."

"Heard of it," said Jackson.

The moment had passed.

"Well, should we make our way there?" I asked.

Dykes nodded, and Jackson and I followed him out of the homicide detectives' bullpen and towards processing and interrogation. We were able to stay indoors the whole way.

Interrogation room zero forty-two was on the main level. We waited out in the lobby for Rampton. We didn't have to wait long. It was not busy yet, but I bet it would be in a couple of hours. First of all it was a Thursday. Most folks would be working tomorrow. Secondly it was only around eleven. That meant folks hadn't had a chance to tie one on long enough yet to cause a ruckus. It also meant the domestics were only starting to simmer in the pot on top of the stove of dissatisfaction.

I sipped my coffee. I'd managed about a quarter of it when Rampton came in. He was leading skinny Jesus whom we'd now come to know as Gilder. His hair looked greasy and he was unshaven. His complexion was sallow and the bags under his eyes were gray and dull. He looked better in the picture. As he came by I put him at around five ten, my height, but maybe twenty pounds lighter. He'd probably be punching at the welterweight division.

He didn't look at us as he passed. His head was slightly lowered. He had on a black tee and black leather jacket with tassels. His pants were black denim and he wore half-high black cowboy boots. He might have passed for goth if he was twenty years younger. His hands were behind his back in silver bracelets courtesy of the Illinois state.

Rampton wore his uniform with pride. It was clean, crisp and ironed. His olive pants were ironed to a razor crease down the front and his khaki shirt under the chocolate jacket looked pressed. He was Master Trooper Rampton. I could tell by the single rocker below a single chevron and the MT insignia on his right lapel. He wore an odd looking hat I knew as a lemon squeezer. It was chocolate brown and had the Montana crease in it. He was tall. A little taller than Dykes as he walked by. He grinned at us and nodded. He probably had thirty or more pounds on Dykes. Mostly muscle. His left hand was holding the bracelets between Gilder's hands. His right hand held a clear plastic baggy with a Ruger SR9 and a smaller plastic baggy with a wedding ring on it. The ring had a smidge of blood on it. Dollars to donuts this had Celia's DNA on it.

Dykes and Jackson and I walked up to the processing desk with him. I stood off to the side for a bit as I watched the handoff from Rampton to Dykes and Jackson. Paperwork was filled out and idle chit chat spouted forth from mouths. I stood and watched and drank my coffee. I was halfway done by the time Gilder was all ours.

Dykes and Jackson walked on each side of Gilder through a magnetically locked door operated by their swipe card. I figured mine wouldn't work down here, so I followed them down a hallway to a small room on the right-hand side. Dykes was holding the baggy with the handgun in it. The magazine was out and the barrel was slid open with a loose bullet in the bag. The plaque on the outside of it read zero forty-two. We walked in and the door closed behind us, locking us in.

Jackson brought the video recorder he'd taken from homicide and put it on a tripod that was leaning up against the corner of the room. To our right was a one way mirror. Nobody was looking in. Well, maybe Lane would be if he got here sometime soon. I figured that was a likely scenario. To our left was a small metal table bolted to the floor. One stool sat on the opposite side of this table also bolted in. On our side were two stools bolted down. I figured I'd be standing. It'd keep me awake.

Dykes took Gilder over to the opposite side with the one stool and sat him down. He unlocked the handcuff on his left hand and slid it under a bar welded to the table. Then he recuffed him. Gilder wasn't going anywhere. He looked up at us with the eyes of a lost, defeated man. They were sad and watery and vacant.

"Do any of yous have a smoke?" he asked.

"There's no smoking in here," said Dykes, returning and sitting down behind him. "Before we start I'm going to read you your rights."

He looked over at Jackson who nodded and started recording. Then he read Gilder his rights. Gilder had probably been read his rights by the trooper, but it didn't hurt to have it on camera. Gilder declined a lawyer. At least for now. Jackson sat down next to Dykes. I leaned up against the far wall opposite the door we'd come in. I crossed my hands in front of me, holding my half empty coffee in one hand. I looked at Gilder. The video recorder was between me and Jackson. Jackson sat closest to me, Dykes closest to the door.

"You know why you're here," said Dykes.

Gilder didn't say anything. He looked down at his hands. I noticed the lighter band of skin where his wedding band used to be. We had that ring now with the vic's blood and DNA all over it. Plus we had the murder weapon. At least ballistics would tell us that within an hour. These guys were working twenty=four seven to wrap this up.

"Now if we get a full confession from you," continued Dykes, "I might be willing to put in a good word with the DA. Tell her how cooperative you were. But we need a full confession, that's why we're taping this. Do you understand?"

Gilder shrugged. He was still looking down. His black, wavy, greasy hair hanging in front of his face like a macabre curtain.

"Don't matter to me. I'm getting life anyways."

"Could be worse," said Dykes. "Where that guy's from you could be looking at the death penalty."

Dykes nodded towards me and Gilder looked up at me. I smiled at him and drew my finger across my throat. He looked away.

"Even so," said Dykes. "We might get leniency. There might be extenuating circumstances. Hell, you might be out before I get retirement."

Gilder looked up at Dykes like a petulant child.

"You fucking cops," he said. "You think you're better 'an us but you ain't. I've seen more crooked cops than my grandma's crooked fingers."

"That may be so," said Dykes, "but you don't look like a man who's been targeted unfairly. Now, if you want me to call IAD I can do that. But then I reckon I should give you something to complain about."

Dykes looked over at Jackson.

"Might want to turn that off for the next part," he said.

Jackson got up to walk over to the video recorder.

"Alright, alright, fuck, let's just be civilized," said Gilder.

Jackson sat back down. Dykes reached into the outer pocket of his jacket and pulled out a roll of Lifesavers. There weren't many left. He unrolled the outer wrapper and put one in his mouth. He offered Jackson one and Jackson took it. He offered me one. I waved my coffee at him. Then he offered one to Gilder. Gilder reached out his hand as best he could. Dykes put one in there.

Gilder put his face down to his hand and took the mint into his mouth.

"Good," said Dykes. "Now that we're all friends, let's have a friendly chat."

Dykes tapped on the handgun through the plastic. The Ruger was close to him on the table. Gilder looked at the gun.

"I'm gonna tell you a story," said Dykes, "and then you can help me fill in the missing pieces."

Gilder looked at him but didn't say anything.

"This Ruger SR9 we've been looking for since earlier this week. It's the weapon that was used to kill James Ensor. Any time now an officer's gonna come in and take this piece of evidence to ballistics and by the time the witching hour comes round we'll have the evidence we need to confirm that."

Dykes slid the gun towards Jackson slightly to show the smaller plastic baggy with his wedding ring in it. Dykes picked it up and waved it in the air like it was something he was trying to dry off.

"And this here," he said, looking at the transparent bag between him and Gilder, "is where the gold is. Not literally of course, I mean it is a gold ring, but this is where we've got your ex-wife's DNA. Bam, two pieces of evidence to tie two murders together in a nice little package with a bow for the district attorney."

Dykes put the baggie down on top of the bag with the gun in it. There was a knock on the door. Dykes got up and answered it. He and another uniform officer exchanged some words. Dykes returned while the officer waited at the door, keeping it ajar with his foot. Dykes picked up the two baggies and then handed them to the officer. The officer disappeared and the door closed behind him.

Dykes came and sat back down. He pulled out his police

notebook and jotted something down. Most likely chain of custody transfer. He closed it up and put it back in his inside jacket pocket. Then he looked back at Gilder.

"Where were we?" he asked. "Ah, I remember. The reason the three of us is here at this drama, this... tragedy, is to understand the plot."

Gilder didn't say anything, his head hung down and every so often he lifted it which seemed like a huge effort and looked at Dykes. Dykes gave him time. He let silence creep into the room like invisible carbon monoxide. But Gilder was happy with it. I got the sense he almost embraced the silence like a petulant child.

"So," said Dykes. It was a question. Gilder looked up at him.

"So what?"

"So why'd you kill Ensor? Why did you kill your ex?"

Gilder looked down. Then he yanked at the bar with his handcuffs, and looked back at Dykes.

"She wasn't my fucking ex. That stupid cunt was my wife, and she thought she could leave me. Nobody leaves me," he shouted.

I looked at him and grinned. It wasn't nice, but sometimes I'm just along to poke the bears and smack the beehives. Clearly here was a guy with abandonment issues.

"I still don't get it. Help me like I'm stupid," said Dykes. "You and Celia..."

"Corinne, her fucking name's Corinne."

Dykes nodded and smiled at him.

"Corinne. Tell me why you killed her when you and her were on a sweet ride bilking the baseball player?"

Gilder looked down and shook his head.

"Man, if I'd meant to have killed her I woulda used the gun, okay? Fuck, it wasn't supposed to happen like that. The whole

271

thing went to shit and she started trying to get out of the deal. We had a deal. We had a fucking deal, me and her. She shoulda just fucking listened to me."

Gilder trailed off, shaking his head slowly.

"Let me try swing for the fences," I said. "See if I can knock this out of the park."

Gilder and Dykes turned to look at me.

"Your old lady leaves you because you're an asshole. You beat your wife. I can understand why'd she'd have enough of a prick like you."

Gilder looked at me and squinted.

"It wasn't like that. She asked for it. The bitch was an arrogant, entitled cunt who thought she was better 'an me. Thought she was better 'an all of us."

"You eat food and kiss babies with that mouth?" I asked rhetorically. "I can see how charming you must be for the ladies."

Gilder ignored me.

"But still, let me see if I can get this straight. Corinne leaves you to try and find a decent life."

"We had a decent life," he interjected halfheartedly.

"But you catch up with her and you put the squeeze on her. I'm thinking you probably threatened to kill her if she didn't go along with you, am I right?"

"Fuck you. You don't know shit about me. You're just a dumb fucking cocksucker. I've known your type."

"That so," I said. "And what type is that?"

"The type who's mother's I fuck and leave crying on the wet sheets."

He shouldn't have said that. I love my mother. More than that she's still alive. And there isn't a human being alive who can get away with talking trash about her. I turned to my left and casually turned off the recorder. Then I walked up to him to real quiet and jabbed him in the nose with my left. His head flicked back reactively and I was just waiting for it to come on back. As it did I smacked him across his left cheek with a hard right. Hurt my hand but I wasn't complaining. I grabbed him with my right hand by the back of the head and crashed his head into the goddamn metal table. I broke his nose. I'm not gonna lie, I wanted to break more than his nose. I might have knocked him out. I wasn't sure.

Before I could think of other things Jackson had grabbed my left arm from behind. Dykes was coming round too.

"Take it easy, AC," said Jackson, "take it easy."

I shrugged my shoulders and took a deep breath. Dykes was in front of me and in front of Gilder. He looked me in the eyes.

"You need to take a time out?"

I shook my head.

"No, I'm good now. Just a family thing."

Dykes put his hand on my right shoulder.

"You sure?"

I nodded.

"'Cos I can't let you do that again," he said.

I nodded again and walked back to the wall were I leaned against it to give it strength. What I got was a sore shoulder. Dykes stayed where he was for a moment looking at me.

"I'm good," I said. "He probably isn't."

Dykes turned around and looked at him. Gilder was slowly lifting up his head. He was dazed. Blood dripped from his nose steadily creating a little maroon pool on the matte aluminum table like a spilt Bordeaux. Jackson walked out of the room. Dykes helped Gilder sit up and put his nose back. He took out a handkerchief he had and wiped up some of the blood from Gilder's nose. It was awful kind of him. I wouldn't have gone anywhere near that asshole. Never know what kind of disease he's carrying.

Jackson came back with a lot of paper towel. A clump of it was wet. He also carried a box of tissues under his arm. He dropped the tissues on the table. He took some of the wet paper towel and mopped up the spilt blood on the table. He used some dry paper towel to clean it further. He gave the rest of the wet towel to Dykes. Dykes used it wipe up the blood on Gilder's nose and around his mouth. He placed it back into the clump that Jackson held out with his one hand. Jackson left with the paper towel. Gilder was moaning and crying and shaking his head slowly.

"What the fuck, man, what the fuck," he kept saying.

"Listen to me," said Dykes. "Listen to me, goddamnit."

Dykes waited for a moment until Gilder settled down. Gilder looked at him out of the corner of his eye with his head tilted back, his hands held in prayer by the table.

"I'm gonna uncuff you. But don't be stupid. Alright?"

Dykes looked at Gilder sternly. Gilder nodded. He didn't look at me. Dykes uncuffed him. He passed the box of tissues towards him. Gilder steadied his head. He inhaled thickly through his nose. You could hear the clotting blood dislodge into the back of his throat. He swallowed. He wasn't happy about it.

"Don't blow your nose," said Dykes. "Just dab at it."

Jackson came back in with a plastic cup of water. He pushed it over by Gilder. Gilder took a sip. Jackson also had some damp paper towel with what looked like ice in it. He handed it Gilder. Dykes and Jackson looked at me. I could tell what they were thinking. I might have messed up this whole case. But I didn't think

I did. We had enough evidence without a confession. But I had a feeling that those couple of blows might've loosened Gilder's tongue.

"Maybe a smoke will make him feel better," I said, looking at Dykes and Jackson. Dykes nodded slowly after a while.

I pulled my pack of cigarettes from the front pocket of my shirt. I tapped one out and leaned in to offer it to Gilder. He shook his head.

"Don't be like that," I said, pushing the pack closer towards him. "You don't talk about my mother and we're gonna get along just swell."

He looked at me with hurt in his eyes. I didn't feel it. He would've gotten worse if we'd just been on the street or in a bar. Slowly he took a cigarette. I took one with my mouth out of the pack and put it away. I reached into my right pocket and took out a booklet of matches I'd taken from the Nite Owl. I tore off a match and struck it on the backside. I lit Gilder's cigarette and then I lit another.

With his one hand, Gilder smoked his cigarette. With the other he kept dabbing at his nose.

"I think you busted my nose, asshole," he said to me. I let him have that one.

"I did," I said. "And I figure the best way to get it fixed is to talk to us about what happened. Talk to us in a decent manner. Use your polite words."

I paused and looked at him. I looked at him hard through eyes like marble. He looked away.

"Or I swear to God I will tear out that tongue you don't know how to use."

I stared at him. He wouldn't look at me.

"Nod if you understand me."

He gave a couple of quick tentative nods. He put the smoke in his mouth and took a long drag. He put the tissue on the table in front of him and picked up the paper towel with the ice in it. He held his head back a bit and placed the iced paper towel over the bridge of his nose. That was smart thinking.

There was a knock at the door and Lane came in. He was clearly upset. He peeked in and curled his finger towards him, aiming at Dykes. Dykes walked round Gilder and out the room. I couldn't hear what they were saying. But I figured I was about to get booted out of the room. A few minutes later Dykes came back in followed by Lane. Lane looked at me, and he was smiling his big easy smile.

"You and I can watch from the other room," he said. It wasn't a suggestion. I nodded. I put my cigarette out on the metal table and walked out. I followed Lane out the one door and in through the other. We were in a darker room. It was more of a rectangular closet. There was nothing in it. Lane was looking out the one way mirror into room zero forty-two. His arms were folded over his chest. He was still immaculately dressed. He didn't look at me.

"I'd be sending you home if we weren't just about done," he said.

I didn't say anything to that. It wasn't a question.

"We don't do police work like that around here. What the hell is wrong with you?"

I wanted to say I wasn't loved enough by my mother. That I had anger problems.

"Just having a bad day," I said, not looking at him either.

Lane glanced over at me and nodded.

"Yeah, you could say that again. Two fights in one day, three in a matter of two days. You'd be fired from my department if you were a cop here. John said you were a little spicy, but come on. This is ridiculous. I can see how you didn't last long in the LAPD."

"Lasted long enough," I said.

"Do you think fighting is the answer to every question?"

"Sometimes," I said.

He shook his head. I could see that out of the corner of my eye. I didn't feel sorry but I figured maybe he was looking for an apology. I swallowed my pride. It was a big wad of gum stuffed full of broken glass.

"Look," I said. "I'm sorry. Won't happen again. I lost control."

Lane looked over at me again before looking out the mirror. He didn't say anything for a while.

"Alright," he said. "But I'm gonna be hard pressed to recommend you."

"I'm not usually like this," I countered.

"You might have just given this murderer a get out of jail free card. You realize that?"

I didn't say anything.

"We've got good evidence. We've got the murder weapon," I said, trying to be helpful. Lane shook his head.

"My guys will have to testify to this shit and it's not gonna help."

"I know," I said.

Lane didn't say anything. He pushed the intercom button on the side of the mirror. We started listening in.

CHAPTER TWENTY-TWO

The Con In Confession

"AND how did you find her?" asked Dykes.

"I've been looking for her these past couple of years. Never found her all this time. But then she goes and marries this rich, successful guy. Saw her in one of them tabloids. Picture of him and 'er. Couldn't believe my luck. Said her name was Celia Ensor. The rest was easy."

"How did you first make contact with her?"

"I came up here and followed her around for a bit. Then one day I followed her into a carpark after she'd been shopping. I sneaked up behind her and grabbed her round the mouth. I had my gun with me. I told her not to make a noise on account I might shoot her."

Dykes nodded. Jackson was taking notes. The video recorder was shooting digital bits, and I was watching the outcome of my good deeds. Gilder sucked on his cigarette. Every so often he'd put the ice-filled paper towel tenderly against his nose. It was swollen.

"So I got into her car. Told her I knew where she lived, who she was married to and that she owed me for leaving me. You gotta understand. At this point I ain't mad at her. I'm pissed, but I ain't mad..."

That made no sense to me. Then again, murder very seldom makes sense to me either.

"But I reckon she owes me. And I'd found my golden chicken..."

"Goose," said Dykes.

"What?"

"It's a goose that lays golden eggs," said Dykes.

Gilder shook his head.

"Whatever. I had my riches staring me in the face and the key to them was that bitch I'd married. I knew she'd never told that player that she was married. So I had leverage."

"How long ago was this?" asked Dykes.

"Maybe about a year. Thereabouts."

Gilder took the last drag of his cigarette. He put it out in the soggy paper towel that once held ice like his childhood might have once held dreams. He took a tissue from the box and dabbed at his nose. The blood had long stopped, but blood was crusted up on his upper lip.

"So what did you have her do for you?"

"I told her that if she wanted to keep living her good life she'd have to buy me out. I'm not unreasonable, I figured we could work this out business-like."

"And she just agreed, just like that?"

"No, but she didn't take much convincing. I had my gun on her, right? And I told her I'd kill 'em both if she tried to screw with me. She didn't have a choice."

"And what did you want from her?"

"I told her she had to get a hundred grand a month to me."

Dykes looked at Gilder. Gilder looked at him and then grinned.

"She said she couldn't get that kind of money without it making him suspicious. She said the most she could get was probably twenty-five thousand. She got me the twenty-five grand pretty regularly over these past few months. But she missed a few of the payments. That got me upset so I went and saw her about it."

"That was at the coffee shop here?" asked Dykes.

He took one of the pictures we had of him from Skeef and placed it facing him on the table."

Gilder nodded, he went to reach for it but Dykes pulled it away.

"She's giving you money here nevertheless," he said.

"Yeah, but not nearly enough. Not nearly what she owed. She owed me something like seventy-five thousand, right? Plus interest. She only got me ten grand here."

"That must've got you pretty upset."

"Yeah, it did. I mean fuck, she owed me. And you've got to pay your debts."

I laughed, Lane looked at me.

"Can you believe this guy, he thinks he's a banker who's owed a legit debt."

Lane wasn't in the mood to joke around with me. I figured he was still sore.

"So you decided to kill James Ensor then. Explain that to me."

"Nah man," said Gilder shaking his head. "It ain't like that, man. I'm not a killa. I mean, I just wanted my golden goose."

He looked at Dykes and grinned. Puffed up pretty proud for getting the name right this time.

"But look here. I'd been following her for a while and I knew she was up to no good. She's just a no good whore. I suspected her of cheating on me and I figured she was cheating on that player with the other player. That black dude with the attitude."

"What attitude?" asked Dykes.

"You know, the attitude black guys have sometimes."

Dykes shook his head slowly. He didn't say anything.

"Well, I told her I knew she was screwing around. Then she got all upset and told me she couldn't be getting me any more money on account that the player she'd married had cut her off and was aiming to divorce her."

"And that's when you got your idea to kill him?" asked Dykes.

Gilder took a sip from the plastic cup of water in front of him. He nodded his head.

"Yeah, but I hadn't planned on killing him see. I went to the ballpark to talk to him. You know to make him see my point and to squeeze him for a bit before getting the hell outta dodge."

"So you found him at Wrigley Field and you just wanted to talk to him?" asked Dykes.

"Yeah, that's right, man. I wanted to have a real serious conversation with him, that's why I brought my gun. That way I figured he'd have to take me real serious. I found him throwing balls and so I went up and talked to him. I tried to be nice about it at first. I introduced myself. Then I told him he was married to my wife. But I told him it wasn't a problem. If he just gave me a million bucks I'd be on my way and he could have her."

"And you figured he'd be happy with that, considering his wife was cheating on him?" asked Dykes.

That's exactly what I wanted to ask. I bet Dykes looked incredulous, but I couldn't see.

"Well sure, man, why not? I figured it was a small price to pay, but hd didn't see it that way. So then I took out Ruger and told him it was either that or I'd kill him and then his whoring wife could get it all and I'd take it from her."

"I see. And I guess he didn't like that option either."

"Well, he might've liked it, 'cept he went for the gun and I shot him in self defense."

Dykes shook his head again. There was no way in hell any court in any county in this country would go for a self defense plea.

"So what did you do?"

"I got the hell outta there man. But then I figured I could still make this goose lay eggs."

"How's that?"

"Well, I knew that all his money, and I knew he was rich, was gonna go to Corinne. So that was my plan. I'd make her give me half. I knew it was a lot."

"Do you know how much?"

"Not for sure," said Gilder, looking down at his hands, "but when I spoke to Corinne she said it was over a hundred million. Can you believe it. I was gonna be rich."

"Except it didn't turn out that way."

"No. See, I went to see her and I brought my gun. I told her I wanted half for taking care of the player. She freaked out. I told her to settle down, we could both be rich. She got real sad and started crying. I told her if she didn't cut it out I'd plant the gun on her and make it look like she killed him and then killed herself."

"But that's not what happened."

Gilder shook his head and squashed the bent cigarette butt further into the soggy paper towel.

"She got mad. Started yelling and screaming at me. She slapped me across the face and told me to get the hell out of the house. I just lost it. I hit her across the face and she fell backwards into the coffee table. I bailed outta there, man. Got scared the neighbors might've heard something and called the cops."

"And your plan of leaving the gun behind?"

"I forgot about that. I just took off man. And now here I am."

And now here you are, I thought. Another asshole just not willing to do the hard yards in order to get a toehold on the cliff face of life called success. I looked at Lane. He was still looking at the three of them through the mirror.

"Another one bites the dust," I said, grinning at him.

He turned to look at me. He wasn't smiling and he still hadn't uncrossed his hands from his chest.

"Looks like your work here is done," he said. "We'll get the money to you next week. I think RG wants to take you out for a beer. There might still be time."

"There's always time for beer with friends," I said.

We exited the observation room just as Dykes and Jackson and Gilder exited the interrogation room.

"Want to go for a beer?" asked Jackson. "Looks like our work is done."

I nodded.

"I think I need one."

Dykes and Jackson nodded.

"You gonna come boss?" Jackson asked.

Lane nodded.

"Somebody's gotta keep you three in line it seems."

He grinned then and I almost felt like we had made up.

"We're gonna be about fifteen," said Dykes. "Gotta get this perp processed. Meet you at The Brass Tap?"

Lane nodded.

"I'll take AC along with me."

Dykes and Jackson nodded and left with the prisoner. Lane looked at me.

"Let's go."

"Listen," I said as we walked along to his fancy beemer, "I'm real sorry about getting too loose. It's not like me."

Lane stopped and looked at me.

"I think it is like you. You're a tough nut, and there's nothing wrong with that. But times have changed. We can't just go banging heads anymore. You're gonna have to find a different way if you want to stay in this game."

"Sage advice," I said, and we walked the rest of the way to his car.

CHAPTER TWENTY-THREE

Salty Sea Salty Me

I'D been home two weeks before the money came through. Twenty-five hundred plus expenses. I'd eat and pay rent the next month, plus have some left over. It wasn't all that bad. Johnny Rotten called me midweek the week I arrived back and told me that things had gone well. Lane had given me a good review, my saltiness and all. Dykes and Jackson had been happy to work with me.

Maybe I would get invited back to Chicago. They hadn't won. That wasn't surprising. The Lovable Losers might still be lovable but they were still losing. I was winning. At least that's what it seemed like.

I got a call from my guy at the gallery. You'll remember I have some art at Triangle Gallery. The art dealer slash owner called early in the first week I was back. He had a sale. Some guy by the name of Dennis Blaney out of Chicago with Blue Ocean LLC. He bought one of my pieces most closely resembling Kandinsky. I called it A Movement In Time Over A Dime. Blaney liked it. It was one of my more expensive pieces. Declan Dawson, that's my guy at the gallery, prices my art by what he thinks they'll sell for. This one was ten grand.

Ten grand is a lot of money. At least for a fella like me. But if there's ever been a legal racket it's gotta be the art galleries. They take fifty percent. Some are trying to take more. Just for hanging pictures on the wall. Don't get me started. Still, adding it all up it'd been a pretty good week's work. Hadn't seen a week like this in, shit, I hadn't ever seen a week like this. Seventy-five hundred. I felt like a millionaire.

I'd watched the final game between the Cubs and Orioles on TV with Pirate curled up next to me opening up his one eye every so often to keep track of the score. It had been an abysmal showing. The Orioles won four in a row. And that was the end of that. I had money on the game, and I lost it all. Naturally. But in the box in front of home plate I saw Dykes and Jackson. They'd taken my tickets for the game, and they'd managed to bring their wives. Israel had come through for me, and I'd given them to RG. Have no idea how they swindled another couple out of Kreyling, but they had.

Sitting there in my apartment with Pirate and watching that last game. Baseball still reminded me of America. Sometimes we're losing but we still see it through. But the money and drugs and politics still put the rotten in the apple's core. But the fans are loyal, brave and true and so long as that remains there's always hope for the red white and blue.

www.ingramcontent.com/pod-product-compliance
Lightning Source LLC
Chambersburg PA
CBHW030959260626
47169CB00002B/614